DIAMONDS
IN AN ARCTIC SKY

(Andi & North, Book 1)

Best Wishes,
Mettauer

Joan Mettauer

ISBN 13: 978-1724295187 (Paperback)
ISBN 10: 1724295187

1. Fiction, Action & Adventure

ALSO BY JOAN METTAUER

NORTH: The Last Great Race
(Andi & North, Book 2)

Honeymoon Bay
(Andi & North, Book 3)

After the Storm
(Andi & North, Book 4)

And for the Littles in your life,
The Adventures of Stripes the Gopher
(An early Readers Chapter Book)

FOR MY SONS

David Strothard
~ I'm so proud of the man, husband and father
You have become ~

And

Michael Strothard
(1985 – 1988)
~ Forever in my heart ~

'We shall find Peace.
We shall hear Angels.
We shall see the sky sparkling with diamonds.'

Anton Chekhov

"Tango Tango Alfa, this is Tuktu base. Do you copy, Jim? Over."

The throaty voice drifted down from Tuktu Aviation's second floor Dispatch Centre, making the nimble woman climbing up the staircase pause. Andrea Jean Nowak, known to almost everyone in her life as Andi, grimaced before she resumed the short climb to her office. She dropped her parka on an empty chair in the coffee room and strode into dispatch. "Hi, Jessica," she said to the woman behind the voice.

Jessica Hartman, otherwise known as 'The Princess Upstairs', or, more often than not just 'The Princess,' was the Chief Dispatcher at Tuktu Aviation. She was attempting to make radio contact with Tuktu Aviation's Twin Otter and was seated at an oversized, cluttered desk bumped up to a grimy window overlooking the runways, taxi-ways, and various aircraft hangars at the Inuvik International Airport. Two multi-line telephones and two shortwave radios were positioned within her reach. Andi leaned against the desk and peered at the mess of papers strewn across its surface. "How are things going this afternoon?"

Jessica frowned and narrowed her blue eyes. "What are you doing here anyway? I thought you were in town at the Chamber of Commerce meeting for the rest of the afternoon."

"That was the plan, but a few of the members had to catch the afternoon flight to Yellowknife, so they cut our meeting short." Andi was getting used to Jessica's disdainful and abrasive manner, but she still didn't like it. After more than a year as Tuktu Aviation's Flight Operations Manager, Andi and her Chief Dispatcher still clashed regularly. "When are Captain Jim and Hank due back from the supply run to Pivot Lake?"

It was a crisp, sunny Friday afternoon in mid-February and the eighteen-passenger turbo-prop Twin Otter, registration C-ITTA, was their only aircraft still out flying.

Jessica flipped long, blond hair out of her eyes and pursed her lips. "Any time now," she muttered. "I was just trying to raise them on the radio." She reached for the high frequency (HF) radio microphone. "Tango Tango Alfa, this is Tuktu base. Do you copy, Jim? Over." This time Jessica's call was crisp and professional, but the radio still remained silent. She lifted the very high frequency (VHF) radio mic from its hook and repeated her call on a higher frequency, to no avail.

Andi picked up the thick black binder that held Tuktu's passenger lists for their scheduled flights to the Arctic communities of Tuktoyaktuk, Paulatuk, Sachs Harbour, Aklavik and Fort McPherson. She leafed through the reservation sheets and was pleased to see that more than half of the seats were already booked for the next week. Tuktu's seven aircraft were always busy. She was proud of their diverse fleet – one Britten-Norman Islander, three de Havilland DHC-6 Twin Otters, one de Havilland DHC-2 Beaver, one Cessna 337 Sky Master, and one Piper T1040 fully equipped medevac-dedicated aircraft.

"What do we have for charters next week?" she asked, setting the reservations binder back on the desk. Jessica had slumped into her chair and stared moodily out of the window at the activity on the tarmac below. She mutely gave an even bulkier binder a one-finger shove across her desk without so much as a glance in her boss's direction. Andi bit back her simmering anger and flipped through the first few pages in the charter reservation book. The bread and butter of Tuktu's winter income came from one customer – Pivot Lake Diamond Mine. In addition to the daily service flights to the mine, Andi was glad to see that there were also several other bookings for the following week.

She carefully set the heavy charter book down in front of Jessica while holding back a strong urge to drop it on her head, then glanced at the dispatch log. Detailed notations were made of each aircraft's trip details and movements. Andi's green eyes narrowed. "It shouldn't take four hours to do a supply run to Pivot Lake. TTA should have been back over an hour ago. Give them another call please, Jessica."

The words were no sooner out of her mouth when Andi felt a sudden, hot tingle flash over her ears. She swallowed a faint gasp that

2

was one more of surprise than discomfort, and reached out to grasp the edge of the desk to steady her suddenly wobbly knees. Andrea Nowak had been born with quirky ears; they often alerted her to the onset of problems or difficult situations even before she had the slightest inkling that anything may be amiss in her life. She came by the trait honestly – for generations it had been passed down from mother to daughter, along with what people often referred to as "The Sixth Sense." Sometimes Andi just *knew* things that she shouldn't.

Oblivious of anything but her own agenda, Jessica keyed the VHF radio mic again: "Tango Tango Alfa, this is Tuktu base. Come in Tango Alfa. Over."

This time the radio crackled to life. "Tuktu base, this is Tango Alfa," Captain Jim O'Neill's deep baritone boomed clearly over the airwaves. "We're inbound Inuvik and should be down in about twenty-five minutes. Do we wrap 'er up for the night, Jess? Over."

"Yes, and take her over to maintenance, Jimmy," Jessica crooned into the microphone. "The engineers need her for the night. Thanks, you're a sweetie. See ya later. Tuktu base out."

Andi clenched her jaw and made a mental note to review professional radio procedures at their next dispatch meeting. She let out a long breath she didn't know she'd been holding. "Do you have any idea why they're so late getting back from Pivot Lake, Jessica? Did the mine book holding time?"

"Nope."

"Well, delays like this could really mess up our flying schedule, especially now that we're doing daily runs to the mine. We can't afford to piss off our other customers."

The lucrative Pivot Lake Diamond Mine flying contract had started over a year ago, when East Three Drilling began diamond drilling in earnest during the winter of 1993. Situated 280 kilometers east of Inuvik, Pivot Lake was remote, isolated, and accessible by land and ice-road for only a brief window of time during the depth of winter.

Tuktu Aviation was reaping the financial benefit of supplying groceries, mail, emergency parts, and small freight to the mine. They also ferried geologists and visitors to and from the Inuvik and Yellowknife airports. Andi needed to find out why the inbound supply trip was late. She reached for the VHF radio mic. "Tango Tango Alfa, this is base. Are you still by, Jim?"

"Yup. Go ahead."

"It's Andi. I'm just wondering what the holdup was on the turn-around on this trip? You're over an hour late."

"Don't worry about it, darling. We'll be home before ya miss us."

Andi's blood pressure took a hike north. *Darling?* He *dared* to call her *darling?* Her ears burned, but this time with a flash of hot anger. She struggled to calm her voice. "It's not *missing you* I'm worried about, Jim, it's our scheduling. I'd prefer if we talk about this in person." The tone of Andi's voice suggested that Jim's presence at the meeting was *not* optional. She quickly flipped through the flight booking sheets, confirming that O'Neill wasn't on Saturday's roster. "Meet me in my office at nine o'clock tomorrow morning. Tuktu out." She tossed the microphone onto the desk and stretched out the tension that had settled between her shoulder blades. Captain James O'Neill had a reputation as a legendary bush pilot, but he really made her skin crawl.

"Okay, Jessica, I'm out of here," Andi said calmly, determined to hide her frustration. "My pager is on if you need me. Have a good weekend." She grabbed her purse and parka and headed toward the staircase, pausing momentarily to throw a guilty glance at her own corner office. The mounds of paperwork on her desk would have to wait another day. After all, she thought, it *was* Friday, even if she couldn't really partake in Inuvik's customary Friday night Happy Hour.

Booze was a bit of a problem for Andi; having an occasional, solitary drink to deaden the pain of loss had quickly bloomed into a full-blown addiction. She absentmindedly rubbed the Alcoholics

4

Anonymous ring of fellowship on her left hand. Fashioned from silver, the ring bore the traditional AA logo of a triangle inside a circle. It was Andi's talisman; she wore it every day to remind herself that she wasn't alone in her struggle with alcohol.

She was halfway down the stairs when a thought brought her to a stop. "Jessica," she called, "has Jim been late coming back from Pivot Lake before?"

"Uh, no. Not that I know of." Jessica's reply was just a tad slow and not entirely convincing.

"Okay, thanks." Andi was perplexed; something wasn't quite right, and her ears had begun to tingle again. Her normally light footsteps were heavy on the stairs. She walked out of the rickety old wooden hangar that housed Tuktu Aviation's dispatch offices and couldn't help but smile when she looked back at the building. She often wondered what people back home would think of her new workplace. It was grungy, cold, drafty and redolent with the odors of fuel, dust, fish, and traces of the incredibly putrid Inuit whale blubber delicacy called 'maktaq.' The main floor of the building housed a freight-forwarding business; anything and everything was shipped through and housed within its cavernous and smelly depths.

By comparison, the Arctic blast that hit her senses when she stepped outside felt like the freshest air in the world, and it very likely was. At minus thirty-three degrees Celsius, winter still hadn't given up its hold above the Arctic Circle but at least daylight still lingered. At this time of the year the days seemed blessedly long with over eight hours of daylight compared to varying shades of darkness for most of December. The sun had set on December sixth and not poked its head above the horizon again for a month, and what a welcomed sight those first rays of sunshine had been.

Andi climbed into the dented old company car that was one of perks of being on Tuktu's Management team. A relic of a beast, she had promptly nicknamed the brown Ford Country Squire station wagon

'The Land Yacht.' Despite being huge and ugly, it had willingly started on many frigid, bone-numbing mornings. Andi let the old car's engine warm up for a few minutes, then slowly pulled out of the parking lot and began the twelve-kilometer drive to Inuvik on a mostly deserted road.

She usually looked forward to a relaxing bath and a good book to fill her evening hours, but today the thought of spending another Friday night alone was discomfiting. At thirty-five years of age, Andi's addiction had pushed her into self-imposed exile.

Another lonely Friday night awaited.

TWO

Andi had just unlocked the door of her company house on Alder Drive when the telephone started ringing. The unexpected call took her by surprise and she decided to let her answering machine pick it up.

"Hey, Andi, it's North Ruben. Just thought I'd see if you're up to going out for a drink tonight. Give me a call when you get in. Talk to you later."

North's message brought a smile to her lips. North, an Inuvialuit from the small village of Paulatuk situated on the coast of the Beaufort Sea, was one of Andi's favourite people. Inuvik's somewhat transient aviation crowd stuck together, seldom mingling with local residents of the city, but North was an exception to the rule. He had befriended Andi when, two days after arriving in Inuvik, she had wandered into his stunning native art gallery, The Qamutik. When she asked him how to pronounce the name of his gallery, he had also told her that qamutik meant 'sled' in his native language. North didn't talk about his family in Paulatuk very much, but Andi didn't talk about her previous life much either. Her life before Inuvik held closely guarded memories – memories kept deeply hidden within the innermost recesses of her mind and aching heart.

Andi pondered North's message. His call both excited and disturbed her. She would love to meet with him to have some fun and a few laughs with a good friend, but for Andi fun could sometimes be a very bad idea. She was torn; the thought of spending another Friday night alone was depressing, but the thought of sitting in a bar with alcohol fumes swirling through the air was terrifying.

She decided to have a bath before she returned North's call, and poured some of her favourite bubble bath under the gushing faucet. As the room filled with the delicate, calming scent of lavender, she stripped out of her clothes and threw them into a wicker laundry hamper. The fragrance of lavender always reminded her of her mother, who had grown the aromatic herb and tucked linen sachets filled with its dried flowers throughout the house.

Andi turned to step into the steaming tub, pausing when she glanced at her own image in the bathroom mirror. She gazed at the woman staring back at her. Sometimes she was afraid that she didn't know that woman at all, and sometimes she wished that she *didn't* know her at all.

The large, almond-shaped emerald eyes reflecting from the mirror knew too many secrets, and held pain that nobody should have to endure. She sighed deeply, dreading the familiar tug of melancholy that threatened to set in. Her eyes slid from her face to assess her naked body, and she found that she was still pleased with the way she looked. Sporadic bouts of exercise and a reasonably healthy diet, with the exception of the occasional cheeseburger, were keeping her belly flat and her arms and legs toned. Her eastern European heritage lent her skin a healthy, slightly bronzed glow without the benefit of sun or a tanning bed. She reached for the hair elastic sitting on the counter and pulled her thick, shoulder-length hair into a high knot on the top of her head. If there was one thing that Andi was vain about, it was the colour of her hair. To call it dark brown didn't do it justice. Her hair captured the colours of the earth, combining rich red, black and brown tones that glowed separately, yet blended as one beneath the rays of a sunny day.

She slipped gratefully beneath the fragrant bubbles, and let her thoughts drift back to North Ruben. He knew that she wouldn't touch alcohol, but he didn't know the truth about *why* she didn't drink. Andi had told him she was allergic to it, and she didn't feel comfortable or secure enough in their new friendship to confide in him.

Half an hour later, wrapped in her favourite fluffy pink robe, Andi made her decision; she just couldn't face another Friday night alone. She picked up the phone and dialed North's number.

"North Ruben."

"Hey, North, I got your message. How are you doing?"

"Just great, Andi! And you? Do you feel like going out tonight or are you doing something with Ken and Margo?"

Margo Thomas was Andi's very best friend. The two women had shared thirteen years of their lives, united through both good and bad times. Margo and Ken were the first friends she'd made when she'd moved to Yellowknife shortly after graduating from high school in Port Alberni, on British Columbia's beautiful Vancouver Island. Andi had been heart-broken when Ken had accepted the position of Chief Engineer at Tuktu Aviation and her best friends had moved to Inuvik. Shortly after their departure from Yellowknife, though, Ken had helped Andi land her own position with Tuktu Aviation, which she'd always be grateful to him for. Within months of Ken and Margo's departure from Yellowknife, Andi had followed them above the Arctic Circle.

"Nope, no plans," Andi said in reply to North's question. "I'd love to go out tonight. Should we meet at the Rail?" Now that her decision was made, she was eager to spend some time with North.

"The Brass Rail it is, but I have to drive into town anyway, so why don't I pick you up? We're in for another cold spell. It's supposed to hit minus forty tonight." North's deep voice was like velvet; rich, smooth and sexy. It was the kind of voice that did things to a woman, especially a young, lonely woman who'd been celibate for way, way too long. An unfamiliar spark of desire stirred somewhere deep within Andi's core.

"Okay, sounds good to me," Andi said. "I'll be ready to go by 7:30. Does that work?"

"Yup. I've already fed the mutts so no problem. See you soon."

Standing before the meager selection of her closet a few minutes later, Andi rejected item after item. She finally gave up trying to find something even remotely sexy and slid into an old pair of comfortable jeans and a black turtleneck sweater.

While she brushed mascara on her long lashes she thought about North and his team of Canadian Eskimo Dogs. He called them his mutts, but Andi knew that the Arctic working dogs were valuable. They were the oldest and rarest purebred, indigenous canine breed in North America, and their history dated back 4000 years.

Andi loved *all* animals, but North's twelve loyal, affectionate, intelligent sled dogs had captured her heart. He had raised them all from pups, nourishing and loving them, and was now training them in harness. North's dogs were his life and family, and his pride and joy. He had confided in Andi that he secretly hoped his team would one day be fast enough and strong enough to compete in the famous Alaskan Iditarod Trail Sled Race, an annual long-distance dog sled race run in early March from Anchorage to Nome. In the gold rush days of the early 1900s, the ancient route was used to deliver mail and assorted goods by dogsled. Now the grueling race helped to keep the north's dogsledding culture alive, and North Ruben wanted a part of it.

The popular Brass Rail Pub was nearly full, which was typical for a Friday night. In fact, it was typical for almost any night in a town where alcohol consumption seemed to be the number one sport. North led Andi through the dim, slightly smoky pub to a small table at the far end of the room. The crowd parted for his imposing 6'1" frame and he stopped several times to exchange greetings and manly slaps on the back with old friends.

After they found a table North went to the bar to get their drinks. Alone for a few minutes, Andi glanced around the dimly lit room. She recognized quite a few faces, and spotted a few of Tuktu Aviation's pilots. She automatically glanced at her watch; Tuktu strictly adhered to the '12-hours from bottle to throttle' standard aviation rule that prevented flying under the influence of alcohol. Or at least it was supposed to. She made a mental note to compare faces to the flight roster the next morning.

Andi wasn't at all surprised to see Captain Jim O'Neill propped up against the long, gleaming bar, with Jessica Hartman glued to his side. Andi's lips twisted in anger; Jessica was well aware that Jim had a wife and two kids waiting for him at home. That little fact didn't seem to have much impact on The Princess though. Anyone with two eyes could see was happening, and it wasn't the first time Andi had seen the two of them hip to hip. She wondered if the rumours were true and they really were having an affair, and made another mental note to remind Jessica of the company's policy on staff socializing. It's no wonder they call me 'The Wicked Witch of The North', she thought with a smile. She wouldn't admit it to anyone, but she was secretly delighted with her moniker.

Andi's face lit up when North returned with their drinks and she firmly set aside all thoughts of work and troubling employees. She took a sip from the glass of Club Soda North handed her while her eyes wandered unbidden to his hand, following his every move as he brought a mug of beer to his lips. He took a long pull of the dark amber brew and licked the foam from his cleanly shaven upper lip. Andi took a deep breath and caught the tantalizing aroma of yeasty, tangy beer. It made her mouth water. She wondered if she would ever be able to look at a drink and not want to guzzle it down. She'd been attending AA meetings faithfully for over two years, but her fight didn't seem to be getting any easier. If anything, she was becoming more and more disgusted with her weakness.

Forcing away the black thoughts that seeped so easily from the recesses of her mind, Andi turned her focus back to the man before her. "So tell me about yourself, North. When did you come to Inuvik?"

North chuckled. "I've been here off and on for about twenty-five years. Guess I'm never leaving."

11

"Where else did you live?"

"Montreal and Toronto. That's about it."

"Montreal?" Andi asked in surprise. "What were you doing there? Do you speak French?"

"I went to McGill. The Faculty of Law. Didn't need to learn French."

"You're a lawyer?" Andi's mouth dropped open before she had the presence of mind to snap it shut again.

"Yes, ma'am," North chuckled. "Guilty as charged. I practiced in Toronto for a few years after I passed the bar and then decided that the high life wasn't for me after all. Came back to Inuvik and opened up the Qamutik."

"I'm ... impressed," Andi stammered.

"Don't be. Lawyers are all crooks," North smiled and lifted his mug of beer mug to his lips – his very well shaped, gorgeous lips.

"That's good to know," Andi laughed. "So what's new in the world of art and artists?"

"Not too much. But I did receive a new shipment of soapstone carvings from Paulatuk today. Some of them look pretty good. Great, actually."

Andi knew that authentic native carvings from North's gallery were in demand worldwide. She'd seen several pieces from The Qamutik on display at the international airports in Edmonton, Alberta and Vancouver, British Columbia. Locked inside glass cabinets, the artwork astounded her, as did the price tags. Even the smaller soapstone or serpentinite pieces were worth thousands of dollars – they were definitely out of her price range.

"You should stop by on Monday and have a look before I ship them out," he continued with a wink. "I'll give you a private viewing. Maybe it's time you started your own collection, eh?"

"I'd love to come by and see them. I adore soapstone carvings, but I don't know about becoming a collector. I think the only carving I could afford would be on a soapstone chip."

"Hey, sorry to change the subject, but did you hear the big news around town today?" North asked. His thickly lashed, espresso-brown eyes widened under heavy black brows.

"No. What?" Andi tried to focus on the conversation, but was distracted by North's bottomless eyes and his strong, square jaw. When he smiled, she knew that a slightly crooked, overly long incisor would reveal itself. The imperfection had earned him the nickname 'Fang', but Andi thought it only added to his sexy mystique. She wriggled on her seat, and unconsciously licked her bottom lip. Her eyes wandered from his jaw to his long, shiny hair; it was jet black, with just a touch of grey at the temples, and was secured in a neat ponytail at the nape of his neck. Andi wondered how old he was, and decided he would be around forty.

"What was that?" she asked, raising her voice above the noise in the pub. She blushed, embarrassed to be caught in her frank assessment of the man sitting across from her.

"East Three Drilling just announced that they've hit the richest kimberlite pipe yet out at Pivot Lake," North repeated, a huge grin on his face. "They say this is likely the biggest diamond find in Canadian history – it's going to put Canadian diamonds on the world map. *And* it's all happening on our doorstep! This town is going to boom." North took another long drink from his sweaty beer mug.

"That's fabulous," Andi grinned. Just thinking about the prospect of additional flying revenue excited her. "Hey, you speak Inuvialuktun don't you?" she asked.

"Sure. That's all we spoke growing up."

"So how do you say 'diamond' in Inuvialuktun?"

"Huh, that's a good question. As far as I know, there's no word for diamond in our language; it just doesn't exist. The closest you'd get would be something that translates to 'stone that sparkles like a star in the sky'. Why?"

"I was just curious, but I find it odd that the biggest diamond discovery in North America has been made in a place where the native people have no word for the gem. It's just like – well, like diamonds shouldn't exist here, or that they really have no value," she mused. "Doesn't that strike you as odd?"

"Yeah, I guess. Never thought about it before."

"Well, I just think it's strange. But the new strike is certainly the best news I've heard in a long time," Andi smiled. "Why don't we celebrate? How about dinner at the Finto? I haven't had Arctic Char for a while." Andi loved the legendary Finto Restaurant; it had both ambiance and wonderful food.

"You're dead on, let's get out of here. I'm starving and it's getting too noisy in here anyway." North grabbed Andi's parka and helped her slide it on. "Dinner's on me, Babe."

THREE

Andi rolled over, hit the alarm clock and took a deep breath. Waking up to the mouth-watering aroma of freshly brewed coffee almost made a cold, dark Saturday morning worth getting up for. She said a silent thank you to Mr. Coffee and its automatic brew feature and crawled out of bed.

By the time she arrived at the airport it was eight o'clock, but the sun wouldn't make an appearance over the horizon for another two hours. Ayame Saito, Tuktu Aviation's petite, twenty-four-year-old Assistant Dispatcher, was already seated at her desk flipping through flight bookings for the coming week.

"Good morning, Ayame," Andi called as she strode into the office. "I thought Jessica was scheduled to work today. Isn't it your Saturday off?"

Ayame rolled her deep brown eyes and smiled. "It was, but you know The Princess. She must have had a blast at the Rail last night because she called me around midnight and literally *begged* me to take her shift today. She was slurring her words so badly I didn't have the heart to say no."

"Yeah, we saw her and Captain Jim at the Rail. I'm not surprised she didn't want to come in today," Andi said with a wry smile.

"We?" Ayame asked inquisitively, a mischievous smile teasing the corners of her lips. "We, as in our friend Fang?"

"Ayame," Andi admonished half-heartedly "Don't call him that." Ayame Saito was not only Andi's Assistant Dispatcher, she was also her friend and ally. Of Japanese-Canadian heritage, she was one of the most intelligent, dedicated and organized women Andi knew. She thanked her lucky stars to have Ayame, whose beautiful name meant 'Iris' in Japanese, on her dispatch team. She didn't think it at all coincidental that the iris also just happened to be her favourite flower. Andi knew that the young woman often took up the slack and cleaned up the messes that Princess Jessica left in her wake. It was Ayame's dream to become an Air Traffic Controller with Nav Canada one day and although Andi wished her only success, she would sorely miss her if she left.

"Well, that's great," Andi sighed. "I suppose that means Jim will either be late for our meeting or not show up at all."

"Meeting?" Ayame repeated, a perplexed frown creasing her brow.

"Just Jim and I."

"Oh?" Ayame's eyes widened. "And what has the great Captain Jim done to piss you off this time?"

"He was late getting back from the Pivot Lake supply run yesterday and I need to find out why. By the way, have you noticed any unusual delays with the Pivot Lake trips lately?"

"Not really, but I have a few days' worth of billings to catch up on so I'll keep my eyes open. I'll let you know if I spot anything."

"Sounds good. I'm going to put a pot of coffee on. Would you like a cup or are you still drinking that herbal cleanse goop?"

"It's not goop!" Ayame laughed. "It's an ancient Japanese cleansing tea. You really should try it sometime. And yes, I'll have a cup as long as you make real coffee and not Jessica's hard-core stuff."

Jessica had returned from her last Vancouver shopping extravaganza with the latest craze – an espresso machine. She parked it next to good old Mr. Coffee and announced, "Finally, I can have a civilized coffee in the office." Much to her disdain, almost everyone else thought Jessica's spurting, hissing machine produced undrinkable tar, and it was judiciously avoided. It seemed to annoy Jessica to no end, which made Andi enjoy her Mr. Coffee machine even more.

She delivered Ayame's coffee to her then settled at her own desk to catch up on paperwork. Quickly engrossed in her tasks, the muted sounds of radio chatter and whine of distant aircraft engines filled the office with comforting background noise.

She jumped when Jim O'Neill banged a cup down on her desk and flopped into one of her two guest chairs. The clock hanging on the wall over his head told her it was close to 10:00; he was an hour late for their meeting.

"So I'm here," O'Neill grumbled, squinting at Andi through a cloud of smoke curling up from his cigarette. The acrid smell assaulted her nose, annoying her even further. "What's up?" Jim was off duty so wasn't sporting his Captain's uniform, but one look at his red-rimmed eyes and sallow, puffy face told Andi the man *was* sporting a wicked hangover. From personal experience, she knew the signs of one all too well.

Andi slowly set her pen down and folded her hands on top of her desk. She took a deep breath. "Well Jim, for starters you're an hour late for our meeting, but don't bother giving me an excuse. I have a pretty damn good idea why you didn't have the courtesy to show up on time."

Jim leaned back in his chair and smirked. With a trembling hand he lifted his cup and took a careful sip of the steaming coffee.

Andi took another deep breath and counted to ten. "I want to talk to you about the Pivot Lake trips. You were at the operations meeting in September when we all discussed the feasibility of fitting the mine's supply runs into our existing schedule. If I'm not mistaken, *you* were the one who said that three hours was, and I quote 'more than enough time to get out there, unload and get back to Inuvik'. So can you please tell me why your trip to Pivot Lake took over four hours yesterday?"

O'Neill jumped to his feet. "That's what this god-damn urgent meeting of yours is about?" he shouted. "I'm frickin' one hour behind schedule and you're on my case?" Coffee sloshed over the side of his cup and onto the floor. "This is bloody ridiculous!" His face darkened and spittle flew from his lips. He waved his cigarette in front of her face. "You know what, shit happens. You're not out there. You have no fucking idea what's really going on out there and now you're giving *me* shit for being an hour late?" Jim's red-rimmed, bloodshot eyes were wild. He slammed his cup down on Andi's desk, spilling yet more coffee on its shiny surface. He took a deep drag and blew the smoke out with more force than necessary. "I'm out of here, darling."

"You stop right there, Captain O'Neill." Andi strode to her office door and slammed it closed. When she turned around she found herself face to face with her nemeses. So close, in fact, that she could smell his sour, boozy breath. "First of all," she said, leaning forward so they were almost nose to nose and enunciating each word slowly and quietly, "I am *not* your darling. I would appreciate it if you never call me that again. And secondly, like it or not, I *am* your Flight Operations Manager.

"In the past year you've made it abundantly clear to not only myself, but everyone else in this operation that you can't stand the idea of a female Ops Manager. Or perhaps it's just me, Jim. Do you have something against me personally? Now's a pretty damn good time to tell me."

O'Neill loomed over her, his beefy hands fisted. Andi fleetingly wondered if he wanted to hit her. She almost wished he would try. Handsome ace pilot or not, he'd be out of a job so fast it would make his swollen head spin.

"Yeah, you think you're pretty good, don't you?" he sneered. "Cute little chick from down south playing with the big boys up north. Well I tell you what, little Miss Operations Manager, you just keep your frickin' nose out of my business and we'll both be better off. Just forget that I was a little late yesterday and we'll let this whole thing blow over. It's not a big deal."

A piece of ash from his cigarette dropped to the floor. Jim looked around for an ashtray and finding none, dropped the smoldering butt into his coffee.

Andi took a step back and crossed her arms at chest level. "I don't like your attitude, Jim, and as far as being a cute little chick playing with the big boys, I've damn well *earned* the right to this position. I've paid my dues in this business and you and your boys don't have to like it, but I'm staying right where I am."

Jim snorted and turned away. He slumped back into the chair he had recently vacated. His face had developed a slightly greenish hue and Andi vehemently hoped he wouldn't puke in her office. Her stomach lurched at the thought.

"So if you're off your soap box now Jim, I still want to know why you were an hour late coming back from Pivot yesterday." Andi stood behind her desk and leaned toward O'Neill, her palms flat on the wooden surface.

"Uh, yeah. What the hell," Jim said slowly. "Well we, uh, Hank thought he saw a herd of caribou on the way out to Pivot so on our way home we went looking for it. Guess we lost track of time."

Hank Brister, a fully qualified co-pilot from British Columbia's lower mainland, had been recently hired at Jim's recommendation and usually flew right seat in the Twin Otter with Jim.

Andi's eyebrows arched and her emerald eyes widened. She reached for her chair. "Caribou? You mean to tell me you burned up an hour's worth of fuel chasing after caribou? You've got to be kidding me."

"Well, you know Hank's new here." O'Neill had the decency to at least appear sheepish about the matter. "He's never seen a caribou before so I thought it would be fun to give him a good look, since we're flying for Caribou Aviation and all. You, uh, you know that tuktu means caribou, right?" He blinked at Andi, giving her his famous puppy dog gaze. It would have had more impact if his eyes weren't bloodshot and red-rimmed. "It seemed like a good idea at the time," he ended weakly when he realized that his best pleading gaze made no impression on his boss.

"It's ... it's just absolutely absurd to burn up an hour's worth of expensive Jet B gawking at caribou," Andi stammered. Her earlier anger had subsided, leaving her exasperated instead. "Don't do anything like that again, Jim. And don't let it get around to the other flight crew either. I don't want them thinking they can use our entire fleet of aircraft for their own personal joy rides. We were lucky yesterday because there wasn't another trip for the Twin, but we may get busier now that they've discovered the new kimberlite pipe out at the diamond mine."

"I heard about that," Jim said, leaning forward in his chair. His eyes brightened and a smile played on his lips. "Man, that's exciting. All those sparkling, lovely diamonds." He cupped his hand while he spoke, curling and rolling his fingers as though diamonds tumbled in his grasp. "Yeah, diamonds on the tundra. Someone's gonna get rich around here." He rubbed the fair stubble on his fleshy chin.

"Well, it's not going to be you and it's not going to be me," Andi said firmly. She rose and strode across her office to the door. "So, let's not do any more sightseeing, okay? Leave that for the paying tourists from now on." She opened the door and looked at the pilot pointedly, indicating that their meeting was over.

O'Neill, his self-confidence seemingly restored, strutted out of Andi's office and into dispatch. He lit another cigarette and peered over Ayame's shoulder "Anything on for me tomorrow, sweetheart?"

Ayame flipped pages. "There's only one Twin Otter trip tomorrow. Another supply run to Pivot Lake, scheduled for thirteen hundred hours. Do you want me to put Hank on with you again?"

"Sure, and tell him to meet me at the hangar at noon." Jim strolled toward the exit. "See you, ladies, and you have yourselves a great day. I'm off for a little nap now." He looked back and winked at Ayame, an innocent enough act that he somehow managed to turn into a lewd assault.

Only when the pilot was safely out of the building did Ayame explode. "Can you believe that louse? He actually had the audacity to ask me out for a little drinky last week!" She grimaced, clearly disgusted at the thought. "I mean, he knows that I know that he's screwing around on his wife. He must think that just because he's messed around with half of the women in town he can get into my pants too. I can't stand him!" She picked up the heavy charter reservations book and threw it to the corner of the desk where it landed with a heavy thud.

Andi was startled by the violent outburst. She couldn't remember the normally shy and reserved Ayame ever getting so worked up over anything before. She was also very surprised that Jim was attempting to charm her assistant dispatcher; Ayame Saito certainly wasn't his type, but perhaps the challenge excited him. Ayame's weekends and days off were no more exciting than her own usually were, although Ayame did a lot of volunteer work in the community. She was also a talented origami crafter, and taught free classes several times a year in the church hall. Many of the Inuvialuit elders were enthralled with the whimsical, colourful paper figures and they had persuaded Ayame to teach her art form during the long, cold winter nights.

"Well, if you start having trouble with him, let me know," Andi said. "I don't want him harassing you."

Ayame smiled and nodded. "I will, but you don't have to worry. I can handle Captain Jim."

"Good. Well I have to get going. "I promised North I'd stop by and meet his new Canadian Eskimo pup this afternoon."

"Oooh, a hot date with the mysterious dog-man himself! Are you sure you can handle him, boss?"

"Ayame, I've told you before – he's just a friend."

"Right. That's your story and you're sticking to it," Ayame nodded her head and grinned.

Andi ignored the comment. "Is everything on time here so far?"

"Yes, everything is right on time. We only have one trip to Aklavik this morning, then the afternoon Tuk flight. Go on and have fun with Fang," she winked. "I'm working tomorrow too, so I'll get caught up on the air bills and let you know on Monday if I find anything unusual with the Pivot Lake trip times."

"Thanks a bunch, Ayame. I've got my pager on so call me if anything comes up. I think Paul is home today too, if you can't reach me." Paul White was Tuktu Aviation's owner and CEO – the man who had lured Andi away from her position as Operations Manager at one of the largest aviation businesses in Yellowknife. Andi, Paul, and Paul's wife Carla had since become great friends.

The phone was ringing again, and the only reply Andi got from the busy dispatcher was a backward wave. She turned and headed out the door, bound for North's secluded cabin.

FOUR

Andi's stomach growled, reminding her that breakfast had been very meager. Guessing that North, if he was a typical bachelor, would have very little to eat in the house, she decided to pick up a few things for their lunch. It meant doubling back a few kilometers since North's cabin was between the airport and town, but she needed to eat.

She raced through the aisles of The Bay Northern Store, throwing a loaf of day-old French bread, gruyere cheese, black forest ham and a few apples into her shopping cart. She added a large bottle of sparkling non-alcohol apple cider. The one thing she really missed about life in the south was fresh, affordable produce and food. Shopping in Inuvik was mindless: you bought whatever the stores stocked that week. There was even less selection during the periods of freeze-up and break-up. For several weeks each fall and spring, the Peel River and Mackenzie River ice-roads or ferries were out of service and all groceries were flown into the small Arctic community. The already inflated price of food took another big hike during these periods.

Andi paid for her small bag of groceries and headed to North's place on Low Road. His driveway was unmarked and the light skiff of snowfall the night before made its entrance hard to see. She finally spotted it and maneuvered the old Ford slowly down the long, curving lane.

When she pulled up in front of North's small home a chorus of barking and yipping greeted her. She had visited North several times before and now his dogs seemed to recognize the sound of her car. They had alerted North to her arrival, and he was waiting on the front step wearing faded jeans, a green plaid flannel shirt and fur-trimmed moccasins. The comfortable, worn clothes only enhanced his virility; the sight of him made Andi's heart skip a beat.

"Come on in," he shouted above the clamour of the dogs. "I just put a pot of coffee on. And you'd better plug your car in." He pointed to a bright orange extension cord hanging over the stair railing.

Andi passed the groceries to North then pulled the extension cord back to her car. She connected it to her car's block heater, which would prevent the engine from freezing up.

North, always courteous, held the cabin door open and followed Andi into the warmth of his home. She shed her layers of heavy winter outerwear, then slipped her feet into the soft, fur-lined moccasins North's sister had made for her. He kept them beside the door for her to wear when she visited him. They fit like a glove.

Shivering, Andi hurried over to the small wood-burning stove that stood against an interior wall of the cabin and held her cold hands to its warmth. Living in a region where wood was scarce, a fire was a real luxury. She sighed with pleasure as the stove's heat quickly drove the chill from her hands and body.

She took a moment, as she always did, to appreciate the simplicity of North's home. From the outside the non-descript building appeared to be a rustic, roughly hewn wood cabin, but inside it was a masterpiece of colour, warmth and texture. Brightly patterned scatter rugs dotted the gleaming pine wood floors, and the home's completely open living, dining and kitchen floor plan gave it a spacious feeling. On one end of the large room an immense forest green braided rug lay beneath a dark brown leather sofa and matching love seat. A scarred, rectangular wooden coffee table lay between them, and a well-worn dark green La-Z-Boy leather recliner stood to one side. Numerous occasional tables and lamps were strategically placed throughout the room. She loved everything about it.

"Whatcha got in the bag?" North asked, peering into the paper sack and breaking into her reverie.

"A light lunch. If you get a couple of plates and knives, I'll set it out. Here, you can cut up some of this bread." She reached into the bag and handed the loaf to him. "We'll need some butter, too."

While they ate North filled Andi in on his progress with the dog team. "I took six of them out on a short run this morning. I'm still having trouble with Juno. He wants to be a lead dog, but Kia definitely has better leader potential." He took another huge bite of thickly sliced bread slathered in butter. "We did have a good training session today, though. Did I ever tell you that I was hoping to be ready for the Alaskan Iditarod next March?"

Andi had just taken a big bite of bread and cheese, and shook her head. "Uh uh."

"Now I'm thinking I might train an extra year and run in the 1997 race which, by the way, is a very special race because it will be the twenty-fifth running. They're going to have a huge celebration, with lots of publicity and stuff. I figure I can wait two years to accomplish my life's dream of running in the 'Last Great Race'."

"I know you can do it, North," Andi beamed. "I've watched the way you interact with your team; it's as if they run just to please you. It's beautiful to watch you mushing."

"Yeah, I love it. But the beasts are starting to eat me out of house and home, now that they're all full grown. I'm gonna have to see if one of my brothers is going on a hunting trip soon. I need some fresh meat for these guys."

"That reminds me, I brought a little treat for the pup. How is she?"

"She's just absolutely wonderful." North beamed like a proud father. "You're gonna love her." He got up and poured two mugs of coffee, setting a cup in front of Andi before sitting down again. "Wait until you see her. She's ten weeks old now and growing like a weed. I'm going to get her used to a collar this week and hopefully be leash walking her by next weekend. She's a smart little thing, that's for sure."

"But why do you need another dog?" Andi asked. "You have a full team of twelve already. Isn't that enough?"

"Nope. I can have up to sixteen in harness for the Iditarod, and I need some extra dogs too in case any of them get sick or go lame. Some guys bring fifty dogs to the race, but I think I'll be happy with about twenty. Any more than that and I'll have to get another job just to feed them!" he laughed.

They sipped their steaming coffee in silence. Andi hadn't missed the fact that North remembered that she took her coffee black. She'd dated men in the past, not that her and North were *dating*, that didn't know how she drank her coffee after they'd been together a year.

"Have you picked out a name for the new pup?" she asked.

"I've been thinking about that. Her coat is staying pure white, which is very unusual for a Canadian Eskimo Dog. Maybe later she'll develop some markings, but right now she looks like a little snowflake. I thought I'd call her Qannik."

"Oh, that's beautiful!" Andi exclaimed. "What does it mean? Is it an Inuvialuktun word?"

"Yes, it means 'snowflake'. I think it suits her."

"Oh, it does!" Andi leaped from her chair, heading for the mountain of boots and parkas by the door. "Let's go see the dogs right now. I can't wait any longer!"

North led Andi out the cabin's back door. High mounds of snow on both sides of the path leading to the dog pen attested to an unusually snowy winter.

Andi was only half way down the path when her ears began to burn. A black shadow slid past her eyes, darkening the path before her for a fragment of a second. She was seized with dread and recoiled at the fetid, sweetish odor of death that drifted by her nose, dissipating as quickly as it had come. She stopped and lifted her eyes to search the cornflower blue sky; there wasn't even a hint of cloud to explain the shadow that had darkened her vision.

North continued down the path, apparently oblivious of his guest's distress. Unsettled and chilled, Andi pulled her prized qiviut scarf closer to her face, appreciating the warmth of the soft muskox wool. She took a few deep breaths of chilly air and tried to shake off her discomfort.

The vocal dogs were overjoyed to see them and yipped in excitement; foggy swirls circled around their heads as their hot breath quickly condensed in the cold air. Their magnificent thick coats were patterned in grey, black, red, brown, and white, and the excited canines raced and lunged in joy around their roomy enclosure, bushy tails curled high over their backs.

"It looks like they're happy to see you, Andi!" North shouted, a wide grin plastered on his handsome face. "Are you ready?"

"I'm ready, open the gate!" she called, pushing the last threads of her previous discomfort aside as they stepped into the compound. She tried in vain to greet each dog by name but soon lost track of the jostling bodies and swinging tails. She recognized Kia, Togo, Suka, Juno, Aleeka and Chinook, and greeted them by name, giving each a rub or scratch. The dogs bumped her affectionately and sometimes too enthusiastically. She fell to her knees once, laughing when Chica took the opportunity to stick her cold, wet nose in her face and give it a sassy lick.

"Okay, I give up. I've officially lost track of them again," Andi laughed. She looked up at North, her emerald eyes sparkling in the brilliant winter sunshine. "How do you keep them straight when they're moving all over the place like this?"

"Oh, it's easy. I've raised them all from pups and spent a lot of time with them. A few of them are quite similar, but they all have their own unique features and markings. See Duska over there?" he pointed to a dark grey dog. "She has a small black spot on her jaw line. And

Mika," he said, indicating a huge, light grey dog, "her coat is a little thicker and shinier than the others. But I think I'd know them just by their personalities, even if they all looked the same. Just like a mother can tell her identical twins apart."

He reached over the nearest dogs to a smaller female lingering behind them. "This one is Chance," he said, scratching the back of her alert ears. "She was the runt of her litter, but she has a big heart and I think she'll turn out just fine. She's one of my favourite girls," He stroked the shy animal's soft, sleek head.

North continued to greet each of the team and then with a small hand signal commanded them to lie down. Almost as a unit they dropped onto the packed snow. Panting in excitement, their hot breath billowed in clouds around their heads.

As he worked with the dogs, North explained his actions. "It's important that I establish authority over the team," he said, "and make them understand that I'm the leader of the pack – the 'top dog'. They have to respect me and accept my commands. Without that I'd just have a howling pack of wild, disobedient beasts."

"Well, you seem to be doing a great job."

"I'll teach you the basics of mushing sometime, if you like," North offered.

"I'd love that!"

"Should we go see Qannik now?"

"Sure. Where is she?" Andi looked around the large pen.

"Inside the kennel," North pointed to a long building forming one wall of the fenced enclosure. "It's been too cold to leave her outside lately. And she's not quite integrated into the pack yet either. I don't trust the others alone with her."

"I've been meaning to ask you, why aren't your dogs chained up separately like all the other sled dogs I see?"

"Well, I got these guys as pups, all around the same time. They grew up together, and so far they seem to respect each other. If they ever start fighting I'll have to chain them up, but until then they have the run of the place," North explained.

"Why don't you go on up to the house and I'll bring Qannik inside for a visit?"

"Sure, I'll meet you inside." Andi gave the nearest dogs a good-bye pat as she made her way to the gate. Snow crunched underfoot on the snowy pathway leading to the cabin, and she glanced around in trepidation. Her ears continued to burn from her earlier experience, and she was still chilled and a little unsettled. She looked forward to warming up by the fire.

A few minutes later North burst through the back door holding a squirming, panting white bundle. "Here she is! Qannik, say hello to Andi Nowak."

Andi held her arms out, eager to snuggle the wiggling pup. "Oh, North, she's beautiful!" Andi gushed. "And she *is* pure white. I think snowflake is a wonderful name for her."

"Hey, sweetheart," Andi crooned when North put the small dog into her arms. She held her close, murmuring, "You're just a little love, aren't you?" Andi was in heaven. She buried her nose in the soft white fur, breathing deeply of the unique scent that only puppies have. The ecstatic, squirming bundle frantically licked Andi's neck, face and hands.

"It looks like she loves you too," North laughed. "Enjoy her while you can, because in another few weeks she's going to join the pack and learn how to be a sled dog. No more babying her when that happens."

"Oh my God, North, she is absolutely beautiful. I just love her." Andi knelt on the floor playing with the rambunctious pup and doing her best to avoid Qannik's razor-sharp milk teeth.

North watched the duo from his favourite recliner, smiling indulgently when they upset a small end table and scattered books and magazines on the floor.

"Is she housebroken?" Andi asked, looking up at North through a veil of brown hair. With her cheeks flushed and hair in tangles, North thought she was the most beautiful woman he'd ever seen.

"No, so keep an eye on her. If it looks like she's gonna squat we have to get her outside ASAP."

Andi pulled a small dog biscuit from her pocket and offered it to the pup. Qannik eagerly grabbed the treat and curled up in front of the sofa to munch on it.

"Another coffee?" North asked, kicking down the footrest on his La-Z-Boy.

Andi glanced at the kitchen clock. She wanted to go to an AA Meeting that evening, but still had lots of time. "Sure, that'd be great. I had a bit of a run-in with Jim O'Neill this morning," she said, making herself at home while North poured their coffee. She stretched out on the well-worn sofa, her head resting on its padded armrest. Waves of thick, shiny hair curled over the side.

North set Andi's mug on the coffee table in front of her and slumped back into his ancient recliner. "What happened?"

"Jim and Hank were an hour late getting back from the Pivot Lake supply run yesterday afternoon," she explained. "I asked Jim to meet me at my office this morning and the jerk was an hour late. When he finally showed up he had a massive hang over."

"I wonder why?" North rolled her eyes, making them both laugh. "I think he earned it, by the looks of him and Jessica last night."

Andi sat up, and reached for her coffee. "Oh, and Jessica didn't show up for work this morning either. She called Ayame about midnight and begged her to take her shift this morning. Ayame didn't have the heart to refuse."

"So what did you learn from Jim?"

"Well, he finally admitted that they were late because they were chasing after caribou with the Twin Otter so Hank could get a good look at them. Joy riding for an hour! I still can't believe it." Andi shook her head. "But before I got the truth out of him he got really pissed at me, and he actually frightened me a little. Not to worry though," she added quickly, seeing the flash of anger in North's dark brown eyes. "I stood up to him and he backed down right away. I won't take that kind of shit from anyone, not even our most illustrious Captain O'Neill. We squared things up and I don't think he'll be taking any more joy rides."

"Jesus, Andi, you know he has a temper," North muttered, his voice edged with concern. "If he ever lifts a finger to you, I'll kill him."

"My hero!" Andi laughed. "Don't get yourself worked up. It's over with, or at least I hope it is." She hesitated a moment before she continued. Her ears still tingled, and she unconsciously tugged on the left one. "Something just doesn't add up, though. I have a feeling he's lying to me, North. He said Hank had never seen caribou before, but Hank's been flying for us for about two months now. It seems to me that almost every time I've been in the air we see caribou, so how could it be that Hank has spent hours and hours flying around the area and has never seen a herd before? I think Jim is hiding something, and I think Jessica knows what's going on."

"Why do you say that?"

"She seemed a bit hesitant when I asked her if other Pivot Lake trips were late returning. And my ears were tingling when I talked to her about it. Remember I told you about my suspicious ears?" Andi's perfectly shaped eyebrows arched over her emerald eyes.

"Right, I remember. But they're still pretty nice ears, tingly or not," he replied with a lazy, crooked smile.

It took a huge amount of effort for Andi to tear her eyes away from North's lips and she did her best to ignore the sudden rush of heat flashing across her belly. She drained the last drops of coffee from her cup, hoping to disguise the pink flush she knew had risen to her cheeks. "Well, I'd better get going. Things to do, people to see, you know."

"Hey, why don't you stay for dinner?" North asked eagerly. He rose in one smooth move from the recliner. "I have some nice muskox steaks in the freezer. It'll be great to have some company tonight." He headed toward the fridge.

"Oh. Thanks for the invite, but I can't tonight. I really have to get going."

North's face dropped. "Oh. That's too bad. Are you sure I can't change your mind?"

"Sorry. I'm sure. Gotta run. But thanks for the fun afternoon. I enjoyed myself and I *loved* seeing the dogs again. And meeting little Qannik, too." She bent to stroke the pup's soft head. Qannik was fast asleep beside the sofa, curled up into a fat, fluffy white ball. "You won't be able to keep me away now," she laughed.

"That's all right with me," North grinned. "I'll run out and start your car. It should warm up for a few minutes." He slipped on his boots and opened the front door.

"Thanks." Andi gazed longingly at North's retreating back. By the time she got her various pieces of outdoor gear on, he was back.

"How about we take the team out next Sunday if the weather is good?" he suggested, stomping snow from his boots. "I'll teach you a few things about mushing."

"Oh, that would be fabulous," Andi agreed eagerly. "You have no idea how much I want to have a ride on a dog sled. It will be so much fun."

"Good. It's a date then."

"Should I bring a lunch?" she asked hesitantly. "Will we be out long enough?"

"Sure, why don't you do that," North grinned. "And I'll bring a thermos of coffee. We'll have a picnic Arctic style."

"Sounds great. I'll talk to you sometime this week then." Andi stood in the open doorway and waved good-bye but realized what she really wanted to do was cover this very charming man's face with kisses.

"And stay away from O'Neill," North warned. "That man is bad news."

He stood on the step until Andi's car disappeared from view, wondering why his heart was beating a little faster than normal.

FIVE

When Andi arrived home she found her housemate's old, beat up Chevy pickup parked by the front door. It was unusual for Coco Montague to be home on a Saturday night; Tuktu Aviation's twenty-year old, red-headed ticket agent loved to party but thankfully she usually did it elsewhere. In spite of that, Andi truly liked the young woman and enjoyed her effervescent personality.

She opened the front door and stepped into the large main-level foyer she shared with Coco. Andi lived on the second floor of the house and Coco rented a smaller suite on the main level.

As the can of chicken noodle soup that constituted dinner heated on the stove, Andi thought about the AA meeting she would attend that evening. The meetings were a mixed blessing; they made her confront her sorrow, fears and addiction, but they also left her feeling drained and immensely sad.

After quickly downing a bowl of soup, Andi began her usual pre-meeting routine. She pulled a photo album from the bookshelf in the living room and sat down on the sofa. Steeling herself both mentally and physically, she opened the cover.

The first page of the album held only one photo – a picture of Andi's newborn baby girl nestled safely in her arms. Andi gazed sadly at her own beaming face and knew that the day Natalie had been born had been the happiest day of her life. It was the day her life had become complete – October 25, 1986.

Her throat burned and tears welled in her eyes. A phantom hand clenched her aching heart. "My baby girl," she whispered, tears blurring the photo before her.

She slowly turned the pages of the album, each one holding a memory more painful than the last. Natalie was in every photo, often with her proud and doting mother or father at her side. She reverently traced the outline of Natalie's face, trying to remember the feel of her soft skin. Six years after her child's death, Andi couldn't remember the sound of her voice, or the smell of her baby-fine hair. Her senses had betrayed her, just as life itself had betrayed her.

She'd been only twenty-two years old when she'd moved to Yellowknife, situated on the shores of Great Slave Lake in the Northwest Territories. Adventurous and eager to grab the world by the tail, she had fallen hard for a young, charismatic geologist named Greg Mountford. Their courtship had been swift, and they soon swore their deep and undying love. Ten months later they were married in a small civil ceremony. They agreed that only one thing could make their perfect life complete – a baby. And so it was that little Natalie was born a year later.

Life doesn't always go as planned, though. When their beautiful child was just three years old, the new parents' happiness was shattered. A speeding truck and an icy road claimed the life of their beloved daughter, redirecting the path of three lives forever.

Six years later, sitting alone in a quickly darkening room, Andi's stomach clenched as she relived the pain of those first indescribable days following her child's death. It had been a debilitating pain – a pain so intense that she had flirted with the idea of taking her own life so she could join her child in everlasting life-after-death.

Andi and Greg did all the right things after their daughter's death. They attended grief counselling, marriage counselling and even took a holiday. Well-meaning family and friends told them that 'time heals all wounds', or 'everything happens for a reason'. Sometimes she had felt like slapping their suitably sorrowful faces.

Greg buried himself in his work and Andi numbed her pain with alcohol, but in the end nothing could save a shattered marriage.

Now, six years later, Andi's AA sponsor encouraged her to vocalize. "Open up your heart and share your fears and feelings," he urged. "Share your pain. Shout out your demons and banish them."

But how does one describe the unbearable pain of losing a child? After two years of attending the meetings, Andi still couldn't find the right words to explain that which cannot be described. And she was still very, very angry at the world.

Dragging her thoughts from the unhappy memories, she glanced at her watch and saw it was time to head to Inuvik's landmark Igloo Church where Alcoholics Anonymous meetings were held every Wednesday and Saturday evening. She absentmindedly thumbed the ring on her finger, tracing the triangle in the circle.

"God grant me the strength to go on," she prayed as she drove through the streets on a dark Arctic night.

SIX

"Okay, people, now that we're all here, grab a coffee and let's get this meeting started." As usual, Paul White was chairing Tuktu Aviation's regular Monday morning management meeting and he was eager to get underway. Jessica's fancy espresso machine gave one final shudder and The Princess picked up her dainty froth-topped cup.

Gathered with Andi and Paul in the Dispatch Centre's rather shabby coffee room were Tuktu Aviation's management team: Steve Mitchell, Chief Pilot; Ken Thomas, Chief Engineer; Jessica Hartman, Chief Dispatcher, and Bob Hart, Medevac Program Director.

"We had a good week," Paul began. He was a solid, compact man, and always in motion. Even in Inuvik, high above the Arctic Circle, Paul White always wore a business suit to the office. His round, unlined face bore a perpetual smile, yet he carried an unmistakable air of authority. Only his thinning hair hinted that he might be approaching middle age. "Anything unusual happening from the operational end of things?" he asked, his quick, dark eyes sparkling behind silver-framed glasses. He glanced around the room, making eye contact with everyone present.

"Nothing from my end," Steve confirmed with a smile and small shake of his well-groomed grey head. The likeable Chief Pilot was a thin, middle-aged man, whose wife still lived in Victoria, on Vancouver Island. Steve was an old friend of Paul's, and was doing him a favour by filling the suddenly-vacated Chief Pilot's position after his predecessor had a rather unfortunate incident involving alcohol.

"Nope. Everything's cool," Jessica offered airily. How her

slightly fleshy body still managed to look firm and toned at almost thirty years of age was a constant source of mystery and aggravation to Andi, who had to work hard at keeping fit. Wearing ragged, torn blue jeans, Jessica sat sideways in a ratty old club chair, her long legs draped over its threadbare arm. A cloud of thick blond hair fell over her shoulder.

"Andi?" Paul asked, tapping his pen on the notebook he balanced on his knees. "Do you have anything for us?"

"Not much. We weren't extremely busy last week so there were no scheduling problems, and I don't foresee any this week." She glanced at the notes she had made prior to the meeting. She'd thought about mentioning Jim's Twin Otter joyride but had decided against it. She was quite sure that O'Neill had received her message and wouldn't be taking any more unauthorized sightseeing tours with company aircraft. She would deal with his bad attitude herself.

"There *is* one thing I think we should talk about though," she said. "You've all heard about the new kimberlite pipe they found out at Pivot Lake?" She glanced around the small room. Everyone, with the exception of Jessica, nodded. The Princess's perpetual pout was evidently unshakable. "I think this could mean more flying for us if we get on it right away. You know the manager out there, don't you Paul?"

"I sure do, but what about scheduling? We're already doing one, and sometimes two supply runs to Pivot Lake every day, aren't we?"

Andi nodded. "Yes, but if we can get enough additional work from the mine, I think it would make sense to dry lease another Twin Otter. I was talking to Charlie Harper in Yellowknife last week and he mentioned that he has one available. He doesn't want to lease it out to us, though, unless we provide the flight crew, fuel and maintenance on it.

Paul nodded his approval. "Okay, that sounds like a damn good plan. Do you have any problems with crewing another Twin Otter full-time, Steve?"

"Well, we've got a few guys who have booked holidays, but

we're all caught up on training and PPC rides," Steve replied, referring to the Transport Canada Pilot Proficiency Check rides which were conducted regularly on each aircraft type. "It shouldn't be too much of a problem to put an extra crew together, but we might have to cancel some holiday time. That might not go over very well." He frowned, making the creases in his weathered face even deeper.

"All right, we'll work through all that. This is good stuff, folks. I'll call my contact at the mine today and see if I can set up some more work. Bob, is there anything from your end?" Paul kept up his agenda and the meeting's momentum.

"Yup. Well." Bob Hart drew out each word with a characteristic sigh as he adjusted his considerable bulk in a decrepit armchair and prepared to update the managers on his pride and joy – the company's medical evacuation program. He spoke slowly, choosing each word carefully while he stroked his short, dark beard. Bob was dressed in his standard off-duty ensemble of faded, loose scrubs. His alert hazel eyes sparkled. "It was a fairly quiet week on the medevac side of things. We had only three trips, and they were uncomplicated pickups from Aklavik and Fort McPherson for the Inuvik hospital." The stocky pilot, in addition to being in charge of the company's medevac program, also captained the medevac-dedicated aircraft. He was a highly experienced bush pilot and could fly any of the aircraft in Tuktu's fleet, and fly them well.

Bob opened his mouth to commence what would likely be a long, drawn-out narrative when Paul jumped in again, cutting him off. "Great. Thanks, Bob." Paul knew all too well the pilot's penchant for rambling stories that were a constant source of wonder to the company's newly-hired pilots, but had little relevance to the issues at hand.

"Ken?" Paul queried, raising his eyebrows at the Chief Engineer. "Anything on your end?"

Andi's old friend Ken Thomas was a serious and dedicated individual. He was a good match for his wife, Margo, who was a fun-loving and carefree spirit; they balanced each other well. Ken took his responsibility as Chief Engineer seriously, and his black brows knit together in concentration as he replied to Paul's query. "We're going to need the 1040 for a few days next week – it's due for a major service."

The Piper T-1040 medevac-dedicated aircraft was a small, fast twin-engine turbo-prop and was equipped with modern, top of the line medical equipment. A two-pilot flight-crew was on call around the clock to ensure rapid response time. At considerable expense, Paul had transformed the Piper's passenger cabin into a mobile clinic, ensuring appropriate care for medical patients. Most of the passenger seats had been removed and a stretcher was secured into the existing seat tracks. The pressurized aircraft was equipped with basic medical equipment, including a respirator, cardiac monitor, defibrillator and various pumps. Since a great majority of their northern medevac patients were expectant mothers, the aircraft was also equipped with an isolette; the incubator provided controlled temperature, humidity and oxygen for premature infants. Even the flight crew had some paramedical training, although a hospital nurse normally accompanied all Medevacs.

"Okay, but give me two-day's notice please, Ken," Bob interjected. "I'll have to call the hospital and let them know we'll be out of service. That will work well for me though; I'll be able to run the flight crew's first aid refresher course then."

"Good," Paul stood up, signaling the meeting's end. "Okay, I guess that's it folks. Andi, could you call Harper and see if that Twin Otter is still available for lease? Tell him we may need it, and we'll let him know for sure within the next day or two. Ask him if he can call us first if anyone else approaches him for it."

"There's just one more thing," Ken smiled sheepishly. "Margo wanted me to remind everyone that we're having a TGIF at our place on Friday. And bring beer."

"Yay!" Andi, Steve and Paul cheered in unison. Bob nodded enthusiastically while Princess Jessica rolled her eyes, managing to look bored and disgusted at the same time.

"I'll let you all know how I make out with the diamond mine," Paul called as he ran down the stairs, leaving the managers to chat over coffee before returning to their respective offices and duties.

Andi had just sat down at her desk when Ayame stuck her head through the doorway. "Call for you on line two. It's Coco Chanel, and she sounds sick."

Andi glanced at her watch; it was past nine o'clock. Their young ticket agent, fondly referred to as 'Coco Chanel' because of her obsession with clothes and fashion, should have been at the airport terminal by now to work the 10 am scheduled flight to Tuktoyaktuk. "Good morning, Coco. How are you?"

"Not too good. I think I've got the flu or something. I feel rotten," Coco's voice was weak and tentative. "I'm, I'm sorry, but I can't come in today."

"Okay. Well no problem. I'll run over and work the ticket counter this morning. Just look after yourself and get well. Give me a call later this afternoon and let me know if I have to get someone to cover for you tomorrow."

"Yeah, all right. Thanks a lot." The phone went dead in Andi's hand before she could said good-bye.

She walked back into dispatch and picked up the passenger reservation sheet for the Tuktoyaktuk flight. There were only seven names; it wouldn't be hard to get the flight away on time. "Ayame, I have to go work the Tuk flight. Coco's got the flu or something. Come to think about it, I don't think she even went out much this weekend."

"Well, I hope she keeps it at home if it *is* the flu," Ayame grumbled. "Here." She reached inside her monstrous purse. "Boil some water and make yourself some tea." She passed a small plastic bag stuffed with greenish-brown leaves and flower petals to Andi.

Andi opened the bag and sniffed cautiously before turning her nose away will an inelegant snort. "What is this stuff? It smells gross. Exactly why do I need it?"

"It's an ancient Japanese herbal tea remedy to ward off colds and flu. It's very good for you."

"It smells bad enough to scare me off, too." She frowned and passed the bag back to Ayame "Thanks, but no thanks. Are you sure it's even legal?"

Ayame threw her dark head back and laughed. "Of course it's legal. You know me better than that!" She lowered her voice. "I'm not The Princess, you know."

"Did you have a chance to look at the Pivot Lake trip times from last week?" Andi whispered, leaning her head closer to the dispatcher.

"Yes, and we need to look at it together, but not right now." Ayame's black ponytail tweaked towards the coffee room, where Jessica and the rest of the team were still talking over coffee.

"Gotcha. I'll be back after I get the Tuk flight away. Thanks, Ayame."

Andi put on her coat and walked out into the pale morning light. Within an hour the Tuktoyaktuk flight had departed and she was back in her office, eager to hear what Ayame had unearthed about the Pivot Lake flights. Luckily, Jessica had left for an early lunch and the two women had the office to themselves. "So what did you find out?"

"Well, I went over the trips from the past month, and about seventy-five per cent of the Pivot Lake runs have taken four hours or more to complete." Ayame scowled and shook her head. "I don't know why I didn't notice this before."

"Don't worry about it. It's not your fault; Jessica usually works the late shift. What else can you tell me?"

"Well, interestingly enough, all of the late trips were flown by our favourite crew – Captain Jim and Hank. It's all right here." With a flourish, Ayame pulled a notepad from her purse and opened it up on the desk. Lines of neatly written data filled the page.

Andi leaned closed. Ayame had compiled a concise summary of trip statistics including dates, trip times, and flight crew names.

"I've itemized all of the Pivot Lake trips from the past thirty days. The ones with a red tick beside them are the ones that have been late returning."

Andi pondered over the list for a few minutes. "Good work, Ayame, this is very interesting. When's the next trip to the mine?"

"Departing at thirteen hundred hours today, and Jim and Hank are flying it."

"You know what? I think I'll just stick around this afternoon and see what happens," Andi said. "Can you do another favour for me, please?"

"Sure thing. What?"

"Could you look back about two months and see if you can find out if Jim's Pivot Lake trips have been consistently late? Would you have time to do that?"

"No problem, I'd love to. This has become quite intriguing."

"Thanks. And mum's the word, eh?"

Ayame scowled for a second then chuckled. Her curved, black brows knit together, forming an almost solid black slash over her flashing eyes. "Hey! Some credit here, please."

The remainder of Andi's day passed swiftly. She called Charlie Harper in Yellowknife and confirmed that his Twin Otter was still available for lease, and he promised he'd hold it for them for the next few days. Then she caught up on paperwork, and worked the air terminal ticket agent desk for afternoon scheduled flights to Tuktoyaktuk and Paulatuk.

By the time she returned to the dispatch office just past four that afternoon, Ayame had left for the day. Andi discreetly glanced at the aircraft trip register sitting in front of Jessica. The log noted that the Pivot Lake flight had been thirty minutes late leaving Inuvik. Andi did a quick mental calculation: if the crew flew a three-hour round trip, they should be back around 4:30.

She spent fifteen minutes shuffling paper on her desk, then told Jessica she was leaving for the day; she didn't want her to forewarn O'Neill that she'd be watching for his arrival.

Since the Twin Otter would be left at the maintenance hangar when it returned, Andi decided to wait upstairs in the pilot's lounge located on its mezzanine level. She drove to the hangar and slipped inside undetected, then silently climbed the steep wooden stairs to the lounge where she settled down to wait with a stale, lukewarm cup of coffee and a *Wings* magazine.

At 5:40 pm – over an hour beyond its three-hour allotted trip window – Andi detected the distinctive whine of a twin turbo-prop aircraft. She threw her Styrofoam cup into the trash can and began suiting up to meet the frigid outside air. She was furious, and had full intentions of confronting Captain Jim about his tardy return.

Most of the maintenance crew had already left for the day, and the hangar was dim and quiet. Her footsteps echoed in its vast interior. She waited just inside the pedestrian door that opened to the airside tarmac until the Twin Otter taxied up to the hangar. Once the engines and props were quiet, she stepped out of the building and strode purposefully through the waning light toward the aircraft. Captain Jim O'Neill had just climbed down from the cockpit, and Andi felt a rush of gratification when she saw his jaw drop.

"What the hell are you doing here?" he barked, dropping his bulky, black flight bag onto the frosty tarmac.

"I'm here to find out why you're over an hour late returning from Pivot Lake again," Andi replied, keeping her voice calm and facial features composed. It was a struggle, considering the anger than seethed within her, inflamed by O'Neill's disrespectful and aggressive attitude.

"Why don't you just leave me alone, Nowak?" Jim shouted. "For Christ's sake, go and spend your time in your little office and leave the flying to me, all right?"

"Why are you late, Jim?"

"Shit happens."

"Not a good enough reason. Why are you late, Jim?"

"Will you just leave it alone, Andi!" he bellowed, taking a few menacing steps toward her. "I have no intention of going over every minute of my day with you, so piss off!"

"This flight was due back over an hour ago. If you will recall our discussion a few days ago, I told you *then* that it is essential that the Pivot Lake trips be kept on schedule. Now for the last time, where the hell have you been, Jim? And if you tell me to piss off again you'll find yourself suspended, O'Neill."

Andi and Jim stood nose-to-nose in the stingingly cold air. A thick layer of cloud had blown in on a strong north wind, darkening the already dim day and bringing with it the chance of more snow.

Hank Brister was staying clear of the sparring couple, quietly going about the business of chocking the wheels, tenting the engines and securing the propellers of the Twin Otter.

"Fuck off, Andi!" Jim bellowed.

Andi smelled his sour breath as her eyes traced the spiderweb of thin, red lines on his cheeks. A vein pulsed angrily along his right temple.

"Leave this alone or you'll end up in trouble," he snarled.

"Okay, that's it!" Andi snapped. She'd finally had enough. "Captain James O'Neill," she barked, "you are suspended from duty. As of this minute, you are off the flight roster." She stepped back a couple of feet and took a shaky breath. "I'll be reporting this incident to Steve and Paul, and if I have any say in it you'll never fly for us again! I'm not putting up with your bullshit any longer."

Without waiting for a response, Andi turned and strode toward the hangar and around the outside corner of the metal building before disappearing from O'Neill's line of sight. Her hand shook as she punched in the four-digit code to open the security gate. The metal gate slammed behind her as she ran toward her car, her limbs weak and boots heavy. Only when she was safely ensconced in the Land Yacht could she relax enough to draw a deep, ragged breath. The fine, moist hair in her nostrils grew heavy with frost and the icy air made her lungs burn.

"You've really done it now," she muttered. A whisper of fear replaced her anger as she turned the key in the old Ford's ignition.

SEVEN

Andi sped home through the rising winds and blowing snow of an approaching winter storm. Hot ribbons of pain ripped through her stomach, a lingering and unwelcome reminder of her confrontation with Jim O'Neill.

As she unlocked the front door to her house, she realized that Coco hadn't called her back. There were no lights on in the girl's suite, but her truck was in the driveway. Andi tapped on Coco's door, waited a few moments, and then knocked harder. "Coco! Are you there? She heard shuffling behind the closed door, then a weak voice.

"Andi, I'm still sick, and I need to rest. I won't be able to go to work tomorrow."

"You don't sound too good, Coco. Can I come in?"

"*No.* Just leave me alone. I'll ... I'll be fine."

"Have you had anything to eat today? Have you seen a doctor? Do you have the flu?" Andi persisted, vaguely aware that her quirky ears were burning.

"I'm not hungry. I just want to go back to bed."

"Well, okay then. But if you need anything just call me. Good night."

On leaden legs, Andi climbed the single flight of stairs to her suite; her ordeal with O'Neill had left her exhausted and unsettled. Coco's behavior bothered her too; it was entirely out of character. The vivacious young woman normally loved to be pampered, and in the past had let Andi fuss over her when she'd had even a simple cold. Andi made a mental note to check in on her young friend before she left for work in the morning.

She was sitting at her kitchen table a few minutes later, dejectedly picking at a plate of leftover pasta, when her phone rang. She answered it reluctantly.

"Andi, its Paul. I have great news! I talked to my buddy over at the diamond mine and he says the extra flying is all ours. I'm meeting with him tomorrow to draw up a new contract, so it looks like we'll need that extra Twin Otter for sure. I want you to get working on it first thing tomorrow morning."

"That's wonderful," Andi said wearily.

"Yeah, it sure is. But, uh, you don't sound too happy. What's up?"

"I'm just tired I guess, but I'm glad you called. There's something I want to talk to you about."

"What's that?"

"Well, it's about Jim O'Neill. He's been completely disregarding our scheduling requirements. I had a talk with him about it a week ago and thought that would solve the problem, but it didn't. He and I had a bit of a run in over it this afternoon. I've, uh, I've suspended him."

"Ouch. That's serious. Did you talk to Steve about this yet?"

"No, it was a situational thing and I just acted on it. Jim and Hank were really late getting back from Pivot Lake again today. This happens routinely, Paul, not just once in a while. So I met them when they landed and O'Neill and I had a run in. I may have acted on the spur of the moment, but he was being a real ass. And he has no plausible reason for being late."

"Okay. Well, let's get together with Steve tomorrow morning and talk about this. He's the Chief Pilot and we need his input. He's really the one who should make the call, but as far as I can see we can't afford to suspend Jim right now, Andi. Not if we're bringing another Twin Otter on line."

"Yeah, I know. You're likely right," Andi sighed heavily. "I'll see you tomorrow morning. Should I set up a nine o'clock meeting?"

"Yup, that works for me. And Andi? Don't worry about it too much. We all know what Jim O'Neill is like. We'll work something out."

"Thanks, Paul. I appreciate your support."

Andi called Tuktu's Chief Pilot and relayed Paul's request for a nine o'clock meeting the next morning. Without going into too much detail, she outlined her confrontation with O'Neill and her subsequent decision to suspend him – a decision that was now looking like it would be overturned. Steve agreed to call Jim and have him attend the meeting. Andi looked forward to hearing Jim's version of the events.

After her customary lavender-scented bubble bath, she settled down in bed with a book. Shortly before midnight she turned out her reading light and tugged the heavy eiderdown over her shoulders.

Outside, the wind had died and snow was softly falling, blanketing the neighbourhood in a cocoon of silence. In the house, even the hot water radiators had given up their creaking and groaning for the night. Andi closed her eyes, sighed contentedly and welcomed the silence.

In those few minutes of semi-consciousness between awareness and sleep, her mind registered a faint, unfamiliar sound. Her eyes snapped open, her heart drumming against her ribs. She stared unseeing into the total blackness of her bedroom and held her breath, listening intently.

There it was again, louder this time, coming from the floor below.

Fully awake now, Andi knew what had woken her. She could clearly hear the heart-wrenching sobs drifting up from Coco's suite. She snapped on the light, stuffed her feet into slippers and reached for her housecoat. Twenty seconds later she was pounding on Coco's door. "Coco, I can hear you. Let me in right now."

She heard a faint shuffling, then silence.

"Open up, Coco. I know you're there."

"Leave me alone."

"I'm not leaving until you open this door, so do it *now*."

After a long pause the deadbolt slid back and the door inched open. Dim light reached from the back of the suite, veiling Coco Montague in shadows.

Andi nudged the door open and stepped into the room. Coco turned away, but not before Andi saw a glimpse of her face.

"Oh, my God, Coco! What happened to you?" Andi cried. She flipped on a small table lamp.

Coco slowly turned into the light. What had so recently been a beautiful visage was now almost unrecognizable amid a multitude of cuts and darkening bruises. Silent tears ran from the young woman's eyes, one of which was swollen shut and ringed in shades of black and purple. Her vibrant red curls were matted and dull.

Deep, gut-wrenching sobs rose from within the damaged young body. Andi gently wrapped her arms around Coco's shivering frame and guided her to the sofa. Beneath her pink robe, Coco felt fragile and weightless.

A long gash marred her left cheek and her lips were cut and swollen. Several smaller abrasions and bruises dotted her forehead and cheeks. Her face resembled a boxer's battered mug.

"Andi, I'm ... I'm *so scared.*" Coco whispered "He hurt me so bad." Her entire body quaked uncontrollably. "*I want to die.*"

Andi slid closer to the girl and wrapped her arms around her thin shoulders, holding her tightly until the trembling subsided.

"Who did this to you, Coco? I'm going to call the police right now. I think you need to see a doctor too." Andi's hands shook with the effort it took to control her sudden rage. She wanted to lash out at whoever had hurt her friend, but knew she had to stay calm and take charge of the situation.

"NO! No cops. You can't call them. I won't let you." Coco held tightly to both of Andi's hands.

"But you can't let him get away with this. Can you tell me what happened? Who did this to you, sweetheart?"

Coco turned her head away, eyes to the floor. "It doesn't matter. I don't want to talk about it."

"You've been beaten," Andi croaked, the sheer effort it took to contain her anger tightening her throat until it ached. "You *can't* let the scumbag who did this to you just walk away," she said slowly, enunciating each word clearly. "Talk to me, Coco. *Who did this?*"

Coco shook her head, a mere hint of movement. "It's too embarrassing," she whispered. She raised her arm, swiping the soft pink material of her robe across her nose

"You should call the police and see a doctor," Andi repeated, "but I can't force you to."

"No police." Coco said firmly. "And I don't need a doctor."

"It's your choice, but can I at least clean up those cuts?"

Coco nodded weakly.

Fifteen minutes later Andi's first-aid was done. She gently applied the last Band-Aid to Coco's cheek, having swabbed and applied antiseptic to the numerous cuts. Band-Aids now covered the worst of the wounds. "Have you taken any pain killers?"

"Yea, I've been taking Tylenol," Coco nodded. "I could use a cup of tea, though, if you'd like to make some for us."

"Sure thing, kid. I could use a cup too."

A few minutes later over steaming cups of herbal tea Coco murmured, "I guess you want to know what happened."

"Only if you want to tell me."

"I'm so ashamed," Coco sobbed. She leaned forward to put her cup on the coffee table, tea sloshing over the rim. Then, for the first time since Andi's arrival, she looked her friend directly in the eye. "Do you understand? I'm just so damn ashamed. What happened was ... *is* entirely my fault."

"No, it isn't," Andi said gently. "Whatever it is that happened, you don't need to feel shame. You were beaten."

Coco shook her head vehemently, lank red curls flying around her head. "But you don't understand! I was so … so," she stammered haltingly, "I was *so drunk*. I barely know myself what happened." Tears ran down her cheeks, staining the plush pink robe.

Andi searched for a box of tissues and pushed several into Coco's hands. "There now, no more tears," she said gently. "Start at the beginning and tell me what happened."

Coco shuddered and took a deep breath. She spoke so softly, Andi had to lean toward her to catch her words. "Last weekend I met a really cute guy at the bar, and then he called me and said he wanted to go out with me on Saturday night."

"Who is he?" Andi asked. "Had you ever seen him before?"

"No," Coco sniffed. "I don't think any of us knew him. His name is Chad something. He told me he was new in town and that he was lonely and that he thought I was so pretty." She blew her nose loudly. "He seemed pretty nice the first time I met him."

"So what happened?"

"He picked me up in his truck. It was a rental, I think."

"Where did you go?"

"Well, first we went to the Rail for a couple of drinks. Then we went to the Zoo with a bunch of his friends, and I guess we closed it down. I can't really remember much except I know we were doing shooters and tequila pops." She closed her eyes for a moment, another shudder raking over her body. "I was so pissed, Andi," she whispered.

"And then what happened after you left the Zoo?"

Coco didn't answer for a minute, then "We went for a drive I think."

Andi frowned. "It was minus forty-five on Saturday night. Where would you have gone for a drive?"

"I don't know! I just remember moving, driving for a while. And then I ... I felt like I was going to get sick so I asked him to stop and I puked by the side of the road." Coco rocked slowly, her arms crossed tightly, clutching her stomach.

"What happened after you got back in the truck?"

"I must have fallen asleep. Passed out, I guess. The next thing I remember is lying on a bed and Chad was taking my clothes off. I told him ... I told him to stop, but he wouldn't. He just wouldn't stop!" she sobbed. "And I was too drunk. I could barely move I was so drunk." Coco began to weep, fat tears rolling from her sorrowful blue eyes. "And then, then he started hitting me. He just hit me and hit me and hit me." She covered her face with trembling hands, sobbing uncontrollably.

"Shhh, you're safe now, Coco. Take deep breaths." Andi tried her best to sooth the distraught girl. After a few minutes the outburst of tears subsided; she wiped her eyes and blew her nose.

"Did he rape you?" Andi asked softly.

Coco's red head nodded slowly, and a torrent of fresh tears erupted. Andi held her tightly but could think of nothing to say to console her friend.

A long time later, Coco's tears stopped flowing and she blew her nose again. "I'm okay. Just a little sore," she whimpered. "And I really don't want to go to the police. They'll just say it was my fault anyway. I've heard how it works."

"Coco, what happened to you is a date-rape. You said 'no', and he didn't listen. It doesn't matter if you were drunk or not, he had no right to have sex with you against your will."

"I just want to forget all about it," Coco wailed.

"Listen to me," Andi beseeched, reaching for Coco's hand. "At least get checked for sexually transmitted diseases. You have no idea what this guy may have given you."

"I will. But not right now."

"Don't wait too long. And please, please think about laying charges against him, okay?"

"No, I won't do it. And you can't tell anyone else about this. I just want to forget about it and get on with my life. And hopefully I'll never see him again. I've had it with the Zoo, too. I'm never, *ever* going into that shit-hole bar again."

Andi nodded consolingly. "So how did you get home?"

"He shoved me into the truck and drove me home. And he told me to keep my mouth shut or I'd be sorry. Oh, Andi, promise me you won't tell anyone," Coco begged.

"I won't. And don't worry about coming to work this week. I'll get someone to cover for you. If anyone asks, I'll tell them you have a vicious, contagious flu, okay?"

A smile flickered over Coco's bruised lips. "All right. Thanks."

Andi stood stiffly. "We'd better get some sleep. If you need anything just call me." She headed to the door, then stopped in mid-stride. She turned to gaze at Coco, a frown on her brow. "I have just one more question. Are you on the pill? Is there any chance you may have gotten pregnant?"

"No," Coco said vehemently, shaking her head "There's no chance I'm pregnant. I'm on the pill."

"Good. Well, goodnight then. Try to get some sleep." Andi heard the bolt click behind her.

With a heavy heart she walked up the stairs to her suite, wondering if her young friend would ever fully recover from her ordeal, and who her savage attacker really was.

EIGHT

Andi arrived at work early the next morning short on sleep and feeling miserable. Jim O'Neill was leaning over Jessica's shoulder, the two engaged in an intense, hushed conversation.

"Good morning," Andi said curtly. They both threw her a foul look. Andi closed the door to her office and made her phone call to Charlie Harper.

Steve and Paul arrived exactly at 9:00, and the meeting went much as Andi had anticipated.

"She's been on my case for nothing," O'Neill claimed in self-defense when confronted with Andi's accusations. "Yeah, we were a little late from a couple of the trips, but it's nothing to worry about. You know what it's like, Steve," Jim chuckled. "Things don't always go according to the dispatchers schedule."

"Right, but nevertheless, Jim, Andi tells us that you've been swearing at her and threatening her. We can't have that kind of behavior." Steve Mitchell was trying to placate both Andi and his beloved Captain Jim, but it was blatantly evident where his loyalty lay.

"Yeah, yeah. Whatever. I'm sorry." Jim threw Andi a begrudging apology.

Jessica had wandered into the coffee room and lingered near her espresso machine. Andi caught her eye and pointed her back to the Dispatch office. Jessica took her time returning to her desk, executing a slow sashay that made her blond hair swing with each step.

"Thank you, Jim," Andi replied calmly. "I accept your apology, but I'm still putting a formal letter of reprimand in your personnel file.

I'll send both of you a copy," she said, nodding at Jim and Steve.

"Okay, then. That's settled," Paul said, a tight smile on his face. "Let's put this behind us and move on. We have good news today. I've met with the Pivot Lake Diamond Mine people and convinced them to give us all of their additional flying. We're drawing up a new contract as we speak and it should be signed by this time tomorrow.

"Steve," Paul continued, "We'll need a third dedicated Twin Otter crew as of this weekend. Andi called Charlie Harper in Yellowknife this morning, and he's going to have an aircraft ready for us on Monday. Andi, make sure you book a couple of seats on the Sunday flight to Yellowknife for the ferry crew," Paul ordered.

"Oh, boy," Steve said dismally.

"What?" Paul asked.

"I checked the holiday schedule this morning and the guys I want to put on the new Twin were both booked out for two weeks holidays, starting this weekend."

"Well, cancel their time off. We can't do anything about it and I'm not going to let holidays screw up our flying. Actually, let's cancel all flight crew holidays until we get a better handle on our flying commitments for the next couple of months. Andi, can you draft up a memo and send it out to the flight crew, please?"

Andi suppressed a groan. The crew would just *love* receiving another 'Wicked Witch of the North' memo from her. "Shouldn't Steve do that?" she ventured "He *is* the Chief Pilot."

"No, no. You go ahead. Get it done this morning. We don't have any time to waste."

Andi nodded resignedly.

"Okay, then, thanks people. I have to run." Paul sprang from his chair, ending the meeting. Steve and Jim followed him down the stairs, but not before O'Neill threw Andi a decidedly self-satisfied smirk.

"Asshole," Andi muttered.

An hour later, she was sitting at her desk, trying to compose Jim

56

O'Neill's disciplinary letter.

"Call for you on line two," Jessica hollered from the adjacent office. "It's your friend, Fang."

Andi grimaced and picked up the phone. "Hi, North."

"Hey, did you forget about me?"

"No, of course not. Why, what's up?"

"You promised to visit the gallery on Monday and give me your opinion on the new shipment of carvings I got in last week."

"Oh right! You know what? I *did* forget all about it. There's been a little too much excitement around here lately."

"Well I have to send most of the carvings out tomorrow. Why don't you come by the gallery today and we'll have some lunch? You can tell me what's so exciting in your life."

"You know what, that sounds like a great idea. I could use a break." Andi glanced at her watch. "I'll be there at twelve."

"Sounds good to me. I'll pick up some food and we can eat in the back, if that's all right with you? I'll make some coffee."

"Perfect. See you soon." The prospect of a visit and lunch with a great guy made her feel a whole lot better.

Andi pushed through the heavy glass double doors of The Qamutik Gallery. "Hi, I'm here," she called.

"Flip over the closed sign and lock the door. I want to eat in peace," North shouted from his office deep in the back of the gallery.

Andi did as he requested and made her way past the rows of beautiful soapstone carvings and statuary. Paintings of every size and medium covered almost every inch of wall space. Exotic and unique caribou hair tuftings, a truly unique northern art form, were scattered throughout the gallery and a large glass case displayed an array of unique, stunning jewelry. The place was a treasure-trove.

"What do I smell? Is that bacon?" Andi called, pulling her gloves and parka off as she made her way to North's office.

"Yup. Went down the street to To-Go's and got us bacon cheddar caribou burgers and fries. Here," he said, pushing a slightly greasy bag toward his guest. "Help yourself. I'll grab the coffee."

"Mmmm, smells wonderful." Andi ripped open a bag and took a huge bite of the burger.

North returned, put two mugs of coffee on his desk and reached for his own lunch. They ate like starving children, sharing shy smiles between bites.

"What are you looking at?" Andi asked after she'd finished her burger and the last French fry. She wriggled in her chair.

"Just thinking about how beautiful you are." North leaned close and, before she could react, licked the side of her mouth. "Especially with ketchup on your lips."

"Oh, jeez," Andi muttered. She grabbed a napkin and scrubbed at her face, marveling at the sensual touch of North's warm tongue. A soft pink blush tinted her cheeks. She picked up her coffee to cover her embarrassment. "Let's go see those carvings. I have to head back out to the airport again soon."

North led her to a spacious storage room where the new soapstone carvings were spread out on a large table. The sculptures were of various sizes; some could fit in the palm of her hand, and some were over three feet tall. Most were of traditional northern figures such as polar bears, geese, seals, walrus, caribou and muskox portrayed in various positions and situations. Another popular theme was the family, and many carvings involved mothers and children, along with fierce hunters. Andi was soon lost in the beauty and wonder of the art, delighting at each new piece.

"So, which one do you want?" North said softly, his warm breath brushing her ear. She jumped, shaken from her reverie, and hastily returned a small carving to the table. She realized that she'd been holding a piece entitled 'Mother with Child' for several minutes, caressing the beautifully carved figures.

"I can't afford any of these," she said hastily, walking around the table and back toward North's office. "But thanks so much for letting me look at them. They truly are amazing. You'll have no trouble selling them."

"You're more than welcome," North said, trailing behind her. "So are we still on for Sunday?"

"Yes, for sure. I'm looking forward to my first sled ride."

"So what are you doing Friday night?" he asked as they walked arm in arm to the front of the gallery.

"Oh, I almost forgot to tell you. Ken and Margo Thomas are having TGIF at their place on Friday. Would you like to join us?"

"Sure, I'd love to. I like Ken and Margo a lot."

"Do you know where they live?"

"Of course; it's a small town," North grinned. "I seem to recall being at one of Margo's famous 'Thank God It's Friday' nights a while back. It was loads of fun."

Andi laughed. "Good. So I'll see you there, then."

"For sure. What are you up to for the rest of the week?"

"Well, I'm planning to hitch a ride out to Pivot Lake one day if there's room on the aircraft," Andi said as she pulled on her woolen hat and looped her purple qiviut scarf loosely around her neck.

"Pivot Lake? Why?" North frowned.

"I want to talk to the Supervisor, Carlos Sante, about the supply runs. Jim O'Neill's trips are taking longer than they should, and I want to see if Carlos has any idea why."

"I see. Well, don't get into any trouble out there with all those miners," North teased. "I know Carlos, and he has a roving eye."

"Don't you worry about me," Andi chuckled. "I can take care of myself."

They'd reached the gallery's front door. North bent over Andi's shoulder to unlock the door and flip up the 'open' sign. As he reached around her, he took the opportunity to nuzzle the soft, sensitive skin below her ear, sending shivers of delight racing up and down her spine.

Andi ran out the door before her emotions betrayed her, throwing a hasty glance back. North leaned casually against the doorframe, a sexy, wicked grin on his face. He seemed to know *exactly* what the hot touch of his lips had done to her.

NINE

The next day Andi manned the dispatch desk during Jessica's lunch break. It was Ayame's day off, but Andi was anxious to find out if she'd completed her research, and took advantage of Jessica's absence to call her.

"I think you're on to something," Ayame replied to Andi's query. "I went back another month and made a chart of all the trips."

Andi chuckled. "Somehow that doesn't surprise me. So what did you find?"

"Well, I've discovered two things. First, Jim O'Neill and Hank Brister are flying over seventy-five percent of the Pivot Lake trips. Second, *all* of their trips are at least an hour longer than the other crews'. Some of them closer to two hours longer."

"And who's in dispatch when their trips return?"

"It's almost always Jessica. But you know that I normally work the early shift, and Jessica works late. So except when we're alone in dispatch for the entire day I'm almost never on duty when the Pivot Lake trips return."

"Right. That makes sense. "You're working tomorrow, right?"

"Yes."

"Can I get the chart from you tomorrow then? I'd like to take a look at it myself."

"I've already made a copy for you. It's in the old filing cabinet, the one we use to store old flight logs and stuff. I filed it under 'Miscellaneous Work To Do'." Ayame giggled. "Figured that's one place Jessica will never look."

"Great. Thank you."

"So what do you think this all means, anyway?"

"I don't really know, Ayame. But I have a feeling that Jim and Hank and possibly Jessica are up to something. I just have no idea what it is."

"This is kind of exciting," Ayame said, her voice tempered to a stage whisper even though they were on a private phone call and there was no need for drama. "Mystery at the Dispatch Office."

"Yes, it is a bit of a mystery."

They ended the call and Andi immediately pulled the new chart from its hiding place, eager to examine it. She was midway through scrutinizing the notations when her ears began to tingle. The more she read, the higher her anxiety grew, until her stomach began to burn. There was a definite and unaccountable pattern to O'Neill's flights to the diamond mine. But why? What was the Ace up to?

She decided there was only one way to find out.

When Jessica returned from lunch and had resumed her post Andi immediately retreated to her office. She closed both doors, the one connecting her office to dispatch and the one entering onto the main lounge and coffee room.

She'd checked the flight roster for the next day and knew that both Jim O'Neill and Hank Brister had the day off. That left her clear to tag along on a trip to Pivot Lake without arousing their suspicion. She called Carlos Sante at the diamond mine and, under the pretense of reviewing their additional flying needs, set up a meeting with him the next day. Carlos was happy to have her visit and told her he would meet the flight himself.

Andi left the office early, the beginnings of a cluster migraine twisting red-hot knives in her head. She made a quick stop for groceries, did a load of laundry and forced herself to eat a slice of toast and a scrambled egg.

She couldn't shake the edgy feeling that had settled upon her earlier in the day, and the sporadic pains in her head threatened to erupt into a full-blown migraine. On her way home from work that afternoon she'd decided to skip her usual mid-week AA meeting that night, but the more her discomfort grew, so did the familiar yearning she was so desperately trying to conquer.

Sitting alone in her quiet, empty home, all she wanted at that exact moment was a drink – any type of alcohol would do. She knew what she had to do. With only minutes left before the 8 pm meeting started, Andi fled her lonely, quiet house on Alder Drive to the safety of the Igloo Church and an AA meeting.

Shivering in the ice-cold Land Yacht as it bumped down the road on square, frozen tires, her chaotic thoughts wandered back to the Pivot Lake flight time discrepancies. The more she thought about the puzzling situation the more suspicious she became. She could think of no good reason for the flights to be consistently late. Perhaps tomorrow Carlos Sante could shed some light on the problem.

Five minutes later she reached *Our Lady of Victory,* the world-famous Catholic Church that resembled an igloo. It was the most photographed building in Inuvik, and she still marveled at its unique structure and beautiful dome roof every time she laid eyes on it. Almost every article or tourist guide written about Inuvik showcased the unique and stunning Igloo Church.

Andi parked on the street, the Yacht's engine running and heater blasting warm air on her face. She watched the last stragglers rush into the bright warmth of the church, fully intending to rush through those welcoming doors herself. Minutes ticked by, but she couldn't seem to mobilize her leaden legs.

The front doors of the Igloo Church had long since closed on the last anonymous alcoholic, but still Andi sat in her car. She couldn't tear her thoughts away from Jim O'Neill and the secret she was sure he was hiding.

When she realized that her suspicious ears were tingling again, she shoved the station wagon's gearshift into drive and headed for the airport. She intended to do a bit of research of her own during the quiet, cold hours of night.

She parked in front of Tuktu Aviation's dark, deserted dispatch building and plugged in the car's block heater. She put a pot of coffee to brew, cleared a workspace on the cluttered desk, and set to work pulling flight logs, air bills and dispatch records.

Two hours and three cups of coffee later she'd completed her task. Her research proved that, without a doubt, Jim O'Neill and Hank Brister were using Tuktu Aviation's Twin Otter for unscheduled flying. Unscheduled *and* unbilled. Aircraft logs don't lie, and there was approximately one hour of unaccountable flight time on each of O'Neill's trips to the Pivot Lake Diamond mine. A few trips showed almost two unauthorized hours.

Andi sat at her desk, contemplating the problem, until exhaustion set in. She glanced at the clock, startled to find she'd been immersed in her research for almost four hours. It was eerily quiet in the old building, and she realized how entirely alone she was. Only the occasional sigh of Arctic wind broke the isolated silence.

The knowledge that over the past two months O'Neill and Brister had flown over fifty hours of unauthorized time left her feeling nauseated and shaken. The cost to the company would be well over $40,000.

What kind of an Operations Manager was she, when a blatant misuse of company resources had taken place right before her very eyes? Jessica Hartman had to be aware that Jim and Hank were consistently late, and that meant Jessica must be a part of whatever was going on. But exactly what *was* going on, and how was she going to get to the bottom of it? What were the three of them hiding, and more importantly, where did the Twin Otter disappear to during those missing hours on the Arctic tundra?

Andi was still in deep thought when a sharp crack pierced the night. She started and let out a shrill scream. The noise seemed to come from the road. Heart thumping, she ran to a window and peered into the night; a single bulb over the old hangar's exterior door did little to dispel the dense black shadows. She searched for movement on the road, anything to account for the disturbance. All she saw was her own old car, sitting alone in a pool of weak light.

She decided that it was definitely time to head home. Working quickly, she replaced the documents she'd been inspecting and restored the dispatch desk to its usual organized clutter.

She locked the front door behind her and started the old Land Yacht, grateful when the engine turned over without hesitation. She began to brush the light film of freshly fallen snow from the car windows, a repetitious, monotonous task she'd always found strangely comforting. The strident strumming of her heart settled and the loud report of a few minutes earlier was almost forgotten when she saw it.

She froze, bright red snow brush in hand, her brain not quite comprehending what lay before her eyes. Her left rear tire was as flat as a pancake. She immediately knew that there was no way the old car was getting her home.

In frustration, Andi kicked the offending tire and looked down the road toward the maintenance hangar. It, too, was in darkness. There wasn't a car in sight. The deserted airport made her realize how alone and entirely vulnerable she really was.

It was well past midnight, and too late to call anyone to come to her aid. There was only one thing to do – go back up to her office and call a cab to take her home.

The next morning Andi hitched a ride to the airport with Paul. He was surprised that she'd been working late the night before, and she considered telling him about her discovery. In the end, she chose to keep her suspicions to herself until she'd decided how to deal with the situation. A head-on confrontation with Jim and Hank right now would likely bring forth a stream of lies.

Ken sent a young apprentice aircraft engineer over to change Andi's flat tire later that morning. When Peter brought her keys up to her office, the young man wore a thoughtful look on his face. "I put your spare on, and left the blown tire in the back," he said, brushing a mop of black hair out of his eyes.

"Great, thanks very much, Peter," Andi smiled, wondering why he looked so uneasy.

"Your spare's not very good either, so I'd get a couple of new tires as soon as possible."

"Okay, I'll do that." Thanks.

"Um, there's one more thing," he said hesitantly, glancing through the open doorway toward the dispatch office.

Andi got up and swung the door shut.

"I can't say for sure, Ms. Nowak, but I'd swear that your tire has a bullet hole in it. It doesn't look like any regular blow-out I've ever seen. You should likely take it to the cops and make a report."

Andi's mouth gaped open. She stared wide-eyed at the uncomfortable youth. "You've got to be kidding," she whispered, disbelief and shock robbing her of her voice. "I'll do that, Peter. Thank you."

He hovered by the door a moment, shuffling his feet and looking like he wanted to say something else. He finally shrugged his thin shoulders and walked out the door.

After Peter left, Andi thought about the sharp noise she'd heard the night before. The more she thought about it, the more she was convinced it had sounded like a gunshot, not that she'd had much experience with guns. But the fact was, there hadn't been a soul around last night. Not that she'd noticed, anyway. So how, and more importantly, *why*, would anyone shoot out her tire?

Now that the idea was in her head, Andi was anxious to find out if her tire really had been shot, or if the suggestion was just the overactive imagination of a young man. Thirty minutes later she lugged her flat tire into Inuvik's RCMP detachment. She set it inside the front door and rang the bell for assistance.

"Hey, Patsy! How are you today?" she greeted the aging clerk who answered her summons. Patsy had been stationed behind the reception desk longer than anyone in Inuvik could remember.

"I'm doing just fine, my dear, but what brings you here?"

Andi pointed at the tire propped up by the door. "I was wondering if someone could have a look at my car tire. One of our engineers thinks it has a bullet hole in it."

"Sure can do," Patsy said, pulling out an incident report form. "Just let me get some details and then you can be on your way. Someone will give you a call just as soon as they can."

Patsy filled in the pertinent information, all the while cheerfully chatting about her five grandchildren and newborn great-grandson.

After hearing more than she wanted to about Patsy's expansive family, Andi was grateful to be on her way. She had a plane to catch, and she didn't want to be late.

TEN

When you live in the Arctic, you either love it or hate it. Andrea Jean Nowak was in love.

As the Twin Otter winged eastward toward Pivot Lake, Andi was mesmerized by the snowy, icebound landscape beneath her. It sparkled like the diamonds hidden deep beneath its surface, glinting and shimmering in the cold sunshine. She smiled in spite of her mission; she loved flying, and she truly loved the Arctic. Even the slight discomfort of the hard, unpadded seat couldn't diminish her joy.

Captain Tim Hudson, a five-year veteran with Tuktu, was sitting in the left seat of the cockpit. Mike Dagasso, a recently hired, though fully qualified pilot, was in the right seat. They were an amicable crew, and seemed pleased to have their Ops Manager on board.

Andi pressed close to the small, frosty window as she peered down at the white expanse, hoping to get a glimpse of caribou or Arctic white fox. On occasion she'd spotted a polar bear, but their preferred habitat was the frozen sea ice further north. The pristine and tranquil beauty of Canada's frozen land was breathtaking, and Andi held herself so very lucky to have it on her doorstep.

The trip to Pivot Lake took a little less than an hour, and they soon commenced their approach to the diamond mine. The aircraft was equipped with wheel-skis, and a few minutes later, they landed safely on the ice-strip and stopped near a small wooden shack.

Two mine employees were waiting for them, eager to help unload the aircraft. Frigid arctic air blasted into the cabin, and Andi quickly zipped up her bulky red parka before carefully climbing down the steep airstair door.

True to his word, Carlos Sante pulled up on a snowmobile, waving as he approached. He killed the engine, and hopped off the machine.

"Hi, Carlos, how are you?" Andi called, extending a gloved hand. "Thanks for meeting me. I hope I'm not taking you away from anything?"

"No, no. Not at all," he smiled. "I'm glad to see you." Then, raising his voice, he yelled up to the flight crew who were already unstrapping the freight. "You guys come up to camp for a coffee when you're done. I'm taking your boss up for a few minutes."

"Sure thing, thanks Carlos," Tim waved.

Carlos raced over the frozen tundra, Andi straddling the long, black leather seat behind him and clinging to the back of his parka for security. The exhilarating trip to the mine complex took only three or four minutes, and they were soon seated in the cafeteria enjoying a mug of hot coffee and a huge slab of the cook's afternoon offering of fresh apple pie.

After a few minutes of gossip about local Inuvik news, Carlos suggested they relocate to his office. They were rising from their table when Carlos pointed across the room and said, "Hey, there's someone I'd like you to meet."

Andi followed Carlos to a table in the farthest corner of the room where four men sat before spreadsheets and calculators. Two of them were clad in business suits and two in casual attire. "Sorry for interrupting, boss," Carlos said, addressing a lean man Andi judged to be in his late forties, his black hair tinged grey at the temples. "I thought you'd like to meet Andrea Nowak. She's the Operations Manager at Tuktu Aviation. Andi, this is Sam Tavernese, our CEO."

Tavernese, wearing a particularly striking dark blue suit, stood and extended his manicured hand. "So pleased to meet you, Miss Nowak. I've heard nothing but good things about the service you and

Tuktu Aviation are providing."

Andi shook his hand firmly. "The pleasure is all mine, Mr. Tavernese. I had no idea you were in camp today." Andi's immediate impression of the lean, compact man was one of strength and composure. She kept her gaze on his steel-grey eyes, fighting an unexpected and irrational urge to inspect his physique more closely.

"Just a quick visit, I'm afraid. We flew in from Yellowknife by chopper this morning." Tavernese held Andi's hand for a moment longer, then gave it a final squeeze before releasing his grip on her. He glanced at his watch. "Unfortunately, we're leaving again in about an hour."

"We won't keep you," Carlos said quickly, "just thought you'd like to meet the person responsible for the excellent service we get from Tuktu."

Tavernese smiled and handed his business card to Andi, his fingers brushing the back of her hand. "It's been a pleasure meeting you, Miss Nowak. I'll be sure to schedule a longer visit to Inuvik next time I'm here."

Andi smiled, feeling guilty. The brief encounter with the mine's charming CEO would made it harder than ever for her to broach the subject that had brought her to Pivot Lake.

Carlos led the way down a narrow hallway, stopping halfway down to unlock a wooden door bearing his name on a silver placard. He flipped a light on, revealing a diminutive, windowless office, and swept a pile of reports from the single guest chair before taking a seat behind the desk. They spent a few minutes discussing the new kimberlite discovery and how it would affect the mine's flight service requirements. Beginning almost immediately, Carlos said, the daily trips to the mine would be boosted by three more flights per week. Once the mine was in full production, it was quite likely that two trips per day would be required.

"We'll have you covered, Carlos," Andi promised. "We've

leased another Twin Otter and we'll have it online this week. Have you been happy with our service so far, and with the flight crews?"

"Oh yeah, everything is great. We couldn't ask for better service, no worries there," he said with a smile. "We're totally happy with Tuktu."

"Good, I'm so glad to hear that." Andi shifted uncomfortably in her chair. "Um, there is one thing that's been bothering me lately," she said hesitantly.

Carlos leaned back in his chair twirling a pen, eyebrows raised expectantly.

Now that she was here, Andi had no idea how to broach the subject that had recently occupied her every waking moment. Finally, she just blurted it out. "Have you had any reason to hold the aircraft here for longer than usual, or send them on any side trips? We've always scheduled an hour for a turnaround, but lately it's often taking two hours or more." Andi cleared her throat and fidgeted in her seat.

The features of Carlos' normally open and friendly face instantly tightened. Andi could sense him closing down. He looked at his desk, and randomly shuffled the papers sitting upon it. "Why do you think that has anything to do with us?" he asked slowly.

Andi glanced back at the open door, then leaned over and pushed it closed. When she turned back to Carlos, his eyebrows had knit together. Deep creases crossed his brow.

"Look," she said, keeping her voice low. "I'll be honest with you. We've had an excellent working relationship with East Three Drilling and Pivot Lake Diamond Mine, and I certainly don't want to jeopardize that."

Carlos crossed his arms and nodded once, his mouth set in a grim line. "Go ahead."

"I've recently discovered that most of your service flights are returning to Inuvik about an hour later than they should," Andi continued, speaking slowly and choosing her words carefully. "We originally blocked a three-hour window for each supply trip, but I've found that a lot of them are taking four hours or more to complete, and those extra hours are unaccounted for. I've questioned the flight crew but they haven't given me a satisfactory explanation. I was hoping that you might be able to help me."

Carlos rested his head against the high back of his chair and closed his eyes. He lifted a large, calloused hand to massage a vein pulsing on his forehead.

Minutes passed in silence, so many minutes that Andi feared she'd angered or insulted the man. Only the constant, dim buzzing from the overhead fluorescent lighting intruded on the total silence of the room.

Eventually Carlos sighed deeply and opened his eyes, turning his gaze toward Andi. She saw something akin to hopelessness in his dark eyes. "I was hoping the problem would go away." He spoke so quietly that Andi had to lean forward to hear him. "I thought maybe I was just imagining it. But if you've noticed that something is wrong, it's only a matter of time before someone else does. Our problems may be tied to each other's." His shoulders slumped and his amicable features suddenly looked fatigued. Elbows on his desk, he propped his head in his hands as if its weight was too much for him to bear.

"Tell me what's wrong," Andi whispered. Her ears were tingling, flaring with heat within seconds.

Carlos abruptly sat up, ramrod straight in his chair. He grabbed the edge of his desk with both hands and leaned forward. "Andi, anything we say in this office is strictly confidential. The success or demise of this mine may depend on it. Do you understand?"

"Yes, of course," she breathed, her wide emerald eyes glued to his.

"Okay. I won't go into a lot of detail but in a nutshell, it looks like the mine has had a breach of security. My outgoing inventory tally has been coming up short in the past few months, and for the hell of me

I can't figure out how or why." Carlos shook his head, lips pursed. "It's getting worse instead of better. My warnings seem to be falling on deaf ears."

Andi looked at him quizzically. "What?" She was totally confused. "What are you saying, Carlos?"

"Diamonds, Andi. Diamonds are disappearing."

A loud knock on the office door signalled an abrupt the end to their disquieting meeting. The aircraft was ready to leave.

During the flight back to Inuvik, Andi barely noticed the beauty of the remote land she loved so much. She used the hour to recall every detail of the meeting in Carlos' office and commit it to memory. Before she left, Carlos had promised to call her soon; she looked forward to talking with him again. They'd left too many questions unanswered.

Andi was too troubled to go back to the office when they landed, and since it was almost 5 pm she decided to go straight home. She was shaken by Carlos's extraordinary news, and wondered if there was even a remote possible that Jim, Hank and Jessica played any part in the missing diamonds. The thought seemed almost too wild to even consider.

As she neared the Centennial Library on Mackenzie Road, Andi spontaneously pulled over and parked the station wagon in front of the library. She ran inside, rummaging in her purse for her library card. She had been planning to educate herself on the history of diamond mining, and today seemed like as good a day as any to start.

When she left half an hour later, her arms were loaded with books on diamonds and diamond mining. She was surprised at the excellent selection available in the small library and was anxious to start her education on the precious stone that was purported to be 'a girl's best friend'."

She spent a few minutes with Coco, dropping off a few items the convalescing young woman had asked for. She was happy to find Coco in much better spirits. Her visible wounds were healing, but she still wouldn't agree to file a police report or visit a doctor. Andi was frustrated, but could do nothing to change the red head's mind.

A few minutes later, over a sandwich and pot of tea in her own living room, Andi began to educate herself on diamonds. It proved to be an engrossing, fascinating subject. The world's love affair with the precious gem started in South Africa in the late 1860s when a teenage shepherd boy found a pretty white rock along the banks of the Orange River. It turned out to be a 21.15 carat diamond, and eventually became one of the most famous stones in the world – The Eureka.

A couple of years later a native African Medicine man found another stone – the 83 carat famed Star of Africa. The diamond rush began, with thousands of fortune seekers and miners from around the world arriving at the Colesberg Kopje area. Much of the area was privately owned farmland. One of the largest farms was owned by two De Beers brothers. The rush also brought a migration of native workers from the entire African continent, and soon the crowds of people found themselves living and working in the most appalling conditions. Newcomers were greeted with stench, squalor, a poor diet and limited clean water.

As there was no governing authority, the prospective miners began negotiating with local farmers and staking out their claims. Around this time, the De Beers brothers, with a concentrated deposit of diamonds on their own land, had partnered up with Cecil Rhodes and started their own mine. And so, the powerhouse of De Beers Diamonds Consolidated was born. They soon found that their biggest liability was theft; diamonds were steadily being smuggled out of the mine by the poorly paid workers. That problem was solved with the immediate creation of segregated, controlled, fenced compounds for the black workers; the first apartheid was created. Searching of houses was established, with all workers being subjected to invasive strip-searches prior to leaving the mine premises.

Wanting to stamp out competition, De Beers founded single channel marketing, which became known as the CSO – a central selling organization. It was, in effect, a cartel controlling over sixty percent of the world's diamonds and limiting the quantity of diamonds put on the market in accordance with the demand, to stabilize trade. It was a stranglehold on supply, upping the value and rarity of the precious diamonds.

But it was the next book that Andi picked up that made her question the world's ongoing love affair with diamonds. She'd heard of the term 'blood diamond', but like most people in North America gave it little thought. What she read next made her stomach turn, and she vowed to never make another casual diamond purchase again.

Blood diamonds, also called conflict diamonds, were mined in African war zones, primarily Angola, Sierra Leone, The Ivory Coast, and the Congo. They were mined and sold to finance rebel groups and the purchase of arms. She had thought that working conditions were bad in South Africa, but the lives of the poor individuals working in the blood diamond mines meant little to the rebels. Mass murder and amputations were methods used to inspire fear and obedience; the family unit meant nothing, and thousands of families were ripped apart. Children were forced into serving the rebels, becoming soldiers before they reached their teen years. So much blood shed, and all in the name of the mighty diamond.

Although it was approaching midnight, Andi was too engrossed to think about sleep. She opened a colourful catalogue of famous diamonds of the world. She read about magnificent, priceless gems such as The Great Star of Africa, weighing 530 carats, and The Orloff at 300 carats. But, according to the book, the most beautiful diamond in the entire world was The Regent, a 140 carat diamond from India currently on display at the Louvre in Paris.

Although Andi had never heard of these renowned stones, she did recognize the next one – The Hope Diamond; this blue gem was reputed to bring bad luck to its owners, and was currently in safekeeping at the Smithsonian in Washington. The photos and descriptions of these diamonds were breathtaking and their values were astronomical, often in the hundreds of millions of dollars.

So much suffering and tragedy, she mused, and all for the sake of some pretty, shiny stones. If only the world put the same value on human life, we would all be living in a much better place. She was becoming increasingly disgusted with the whole idea of diamonds, but it didn't seem very likely that she would be able to escape them any time in the near future.

Andi had a vague idea of how the value of a diamond was assessed. As anyone who's been in a jewellery store on a diamond buying expedition, or been the lucky recipient of diamond jewellery knows, 'The Four C's' matter: clarity, colour, cut and carat weight.

Reading further, she found the facts on diamond pricing equally fascinating. Who knew there was a diamond cartel that single handedly fixed the price per carat weight of diamonds? And that this same cartel withheld diamonds from the market at will, to increase the amount they could charge? It all seemed rather like mob-mentality.

Flipping through the next book in her pile, Andi saw that it focused on the transformation path of rough stones to finished product. It seemed that most rough diamonds, in fact about eighty percent of them, passed through one single location in Antwerp, Belgium. It was known as 'The Diamond Quarter', and dubbed the 'Square Mile' because the district covered about one square mile. There, the stones were assessed and cut into rough diamonds, batched according to size and potential value. At this point, batches of rough-cut diamonds were usually sold in lots to manufacturers who cut and polished them, often in India. It was a multi-billion-dollar market.

Andi's eyes were heavy. She yawned and glanced at her watch. It was time to turn in. Now that she knew the history of diamonds, she vowed to learn more about the fledgling Canadian diamond mining industry next.

ELEVEN

Andi awoke with a start to the shrill ring of her telephone. She rolled over and groped through the darkness. "Yeah."

"Andi, Paul here. We have trouble. Louis Teto wants to see us both in his office at 7:30 sharp."

Paul's tense voice and the mention of Louis Teto's name drove the last bit of sleep from Andi's foggy brain. "What! Why?"

"I don't know for sure, but it has something to do with Pivot Lake Mine. And he is *pissed*. I'll see you there at 7:30." Before she could reply, a dial tone buzzed in her ear.

Her alarm clock read 6:15 am. She raced through a shower, gulped down a scalding cup of coffee and at 7:25 stood in the reception area of the Inuvialuit Regional Corporation (IRC) office. The imposing metal and glass tower stood regally in the centre of Inuvik's small downtown core. Louis Teto was the Director of the IRC, and hence the most influential and powerful man in both Inuvik and the entire western Arctic. Andi grimly wondered what *faux pas* she could had possibly committed to earn his attention.

Although the hour was early, the Director's receptionist was already behind her desk in the lavishly appointed seventh floor office. Throughout the roomy reception area authentic and priceless Northern paintings and sculptures were strategically positioned for maximum impact.

"Ms. Andrea Nowak to see you, sir." The receptionist announced demurely as she led Andi into the Director's inner office. The door closed behind her with a soft click.

Paul White, his expression grim, was already seated before a vast desk. Andi sat down in the vacant chair at his side, the fingers of her right hand unconsciously worrying the silver ring on her left ring finger. Behind the desk, Teto's fleshy face was set in angry lines. Andi's stomach dropped.

"I have a nine o'clock flight to Edmonton," Louis barked without preamble, "but this couldn't wait, so I'll be quick. I got a phone call last night from an associate at Pivot Lake Mines." The Director's voice was deep and gravelly. "He was mad as hell, which means *I* am mad as hell. He wants to know what the hell *you*," he leaned over the desk and stabbed a stubby, fat finger in Andi's astonished face, "were doing at the mine yesterday. He said you were poking your nose into confidential and sensitive matters." Perspiration glistened on Louis Teto's broad forehead. "And I wanna know, too, girl. What in the *hell* were you doing out there?"

Andi was speechless, stunned by both the Director's offensive attitude and by the nature of the complaint against her. She had not seen this coming, and was at a complete loss for words. "Um," she stuttered, "I needed to talk with Carlos Sante about trip scheduling, and since there was room on the service flight I tagged along. Look, what's this all about?"

Louis glared at her, his eyes accusatory. "And what else did you do out there? Who else did you meet with?"

"Nobody! I had coffee with Carlos in the cafeteria, then we went to his office to review the upcoming flight requirements. Oh, Carlos introduced me to Sam Tavernese. That's it." Andi felt sick to her stomach and wondered if somehow the information Carlos had shared with her was at the root of this complaint. "Why?" she asked. "What's happened?"

"What's happened is that my contact at the mine has reported that you've been out there snooping around and sticking your nose into confidential matters." Louis screamed. "Matters that are none of your god damn business! I want you both to listen to me, and listen good. You stick your nose into that mine's business and it will spell trouble for you, Tuktu Aviation *and* the corporation. *That's* what's happened." He stabbed the desk with a pudgy finger, accentuating each verminous word.

Andi shook her head vehemently. "No! No, I only-"

"They say you breached security," Teto interrupted, "and they're afraid that confidential information about the new kimberlite pipe may have been leaked. And that maybe you're selling it to their competitors or the *Russians*!" he ranted. "They're talking about suing you and you and Tuktu Aviation," he roared, stabbing a finger at Andi and Paul. "So explain yourself, girl, and make it quick!" He pulled back the sleeve of his dark blue suit jacket and glared at the large gold Rolex on his wrist.

Andi stood up. Her knees were weak, and she needed air, but she was determined to do whatever she could to mitigate the situation. In a calm, firm voice and looking directly into the Director's blazing eyes, she said, "Mr. Teto, I can only assure you that none of this is true. I went out there to talk to Carlos about service flight scheduling and we had a cup of coffee. I don't know who's feeding you this load of crap, but I did *not* breach their security. I do *not* have any information about the mine's operations, and I am *not* a communist spy! In fact, I'm insulted by these insinuations."

The Director glared at her for a long moment. Andi looked at Paul, her shimmering green eyes entreating support from her boss.

After what seemed like a short eternity, Paul looked at the Director and said, "I know Andi, Louis, and I'll vouch for her. I trust her. She wouldn't do anything to jeopardize our working relationship with Pivot Lake Mines; she's as honest as they come. If there's been a breach of security at the mine, tell them to look elsewhere."

Andi's knees buckled. She collapsed into the deep leather chair, not trusting herself to continue standing.

Director Teto's nostrils flared. Breathing hard, he glared at Paul and Andi for a long moment, then shoved his chair back from his desk. It took more than a little effort to lift his cumbersome bulk from the thickly padded leather seat. "All right. But you make sure I never, *ever* hear that Tuktu is mixed up in any shady dealings out at that mine site." He pointed an admonishing finger at Paul. "Just remember that *I* was the one who approved your application to operate on Inuvialuit land, and I can rescind it just as quick. Don't make me regret my decision. Now get out of here."

Speechless, Andi walked out of the Director's office on shaky legs. Neither of them spoke on the short elevator ride to the main floor of the Inuvialuit Regional Corporation building. It was just as well. Her thoughts were focused on the question of who could possibly want her to stay away from the diamond mine. She had somehow made an enemy, but who was it?

Her quirky ears told her that, without a doubt, trouble was once again brewing in her life.

By 11 am Andi's grumbling stomach reminded her that she'd missed breakfast. After such a rude start to her day she thought it would be nice to meet North for lunch. He readily agreed to join her at the Greenbriar Restaurant.

She was already seated in the hotel restaurant studying the short menu when North arrived a few minutes later. "Sorry, Babe," he said, stopping to drop a chaste kiss on Andi's cheek before settling in the chair opposite her.

Their intimate lunch at the Qamutik a few days earlier had somehow changed their relationship. Andi was both bemused and flustered by the unexpected emotions she felt for the dark, mysterious man sitting across from her.

"I had a client from California on the phone and couldn't shake him."

"That's fine; I'm not in a hurry. I hope your Californian placed a very large order?"

"As a matter of fact, he did," North grinned. "It was a *very* profitable morning, so lunch is on me."

An attractive young waitress appeared, her blond ponytail bouncing jauntily with each step. She poured coffee and took their lunch orders. "You sounded kind of tense on the phone. What's up?" North asked, blowing on his steaming mug.

Andi hadn't intended to dump her problems on North, but she instinctively decided to confide in him. "Well, remember I told you that I thought something strange was going on with our Pivot Lake supply runs? They're taking way too long."

North nodded.

"Well, I went out to the diamond mine yesterday, and now I know *for sure* there's something going on. You have to swear not to say a word to anyone, okay? This is totally confidential."

"Of course. What's up?"

"Well, when I was there I had coffee with Carlos Sante. You know him, don't you?"

"Yea, sure. I've known him for years. He's part Inuvialuit, from Holman Island. A good guy."

"Well, when I asked Carlos if he had any idea why our service flights were often late returning to Inuvik, he kind of clammed up. Then he finally told me that they've been losing diamonds!" she whispered, although there were no other diners within earshot.

North's eyes widened. "Losing diamonds? What does that mean?"

"Just that. He said their outgoing inventory, as he put it, has been short for the last few months." Andi's muted voice squeaked with excitement. "Someone at the mine is stealing diamonds!"

The perky blond waitress appeared with their lunch, spending more time than necessary ensuring that North had everything he needed and that his steak sandwich was cooked to order. Andi glared at her.

North grinned at both women. The waitress sauntered away, slender hips and short skirt swinging.

"Are you done fraternizing with the waitress?" Andi snapped, jabbing a French fry with her fork.

"I love it when you're jealous, Babe. You look so hot."

"I am *not* jealous. I just think it's just ... it's very immature behavior." She took a bite of her beef dip sandwich. "This is great," she mumbled.

"So what else did Carlos say?"

"Not a lot. He'd just dropped that bombshell when our co-pilot came to get me and I had to leave. But Carlos made me promise to keep it to myself. He looked *scared*, North – I'm worried about him. I got the distinct impression that he definitely thought there was a connection between their missing diamonds and our late flights."

North chewed thoughtfully for a few seconds. "Well, if Carlos thinks something funny is going on, then there likely is. He's a solid guy. Have you talked to him again?"

"No. He said I wasn't to try and contact him, and that he'd get in touch when he could." Andi dipped the crusty loaf into dark brown *au jus* and took another big bite. "I think he's afraid their phones are bugged or something."

"Ha! That's hilarious. Who'd bug a phone up in Pivot Lake? I think your imagination is getting away with you, Babe."

Andi stopped chewing and threw green daggers across the table.

North cleared his throat. His countenance turned solemn. "Sorry. So your quirky ears and highly evolved senses are telling you that the missing diamonds and your late flights are somehow connected?" He sliced off an enormous piece of rare steak and forked it into his mouth.

"Yes, I'm positive. I just don't know how to go about proving it." She laid her fork down, suddenly uninterested in her lunch. "And something else happened."

"There's more?"

"Yes. Louis Teto called Paul White and me into his office at 7:30 this morning. He said someone at the mine called him last night and complained about my visit. They told him I breached some kind of security, so I got raked over the coals pretty good."

"What? You've got to be joking."

"I wish I was. Paul vouched for me, and I think we finally convinced Teto that my visit was perfectly innocent, but it was nerve-wracking."

"And does Paul know about the, uh-"

"No. I didn't mention the missing diamonds to him."

"Hmph. I really don't know what to make of this."

They finished their meals in silence. North pushed his plate away, his dark brows knit together. "I tell you what. I think it's about time I got out on the land again. When's O'Neill's next trip to the mine?"

"Tomorrow afternoon. It leaves Inuvik at one o'clock. Why?"

North's sly smile gave Andi just a glance of his long eyetooth. "I think it's time we found out just what the hell your Captain O'Neill is up to out there. Don't you?"

TWELVE

She knew she was late, and judging by the number of vehicles parked haphazardly in Ken and Margo Thomas' driveway and along the street, their TGIF party was in full swing. When she spotted North Ruben's old Chevrolet pickup her mutinous heart missed a beat.

Snow crunched underfoot as Andi walked up the short driveway. She was almost to the front door when a speeding bullet of white and tan fur tackled her. Andi had known Toffee, the Thomas' three-year old Siberian husky, since the dog was a pup. Every time they saw each other the sassy dog greeted her with a furiously wagging tail and enthusiastic Toffee-talk. Andi knelt on the snow and spent a few moments scratching the thick fur around the dog's neck and engaging her in their private version of a conversation.

Even outside the Thomas' blue, one-storey wooden house the familiar tune of Garth Brooks' *Friends in Low Places* was remarkably loud. Andi hummed along to the familiar tune and snickered; Margo's favourite song was cranked up loud, which meant she would likely be on her third or fourth beer already.

After giving Toffee a final pat Andi let herself into the familiar dwelling, slipped off her boots and threw her red parka onto the mound of coats by the door. The air in the house was warm and heavy with the odours of cigarettes and beer. The latter's yeasty aroma instantly tantalized her senses and awakened the old cravings she'd been so valiantly fighting to conquer. She twirled the AA ring on her hand, her fingers automatically gravitating to the silver band that exuded support and bolstered her resolve to stay sober.

"Hello, everyone!" She waved to the occupants of the crowded living room and had to shout to be heard above the deafening music. Most of the dozen faces were familiar; several were Ken's coworkers from the maintenance department and the balance either worked with Margo at the Inuvialuit Regional Development Corporation or knew their hosts from other social activities around the city. There was no such thing as a 'stranger' in a small place like Inuvik.

Ken, clutching a bottle of beer, wandered to the door to greet her. He had to lean close to be heard above the din in the room and was beaming from ear to ear. "Hey, glad you could make it. We were wondering where you were." Ken, like Ayame, was of Japanese descent, and while he was typically focussed and serious on the job, after work he was usually game for a bit of fun.

Andi chatted with Ken for a minute, then made her way through the crowd and into the kitchen in search of Margo and North. Garth was still singing his heart out about fear and champagne. She stopped for a minute to visit with Steve Mitchell and Bob Hart (who was still dressed in his trademark green scrubs).

When she finally made it into the kitchen, she found it too was packed with familiar faces. Everyone had a bottle of beer or a glass of something in their hand. Margo and North were sitting at the round, wooden kitchen table, frosty mugs of beer in front of them.

"Hi guys," Andi smiled. She bent down to give Margo a quick hug before edging over to the fridge in search of a can of the alcohol-free beer Margo always kept on hand for her. Margo knew Andi's history, and about her battle with booze. She was, after all, Andi's best friend. Nobody but Margo, Ken and Andi ever knew that the golden, foaming liquid in Andi's mug contained zero alcohol.

Someone in the living room, most likely Ken, abruptly turned *Friends in Low Places* down a few decibels.

Andi wandered back to the table. "We were starting to wonder about you!" Margo admonished with a lop-sided grin. A cigarette burned in one hand while the other clutched a half-empty beer mug. "Where've you been?"

"I decided to have a nap after work," Andi replied, taking a long pull of the tangy, cold alcohol-free beer. It was a surprisingly good substitute for the real thing. "I was up late last night, reading," she added.

There was standing room only at the table and before Andi realized what was happening North wrapped an arm around her waist and pulled her onto his lap. "North, what are you doing?" she gasped.

"Making you comfortable and me happy, Babe." His full lips broke into a grin that made his dark eyes sparkle. He shifted and settled his arms more securely around his prize.

Margo broke out in boisterous, contagious laughter that, despite Andi's embarrassment, soon had her laughing too. Margo Thomas was the reason Andi had survived those dark and dismal days and nights after the tragedy in Yellowknife. She knew that she could count on her dearest friend – her laughter, her endearing personality and her caring nature – to inspire and support her for rest of her life. She loved her friend dearly.

"Hey, Andi, you'd better not let Ruben gets his fangs into you," Paul chortled as he made his way passed the table clutching four full bottles of beer. Even North had to laugh. Like Ken, at the office Paul White was the boss. He was efficient, organized and respected. After hours, he was the life of the party, providing hours of laughter and camaraderie to a motley crew of friends and co-workers.

Andi rolled her eyes and feigned exasperation, but couldn't suppress a smile. She contemplated the individuals in the increasingly smoky kitchen and realized that she loved the entire crowd. There were more people in this house, and in Inuvik itself, that she could honestly call *friends* than she'd had at any other point in her life. She felt like she was finally becoming a normal human being again, and not an empty shell of a person functioning on autopilot. It was a damn good feeling.

"Where are Krystal and Kimberly?" she asked Margo. She sat crosswise on North's knees, one arm casually draped over his broad flannel-clad shoulders. A slow blooming of heat had begun to spread within her inner core, slowly driving out the numbness that had lodged there years ago.

She unconsciously reacted to this long-forgotten hint of longing and leaned closer to the warm, hard solidity of North's body, hugging his shoulders a little harder and wiggling down into his lap. He must have noticed too, since he suddenly choked on the swig of beer he'd been about to swallow.

"They're in our room," Margo replied, a faint smile on her lips. Nothing escaped Margo's sharp hazel eyes. "We got them a pizza from To-Go's for dinner, so they're eating and playing Nintendo."

North reached into a large bowl of potato chips sitting in the middle of the table and stuffed a handful into his mouth. Andi looked at him innocently and batted her long eyelashes just inches from his. "You okay, North?" She was starting to enjoy the close proximity to this dashingly handsome man.

"Just fine, Babe. How about you?" He didn't wait for a reply, but planted a long, salty kiss on her lips. They both laughed when he finally released her, realizing they'd come to an impasse.

The smoke in the house grew thicker and conversations grew louder as the night wore on. Generous amounts of alcohol were consumed. At some point during the evening Margo set out trays heaped with cold cuts, cheese, pickles, vegetables and dip, crackers, and buns. Most of the crowd, if not everyone, had arrived at the Thomas' home directly after work, skipping dinner in favour of Friday night drinks and fun.

Garth Brooks performed for them a second time, even louder than the first. Margo and Andi sang along with him enthusiastically. Their rather off-key duet had everyone howling with laughter.

Paul, with his friendly and outgoing wife Carla at his side, was entertaining the crowd with a long, rambling joke about *La Camel in La Desert* when Andi and North decided to relocate to the living room floor. Paul didn't just *tell* a joke; he embellished it with movement, gestures, and exaggerations that usually had even the most stoic listener in stitches. Tonight was no different, and the gathering of friends roared at the joke's hilarious conclusion.

Sometime later Andi stifled a yawn and glanced at the clock hanging above the entertainment unit. It was closing in on midnight. She turned to North, who had grown quiet, only to find his deep brown eyes staring at her with an expression she couldn't quite identify. Was it lust, she wondered, or just smoke and fatigue that narrowed his eyes? He hugged her closer, brushed his lips along her ear, and softly sang a few bars of Garth's popular song. His deep, baritone voice and hot breath sent shivers down her spine. "You coming with me to my oasis tonight, Babe?" he whispered, nuzzling her neck and trailing the tip of his tongue down its length.

Andi gasped. Fire shot through her veins and into her loins. It took her a moment to regain her composure. "I'd love to, but I think I'd better get home," she murmured. What she *really* wanted to do was go home with North and rip his clothes off, but she knew that would be a decision she'd never be able to take back. And it was just too soon.

"Yeah, me too," he agreed reluctantly, giving her another quick hug before releasing her. "I'd better see what kind of trouble my mutts are getting up to." He rose from the blue shag rug and stretched his long legs. "What are you doing tomorrow?"

"I'm going in to the office. I have tons of work to catch up on. Ayame will be there, so it will be a good day. Are you still going out to your dad's cabin to do the recon?"

"Yup, bright and early. Soap said he'd be ready to leave at daybreak. Lucky me." North's lips curved into a slightly lopsided grin that stirred Andi's yearnings again. "I'm not used to drinking this much so I hope I don't have a hangover. I'll call you as soon as I get back tomorrow, okay?"

"I'll be waiting for your call."

Andi and North made their way back to the kitchen through the remaining happy Friday crowd. They said goodbye, and Andi gave both Margo and Ken a hug, then went to seek out their daughters. The girls were still happily playing Nintendo, hopping around on some kind of floor mat connected to the game.

North had gone out ahead of Andi and started their vehicles. By the time she got to the Land Yacht the frost on its windows had begun to thaw and the interior temperature was just short of freezing. He was waiting for her by the car, and their long and steamy good night kisses left no doubt in her mind of North's desire.

Later that night, Andi awoke from her solitary dreams feeling restless and yearning for something she didn't have, but evidently needed.

It was already after 9 am, but dawn had only begun to tint the eastern horizon with a warm, pink glow when North backed his old Chevrolet truck up to a hard, windswept snow bank at the Shell Lake water Aerodrome. Situated on the banks of the Mackenzie River eight kilometers southeast of Inuvik, the small airport was technically in operation only during the short summer months, when floatplanes landed on the river.

He reached for the large backpack and rifle sitting on the bench seat beside him. Inside the Chevy's dented, rusted box sat his reliable old Arctic Cat snowmobile. North pulled the starter cord once and the machine roared to life. He gunned the two-stroke engine and eased the sled out of the truck and down the natural ramp, balancing a small plastic jerry can of extra gas on the seat in front of him.

A ski-equipped de Havilland DHC-2 Beaver sat on the frozen ice of the Mackenzie River, awaiting its load. North roared up to the five-passenger aircraft, skidding to a stop just a few feet away from it and spraying a sheet of snow into its open cargo door.

A shout erupted from within the aircraft. "Hey, what the hell are you doing?" A second later a compact, burly figure clad in a tattered and grimy dark blue parka appeared at the door. The aged Eskimo's dark, heavily lined face broke into a wide grin when he spotted the perpetrator. A sparse and shaggy moustache exposed more gaps than teeth in his mouth. "North! Hey you young pup, it's good to see you again."

"Soap, old man, it's good to see you too. It's been too long. You keeping busy?"

"As busy as I wanna be. These old bones need more rest than they used to."

"I hear ya. Hey, I really appreciate the lift on such short notice." North climbed off the snowmobile and reached up into the cargo hold of the ancient Beaver to grasp the old man's hand, surprised at the strength of his grip.

Nobody knew Soap's real name. His talented family and ancestors had been soapstone carvers for generations and he had eventually quit using his given name years ago. Now everyone, including his closest relatives, just called him Soap.

"No problem. Like I said last night, any time you ever need anything, you call me. Our families go back a long way – you know that. Now let's get this smelly beast of yours loaded up and get out of here."

The aircraft's skis skated easily over the ice and packed snow, and within minutes they were winging eastward into the lightening, pink-streaked sky. The Beaver's single Pratt & Whitney radial engine, though powerful and dependable, made conversation in the cockpit difficult. North sat in the right-hand cockpit seat, donned a green David Clark headset and settled in to enjoy the short flight.

"You have the co-ordinates?" Soap's deep voice rumbled through the headset.

North pulled a crumpled piece of paper out of his pocket and handed it over to the pilot, then keyed his microphone. "Here they are. Do you remember where my dad's old hunting cabin is?"

"Yeah. Been there many times."

"You can drop me off about five kilometers east of the cabin."

"What are ya gonna be doing out there? Hunting?"

"No. I just wanted a day out on the land again. I thought I'd take a look at the old place again and see if I can spot any caribou. It's been a while."

Soap nodded, his wise, watery brown eyes fixed on North. A web of deep wrinkles ringed his eyes from countless hours spent peering into the strong Arctic sun without benefit of sunglasses. "Uh huh. And you really expect me to believe that bull shit?" He grinned at North, apparently comfortable and unembarrassed at his toothlessness. "What time you want me to pick you up, son?"

North shifted uneasily in his seat, caught in his lie. "About 17:00 hours. That should give us plenty of time to get back to Inuvik before civil twilight. You said you're going to fly over to Paulatuk and visit some folks there?"

The old bush pilot nodded. "Yup. It's only about forty-five minutes over to Paulatuk and I kinda like that Auntie of yours who runs the airport. Maybe she'll buy me a coffee."

North grinned and didn't say a word.

"You just be ready and waitin' right where I leave you," Soap warned. "I won't have any time to spend lollygagging around lookin' for you."

"Roger that. I'll be ready at 17:00 hours." The two men chatted about days gone by and old relatives for the remainder of the short flight, and before long North was watching the small aircraft disappear from sight. He had spent many hours on the land, hunting first with his father and dog teams and then with his brothers on snowmobiles. A few family members still lived in the small Inuvialuit village of Paulatuk, situated on Darnley Bay off the Amundsen Gulf.

He hopped on his black Cat and sped over the frozen tundra in the general direction of Pivot Lake. Within an hour he spotted the mine's communication towers. He circled the mine site until he found the landing strip, careful to stay out of sight of the buildings. The ice strip angled northeast to take advantage of the prevailing winds.

North searched until he found a small bluff where he could remain hidden from an aircraft's approach. He banked snow around the Arctic Cat and covered the machine with a thin white blanket he'd brought along for that purpose. That done, he burrowed into the side of the bluff, made himself comfortable and poured a cup of coffee from his thermos. With a bag of bacon and egg sandwiches and his rifle at his side, he settled in to wait for Tuktu Aviation's Twin Otter to make its appearance.

North jerked awake to the distant drone of an engine, startled to discover that he'd dozed off. He shook his head to clear the cobwebs and glanced at his watch; it was 2:15. The service flight was right on time.

When he heard the aircraft taxi toward the makeshift terminal shack, he stole a cautious peek over the snowbank. Four men and two bright yellow pickup trucks were waiting to offload the plane's cargo. As far as he could tell, the pilots never left the aircraft.

Thirty minutes later the twin turbine engines whined back to life and the yellow trucks began the short trek to camp. North hastily repacked his thermos and lunch bag into his backpack and readied himself for pursuit. He waited until the Twin Otter lifted off, snow billowing in its wake, before pulling the camouflage blanket from his snow machine. He hastily stowed it in the cargo hold beneath the Cat's long seat.

Instead of banking west, toward Inuvik, North was surprised to see the aircraft continue almost due north. He trailed behind it, pushing his machine to its limit to keep the Twin Otter in sight. Skimming over the uneven, concrete hard snow at speeds of up to 110 kilometers per hour, the rough ride jarred his spine in spite of the heavily padded seat. Wherever the pilots were heading, it definitely wasn't back to Inuvik.

The Twin Otter, flying faster than North could drive, pulled away from him. He was slowly losing sight of it and couldn't coax any more speed from his machine. When the aircraft finally disappeared behind a low range of hills North knew he was defeated. It was useless to continue his pursuit. He stopped and shut the noisy snowmobile off, kicking out at a drift of hard snow in frustration.

Determined not to let the entire trip be a monumental waste of time, he spent a few minutes imprinting the area's landmarks in his mind. He had never lost his hunter's instincts – those lessons drilled into him from spending weeks on the land with his father, an unrelenting and unforgiving tutor – and was confident that he could trace the route again. Then he got back on the Cat and followed his tracks to the diamond mine before continuing on to his rendezvous with Soap.

North was disappointed in the day's results, but at least he had confirmed Andi's suspicions; the Twin Otter was definitely not returning directly to its Inuvik base after leaving Pivot Lake. He cursed under his breath, the low words lost in the racket created by the powerful machine beneath him. He would much rather have gone back to Inuvik with an explanation for the deviation in Captain Jim O'Neill's itinerary.

Behind the clear acrylic shield of North's snowmobile helmet, his mouth twisted into a wry grin. The reason for the Ace's diversion was still unknown, but there was nothing North Ruben liked better than solving a mystery.

He couldn't wait to get home and tell Andi the news.

THIRTEEN

Sunday morning arrived at long last. Andi awoke early and, even before pouring her first cup of coffee, checked the weather forecast. She smiled at the promise of clear, calm skies. It would be a perfect day for a mushing lesson, a sled ride and a picnic.

She curled back up in her warm bed and lingered over a cup of coffee before calling North to confirm their date. Then she sprang into action. By nine-thirty she had made a picnic lunch and was ready to leave. Before she left, though, she made her customary Sunday phone call to her dad, cutting their usual long conversation rather short. Then she called the office. Ayame was on duty, and she assured her boss that the operations were running smoothly and on schedule.

She had only one more thing to do before she left for her outing – check on Coco. Andi picked up the tray of extra picnic fare she'd set aside for the recovering young woman and carefully walked down the steep stairs from her suite to the main floor.

It didn't take Coco long to answer Andi's knock. "Good morning," Coco chirped. "Oh, what's this? For me?"

"Yes, I made more than enough lunch for North and me. We're going out mushing today," Andi announced with a wide smile. "How are you doing, anyway?" she peered closely at Coco's fading bruises.

"I'm healing. I feel almost normal again. I'm damn mad, but I feel okay."

"Yeah, I don't blame you. Have you heard anything from him?"

"No, thank God. He hasn't called, and he'd better not if he knows what's good for him."

"Well I don't want to rush you, but do you think you're going to be able to come back to work tomorrow?"

"Yes, definitely. I was practicing with makeup yesterday and I can pretty much hide the worst of it," Coco said. "I'm bored stiff anyway."

"Great. So, my story has been that you've had a nasty, contagious flu bug. Are we sticking to that?"

"Yup, that's what I've been telling people too. It's kept everyone away. Except Ayame," Coco laughed. "She's like a mother hen and insisted on bringing me some kind of Japanese herbal shit to drink."

Andi snickered. "I know what you mean. Some of that stuff smells vile, but she insists that it really works and she really means well. If you ever *do* get the flu, you've got a sure-fire cure on hand."

Andi gave Coco a quick hug before running back up to her own suite. She dressed in warm layers for her big day out on the tundra, and added her well-worn purple Qiviut neck warmer and scarf. Two Hot Shots shoved into her mitts guaranteed her hands would stay warm all day. After one last wardrobe inventory she picked up the heavy, padded lunch bag and headed out the door with a light step and even lighter heart.

She had a feeling it was going to be a most memorable day.

When she arrived at North's he already had a six-dog team in harness. He had chosen the calmest, most obedient dogs for their day out: Kia, Nanuk, Togo, Aleeka, Ikkuma and Chance were tugging at the towline, eager to run. Canadian Eskimo Dogs were by nature not only athletic, but mischievous and sneaky, too. He didn't want any trouble with the pack while Andi was learning to mush.

Juno, who North had recently been training as a 'lead dog', a position the self-assured canine was quite suitable for, was raising havoc at being left behind in the pen. Lead dogs run at the front of the tow line, and generally must be both intelligent and fast; mushers only use spoken commands to direct the dogs and at times there appears to be ESP between a musher and a well-trained lead. Now Juno was frantically racing around the enclosure, yipping and nipping at the other dogs, clearly unhappy with the current turn of events. North said it was good training for the bossy, determined dog. Juno wasn't always going to be lead dog on a team, and he couldn't always get his own way.

Before they set out, North taught Andi some basic mushing lingo and commands. He had an easy, natural teaching style and before long Andi was able to start and stop the team by herself. He showed her how to stand safely and securely on the sled's runners, how to hold the arched wooden handlebar, and how to manage the long mushing whip. The whip was the part Andi liked the least and she was relieved when she learned that it never touched the dogs. It was the sharp crack as the whip snapped the air above or beside them that got the dogs attention.

The bright winter sun had risen swiftly in the azure blue sky by the time they were ready to leave, as it tends to do so far from the equator. The temperature was a balmy minus twenty Celsius and perfect for dog sledding. North told Andi that he planned to take them out onto the McKenzie River Delta and continue her lesson while they travelled. He had already lined the small, narrow qamutik sled with a warm bearskin rug, and he instructed her to sit in the sled with her legs extended in front of her and her back resting against the rear wall.

It was a surprisingly comfortable position, and Andi felt like an Eskimo princess. "North, I'm so excited I can barely breathe!"

"Here, let me wrap this around you. I don't want my princess getting cold." North, an imposing figure clad from head to foot in the traditional Inuit winter garments of fur-trimmed caribou skin anorak, pants and kamiks, knelt on the snow beside the sled and wrapped a striped Hudson Bay Northern Store blanket around Andi's legs. He brushed her cool lips with a kiss before he rose, then he secured their picnic lunch and thermos beside the survival gear in the sled's cargo area.

With a chorus of barking and sharp yelps the six eager dogs joyously responded to North's loud command of '*MUSH*'. The team surged ahead, the towline, or gangline as it was often called in the mushing world, straining momentarily before the sled's skis broke free from the ice beneath them. And then they were off.

North ran behind the sled for a few moments, allowing the dogs to gain a bit of speed before he jumped onto the runners behind the sled basket. He made it look so easy; Andi wondered if she could ever look that natural and graceful working with a team.

The dogs ran in apparent bliss for half an hour, pink tongues lolling, each hot breath a puff of white in the cold air. Andi swore they were grinning. These dogs were built and bred to run and they loved doing it. Each animal was in the prime of life, sleek and fit. Beneath their thick pelt, each dog was pure muscle, weighing about twenty-five kilos each.

North ran the team along the frozen Mackenzie River until they were well away from town, then he turned onto the snow-covered tundra. A few hardy bushes and stunted black spruce, birch and jack pine trees dotted the snowy winter landscape. Andi knew that in spring a touch of magic would light up the tundra. Although small and lowly, the abundant grasses, lichen, heath, crocus, arctic poppy, and wallflower would burst forth with colour. Today, though, still frozen in the midst of a long winter, the pristine snow and ice sparkled and glimmered in the sun, almost blinding to the naked eye. Andi was glad North had given her tinted ski goggles to protect her eyes from the sun and wind.

North finally called the team to a halt atop a small rise overlooking the majestic Mackenzie River Delta. The vast, untamed beauty of the Arctic was an awe-inspiring sight. While Andi chose a spot for their lunch, North tended to the dogs. He loosened the tugs that connected their harnesses to the towline, giving them more freedom to lay down, then threw them a frozen meat snack.

When Andi found the perfect spot she stomped on the inevitable drifts and clumps of snow, turning the area into a reasonably level picnic site. She spread out the bright Bay blanket and fetched the picnic bag from the qamutik. She had prepared a veritable feast; smoked arctic char and crackers for a starter, potato salad, thick ham slices, devilled eggs, fresh homemade rye bread and pickled beets. Dessert would be her famous lemon loaf – her own beloved mother's recipe.

North's eyes widened at the spread of delectable fare. "Whoa, looking good, Babe." He wrapped his arms around Andi's bulky, parka-clad body, lifting her off her feet as though she weighed no more than a feather. Holding her close, he twirled around until they both collapsed on the snow, dizzy and howling in laughter. His eyes caught hers and the laughter died on their lips. Andi had landed on her back, and squinted into the dazzling sunshine. North slowly lowered his head and brushed her lips lightly with his. When he raised his head again there was a silent question in his dark, espresso eyes.

Andi reached up with a cold, gloveless hand and cupped a smooth cheek. Their next kiss was not as restrained. North's demanding lips and tongue robbed her of any breath that happened to remain in her lungs. It had been too long since she had been kissed that way, and she didn't want it to stop. Andi willingly gave herself to North's lead, opening her lips and heart and soul to him. Too soon, though, he drew away and pulled her to her feet. She found herself too weak to stand on her own, and leaned into his solid bulk a moment to steady herself.

"Let's eat," he announced with a grin, apparently oblivious of Andi's feverish state. He certainly didn't know that, beneath her purple toque, her ears were on fire. "We don't want this fantastic lunch to freeze."

They sat side by side in the companionable silence that only true friends or old couples share. With no need for words, they savoured every bite of the delicious food, exchanging an occasional shy glance. They both realized that everything had changed between them. They were no longer 'just friends'. A deeper, more meaningful relationship had bloomed between them and they both sensed it was just the beginning.

When their meal was finished North poured coffee into insulated stainless-steel mugs while Andi packed up the meager leftovers. "That was amazing," he sighed, patting his belly. "My compliments to the cook." He passed her a mug of coffee, holding up a Mickey bottle of Southern Comfort in his other hand. "I'm having a shot. You want some in your cup, too? It warms you right up."

"No thanks, I'm good."

With a cup of coffee in one hand and a thick slice of lemon loaf in the other, they wandered to the edge of their majestic, secluded viewpoint.

"At night, you can see the lights of Inuvik," North said, gesturing south, down the delta. "And if we continued up this way," he pointed northwest, "we'd eventually hit Tuktoyaktuk."

Andi gazed at the empty, vast expanse around her. It was hard to believe there was actually civilization anywhere nearby. She felt humble in the knowledge that the very ground she walked on may have never before seen human footsteps. The very air felt ancient and mysterious and frightening, and the silence was absolute. The silence was deafening.

In the serenity and companionship of the moment, Andi made an abrupt decision. "North," whispered, although there was no one else to hear her words. "I have something to tell you."

"What? Do you have to pee?" he whispered back, a crooked smile on his lips and the tip of his long eyetooth peeking at her.

"No!" she said loudly. "Well, not yet anyway. This is *serious*, North."

"What is it?"

"Well, you know that I don't drink alcohol."

North nodded, and took another sip of his Southern Comfort-laced coffee. "I know that. You told me you're allergic to alcohol."

"Well, that's not exactly true. I, um, I'm a recovering alcoholic, North. I go to AA meetings at least once a week." Andi lost the ability to breathe. Her throat clenched, the air in her lungs trapped with no escape route. She knew that North's reaction to her announcement would be the deciding factor in the next chapter of their relationship, and quite possibly in the rest of her life.

"I know," he said softly, gazing down at her with an unfathomable smile on his lips. "I know, Babe, and I'm okay with that. I've been waiting for you to tell me. *Wanting* you to tell me." He leaned down and kissed her cheek, his breath scorching her cool skin.

Her mouth fell open. "You *knew*? How did you know?"

"It's a small town, Babe. Never forget, everyone knows pretty much everything about everyone else. And especially about the hottest new chick in town." The object of Andi's bemusement winked at her with a wicked grin.

"Oh my god! Don't tell me *everyone* knows I'm AA?" The very thought appalled her, instant tears glinting in her emerald eyes.

"Hey, easy now, sweetheart." North pulled her close and looked deeply into her brimming eyes. "I made a point of finding out everything I could about you, that's why I know. From the first day I met you, Andrea Nowak, I knew I wanted you to be part of my life. A *big* part."

Andi sniffled and blinked rapidly in a futile attempt to prevent her tears from falling.

"I was just joking earlier, but I guess it was a damn bad joke. No one has ever mentioned that you go to AA meetings, Andi." North reached up to brush the tears from her cheeks. "And besides, there's no shame in it. Going to those meetings proves that you have courage, and I admire you for that."

He wrapped his arms around her in an enveloping hug and Andi's arms responded as if they had a mind of their own. She felt like she was finally at home, in his arms. On her left hand the silver AA ring warmed her finger, making her aware of its mystical presence. She was acutely aware of its healing powers – the powers that guided her every day and delivered continuous support and strength.

They stood together for long minutes, holding each other as closely as their bulky outerwear would let them. The light of the Arctic day was quickly fading, but neither of them noticed.

FOURTEEN

"It's a lemon!" Andi shrieked, the force of her words lost within the vast reaches of the cavernous maintenance hangar. With a few minutes to spare before their Monday morning management meeting, she'd stopped to take a look at the Twin Otter they'd leased from Charlie Harper. The aircraft had arrived from Yellowknife the night before and Ken's engineers were already buzzing around the machine. They would give it a thorough safety check before it was put it into service for Tuktu.

She stood rooted to the concrete floor, staring in dismay at the gaudy aircraft. Painted lemon yellow with a band of black bisecting the fuselage and continuing up the tail, the aircraft was shockingly bright. "Well that thing sure won't sneak anywhere undetected," she muttered, shaking her head. She definitely preferred Tuktu's colour scheme of white with discreet azure blue pinstripes and the Tuktu Aviation caribou head logo emblazoned high on the tail. It was much more pleasing to the eye.

Andi glanced at her watch and hurried out the door; she didn't want to be late for Paul's Monday morning management meeting. On her way to the office she tried to decide if she should tell Paul about North's scouting trip to Pivot Lake. After giving it some consideration, she decided that concrete evidence, instead of mere speculation, was needed before she would share her suspicions about Jim O'Neill. The fact that her own trip to the diamond mine had hit a sore spot with someone confirmed, at least in her own mind that something was going on. Her instincts, which usually proved to be 100% accurate, told her that Tuktu's illustrious Captain O'Neill was at the centre of it all, but

103

she needed to find out what 'it' was before she voiced her suspicions.

She ran up the dusty old stairs to her office, not at all surprised to find Ayame manning dispatch. "Good morning, Ayame. Let me guess. Jessica didn't make it back from her trip to Vancouver?"

"Hi, yourself. No, she's not back but I'm fine with it," Ayame chuckled. "I totally expected her to call and ask me to cover for her today. I'll get an extra day off later this week. So how are *you*? How was your big day out with Fang?" She wiggled her eyebrows up and down.

"Ayame, stop it. You know he doesn't like to be called that. And by the way my day was just *amazing*. I haven't had that much fun in … well, I can't remember when." Andi's face and eyes lit up. "It was an absolutely wonderful day."

"I'm so glad for you," Ayame smiled. "You deserve a little happiness in your life. I want to hear all about your day, but I guess it will have to wait." Two phone lines rang in unison; the typical Monday morning rush had begun.

Andi put a pot of coffee to brew and dug out the notes she'd hastily prepared for their meeting. She'd just poured herself and Ayame a cup when footsteps thundered up the stairs.

There was more on Paul's agenda than usual, and their meeting stretched from one hour to two. No mention was made of Jim O'Neill's past behavior, or present indiscretions, and Andi didn't bring the subject up either.

When the meeting was finally over she decided to call Carlos Sante. It had been four days since she'd been to the mine and, contrary to his promise, she hadn't heard a word from him since. She pulled out his business card and called his direct phone line at the diamond mine. There was no answer, and her call wasn't picked up by an answering machine. She left his card on her desk to remind herself to try again later in the day.

Engrossed in her work and with the constant background noise of radios and ringing phones, Andi didn't hear booted feet running up the stairs. She started when a deep, familiar voice called out, "Hello, ladies!"

"North!" both Andi and Ayame exclaimed. "I wasn't expecting to see you here today," Andi frowned. "Let me make some fresh coffee."

"Sounds great, I can use a cup." North rubbed his bare hands together. "It's damn cold out there today."

Andi engaged North with casual chatter while the coffee brewed. Ayame joined them for a few minutes during a lull in phone calls. When the coffee was ready North followed Andi into her office and closed both doors. She sat behind her desk and North sank into one of the guest chairs across from her.

They grinned at each other like mischievous children. "What's up?" Andi asked over the rim of her steaming mug.

North leaned back, looking like a cat that had swallowed a canary. "I have a plan," he grinned.

"What kind of plan?"

"I'm going to get Soap to take me back out to the hunting cabin tomorrow, but this time I'm taking enough gear to spend a few days. I'll tell everyone I've gone hunting – back out on the land to reconnect with my roots." He seemed so amused and satisfied with his plan that Andi had to smile too. "I'm going to need your help though," he added.

"Of course, I'll do whatever I can. This *is* my problem, after all. Not yours."

"Well, I'm making it my problem, Babe. From now on, anything that concerns you, concerns me." North's features softened when he saw a delicate blush creep up Andi's neck and spread to her cheeks. "From now on, it's you and me."

"North, you don't have to do this."

"I know I don't have to. But I *want* to."

Andi smiled shyly. "So, what do I do while you're out on the land?"

"You have to stay at my place and look after the mutts."

"Oh, I can totally do that!" she cried, leaning forward eagerly. "I'd love to spend some time with them. You'll have to show me what to do before you leave, though. I don't have a clue how to look after them."

North nodded. "I'll prepare my gear today, and I've already called Ruby to cover the gallery for me. Why don't you come out after work and help me with the evening feeding? That would be a good way to get familiar with the procedure. You can make some notes too."

Sure, that'll work. About 5:30?"

"Yup, that's good. Can you stay for dinner, too? It'll give us more time to talk about the plan I have for my little recon trip. I'd rather talk in private."

"Sounds great. Can I bring anything?"

"Just your beautiful self, Babe." In one fluid motion North rose from his chair, leaned over Andi's desk and kissed her. "Later, then." He winked and walked out of her office, leaving a bemused Operations Manager staring blindly through her office window, deep in thought.

FIFTEEN

North swept the last flakes of snow from his father's abandoned hunting cabin and pulled the flimsy plywood door closed. Outside the cabin an occasional gust of wind stirred up whirling eddies of dry, loose snow.

Soap had once again had the Beaver ready to depart at dawn. By 11 am he had deposited North, along with his snowmobile and gear, at his old friend's cabin. Promising to return at 5pm on Thursday, two days hence, Soap took off in a flurry of white, bound for Inuvik.

North lit the small kerosene heater he brought with him, quickly forcing the worst of the bone chilling cold from the building. There were so many cracks and crevasses in the old wooden structure that North wasn't concerned about poisoning himself with toxic fumes.

He set up a two-burner Coleman stove and a kerosene lantern, feeling slightly guilty about 'cheating', as his dad would have called it. Going out on the land with an assortment of modern camping gear was not really roughing it like they used to, but it sure as hell made life a lot more comfortable.

North reached into his Coleman cooler and pulled out eggs and bacon to cook up a late breakfast. He hadn't had time to eat before he left Inuvik, and wanted to do his reconnoitering on a full belly.

Thirty minutes later he packed a small thermos of coffee, two bacon sandwiches, maps, and a box of bullets into his backpack. He strapped the pack and an extra plastic jerry can of gas to the back of the Arctic Cat, stowed a satellite phone under the seat and slung his rifle across his back. Then he headed out onto the tundra, aiming north of the small range of hills that had defeated him on his last foray.

Even though he was on a mission, North couldn't ignore the beauty of his unspoiled native land. It was a stroke of luck that the weather was cooperating. The sky was a clear, vibrant azure blue, the winds were light, and the temperature was a balmy minus fifteen Celsius. Most Northerners would be unzipping their heavy parkas in this weather, complaining that it was getting too warm.

His internal navigation system didn't fail him and about an hour later he spotted a bump in the land that looked familiar – the hills that were his target. When he arrived at his destination he immediately began a grid search, looking for trails or unusual marks in the snow. By his calculations he could spend about four hours snooping around before heading back to camp during daylight. Being caught on the land in the dark could spell disaster.

He was looking for signs of recent disturbance, such as aircraft landing marks or a snowmobile trail. If his hunch was right, the Twin Otter would be landing close enough to the diamond mine to allow a snowmobile to easily reach the site.

The afternoon wore on. North found nothing of interest. He stopped only once to top up the gas tank and wolf down a sandwich and cup of lukewarm coffee. His enthusiasm waned with each passing hour.

When the sun hovered near the western horizon North resigned himself to the fact that his day was an abject failure. He was bone-tired and his shoulders and neck muscles ached from the physical effort required to manhandle the snowmobile over the rough terrain. He had decided to abandon his search for the day when a nearby glint caught his eye. It was more than a glimmer of sun on ice; he'd seen enough of that to know that this was something different. His interest peaked, and he gunned the Arctic Cat forward.

A few seconds later North was looking at a half-buried piece of foil liner from a pack of cigarettes. The immediate area was covered in a multitude of boot prints, as well as several sets of snowmobile ski tracks.

"Bingo," he whispered through frozen lips that just managed to curve into a smile. His exhaustion vanished. With renewed zeal he expanded his search for signs of an aircraft landing site. He wasn't disappointed. Several tracks left by a set of Twin Otter skis were clearly etched into the nearby terrain. It was evident they'd landed in this spot more than once.

Daylight was fading quickly; North knew he had to work fast or be caught in the approaching blackness of an Arctic night. He noted his location on his map and turned the Cat toward the cabin, opening the throttle wide. The finely tuned machine responded with a satisfying burst of speed. Exultant over his discovery, he whooped in triumph.

He couldn't wait to tell Andi the good news.

By the time North reached the cabin early stars winked in the night sky. He fired up the heater and put a pot of coffee on the stove, then prepared a hasty and well-earned dinner. Minutes later he swallowed the last morsel of his sister's succulent caribou stew. He wiped up the last bits of brown gravy from his plate and shoved the bread in his mouth, sighing in contentment. The meal had been a delicious treat that brought back memories of his mother's cooking, and one he seldom got to enjoy any more.

A glance at his watch told him it was time to turn on the satellite phone. Andi had made him promise to check in every evening, and at eight o'clock sharp her call broke the silence. "Hi Andi, how are you doing?"

"I'm great, and how are you? Is everything okay out there?"

"Yup, I'm fine. Had a good day today. Got some great shots for my gallery. They'll be real winners."

Aware that satellite phone conversations are vulnerable to eavesdropping and wanting to keep North's mission a secret, the pair had devised a code for their conversations. He had just told Andi that he had found the Twin Otter's secret landing site. If he had said, "Had some trouble with the Cat," she would know that he'd had no luck finding it yet.

"That's wonderful! I can't wait to see them. I'll call you again at one o'clock tomorrow, okay?" Andi had just advised North that the Twin Otter service flight, captained by Jim O'Neill, would be landing at Pivot Lake about one o'clock the next day.

"Sounds good. I'll talk to you again tomorrow. Have a good night."

"Thanks, you too. Take care out there."

North turned the phone off to conserve its battery, then slipped on his boots. He had to pay a visit to Mother Nature. There was no convenient indoor plumbing on the land, which was the one thing he missed the most.

The moment he opened the cabin door he forgot his pressing need. The sky above was alive with colour, wide bands that danced and glowed with the beauty of the Northern Lights. It had been a long while since he'd taken the time to appreciate the night sky, and he'd forgotten how breathtaking and majestic the Aurora Borealis were. Yellow and green flares, touched with a hint of red, purple and white danced across the sky, leaping and flaring in a turmoil of colour. The air fairly crackled with energy. It was an awe-inspiring sight – one that made him glad to be alive.

When he finally crawled into his heavy Wood's Three Star sleeping bag a little later, he quickly fell into a deep and dreamless sleep. Exhaustion, both mental and physical, had taken its toll on him.

While he slept the Aurora continued to paint the heavens above, the magical, mysterious colours illuminated the way for Arctic fox, hares, wolves, caribou and countless other creatures that wandered the frozen tundra.

"Shit!" North exclaimed, foggy breath trailing in his wake as he hurried back to the relative warmth of the cabin. Although the temperature had

plunged during the night, he'd slept comfortably enough in the heated cabin. Braving the frigid pre-dawn air with his pants down, however, wasn't an enjoyable way to wake up, even for a seasoned Arctic hunter.

Grumbling and cursing, he lit the Coleman stove and put coffee to perk in an old-fashioned, blue enamel coffee pot. He rubbed his hands together near the small flue flame, attempting to restore feeling to his frozen digits.

His mood didn't improve much when, in his haste for a much-needed jolt of caffeine, he scalded his tongue a few minutes later. Miserable and hurting, North decided that bacon, eggs and hash browns would make him feel better. He'd think about his plan of attack when his breakfast was done.

Camouflaged behind a small knoll overlooking the site he'd discovered the previous day, North hunched in his makeshift snow den. He was cold, cramped, and miserable. With his long hunting knife, he'd carved out a depression for his body and hidden himself and the Arctic Cat beneath the white blanket, banking it up with snow.

He'd been waiting for well over an hour and, although he was protected from the wind, he sensed that the temperature was still falling. A shake of his coffee thermos told him it was almost empty. The bitter cold had made him ravenous, so his bacon sandwiches were long gone, too. By his calculations the Twin Otter should have arrived about thirty minutes ago – if it was coming at all.

The wind picked up and gusted overhead. Dark, snow-laden clouds had been looming on the horizon when North arrived at the site. He knew that if the weather was bad in Inuvik the Twin Otter may still be sitting there. Or maybe he was waiting in the wrong place after all.

He'd just stood up for a much-needed stretch when he heard the distant hum of turbine engines. He dove back into his den, and settled the white blanket over the entrance. It sounded like the aircraft was headed directly toward him. A rush of adrenalin coursed through his veins. No longer cold, cramped and hurting, North became fully alert, his heart pumped with renewed energy and purpose.

Every second seemed like an eternity as the aircraft made a slow approach. At last it landed. The snarl of twin propellers grew louder as the aircraft taxied closer.

Keeping his head low, North cautiously peered under the edge of the blanket. Over the rim of his hideout he saw a white and blue Tuktu Aviation Twin Otter taxiing toward him, its spinning propellers kicking up a thick flurry of white snow. He ducked down again, breathing heavily. A few seconds later the engines whined down and the props stilled.

Minutes passed in utter silence. Even the wind had suddenly dropped, reserving its voice for another hour or another day.

In the ensuing silence North strained to listen for a clue of what lay ahead, but the only sound he detected was the beating of his own straining heart. He became restless, eager to use his new boost of energy for something other than hiding cowardly in a frozen cocoon.

Finally a faint sound broke the silence. North grinned. Just as he'd predicted – a snowmobile was approaching. The machine's high-pitched whine steadily and quickly grew louder. He dared not poke his head up again. Patience was one thing he'd learned from his dad. A good hunter must learn to have patience, or become the hunted.

A few minutes later the second visitor to the party arrived. As soon as the snowmobile's engine fell silent North heard the dull clank of frozen metal; a door was being opened on the aircraft. He risked a quick peek and was rewarded with a broadside view of the Twin Otter, which had come to a stop no more than 50 paces away. The driver of the snowmobile, clad in a black one-piece snowsuit and black helmet with a full black visor, was standing in front of the open airstair door. A powerful looking bright yellow Ski-Doo was parked behind him, a rifle strapped to its side.

A familiar figure descended from the aircraft, zipping up his bulky dark blue parka. His head was bare, save his yellow-tinted aviator glasses. Captain Jim O'Neill in the flesh.

The driver of the snowmobile tugged off his bulky gloves and the two men briefly shook hands. A gust of wind sprang from nowhere, teasing the pure white snow beneath their feet. O'Neill turned and climbed back up the airstair, followed by his mysterious visitor. Moments later the door was pulled closed with a resounding *clunk*.

Inside his frigid white lair North quickly became frustrated. He needed to find out what was going on inside that Twin Otter. He wanted to know who was driving that snow machine.

He had no choice, though, but to sit huddled behind a snow bank, feeling increasingly helpless. His initial adrenalin rush was fading and he began to grow cold again. His heightened senses dulled. His joints grew stiff. He had to take a piss but couldn't risk moving or standing. If he knew one thing for certain it was that showing himself now could be dangerous to his health. It could be fatal. *Damn*, he cursed under his breath. He felt trapped, like a hare in a hole.

As the long minutes dragged by only the freshening wind broke the silence. North became increasingly restless. He knew that the plummeting mercury would be on his side; the flight crew couldn't remain parked on the tundra long and risk freezing the Twin Otter's Ni-Cad starting battery.

Ten long, cold minutes later the airstair door flipped down again. The figure in black walked down the stairs and directly to his waiting machine without a backward glance. O'Neill pulled the aircraft door shut as soon as his visitor's last booted foot left the airstair.

The yellow Ski-Doo roared to life and sped off, leaving a blanket of white in its wake. North could only assume it was returning to the Pivot Lake diamond mine site – the only place of inhabitation within a fifty-kilometer radius.

He desperately wanted to follow the mysterious rider but instead forced himself to wait for the Twin Otter to leave. When the aircraft finally started to taxi away, he began digging his snowmobile out of its blind. Keeping a wary eye on the aircraft, which had quickly taken off and was now heading in the general direction of Inuvik, North stowed his gear and fired up the Arctic Cat.

By this time the unknown visitor was nowhere in sight but North had no trouble following his tracks. Once he knew what he was looking at, a well-worn trail was quite evident amongst the drifts and chunks of frozen ice and snow. North skimmed over the trail, not surprised to confirm that the route was taking him around the range of low hills and in the general direction of Pivot Lake.

He plowed on through the opaque light of the cloudy day, coaxing every bit of speed he could out of his well-tuned machine. He had yet to spot his quarry. When he veered around the last small knoll he stopped short, releasing his grip on the throttle. The man, or woman, in black had come to a stop forty meters away and was standing beside the yellow and black Ski-Doo. North swore when he spotted a rifle pointed in his direction.

Before he could react the loud report of gunfire pierced the air. North gunned his Cat again, leaning hard into a tight right-hand turn. Snow arced behind him, providing a thin white screen. He fumbling for the rifle he'd strapped to his back. Another shot ruffled the snow beside his machine.

So much for just a warning shot, North thought, his mind racing. *This guy means business.*

He headed back to the squat hill he'd just rounded. On the other side of it and out of sight of the shooter he slowed and reached for his own rifle, his father's lovingly preserved .22 Long Range Rimfire. A second later the other rider raced around the hill and into range.

Confident that his well-tuned Arctic Cat could outrun anything else on skis, North took a second to steady a return shot. He fired, plugging the snow a hand span from the Ski-Doo, but the snow machine continued toward him. North fired a second shot, once again missing his speeding target. He decided it was time to make a run for it and cranked the Arctic Cat's throttle. His compliant machine surged ahead, but not soon enough.

He heard another crack and felt a sharp sting high on his left arm. Within a breath the sting morphed into intense, overwhelming pain. He bellowed in rage, his first instinct being to grasp the injured arm hanging at his side. His mind raced, looking for a solution to his quandary. His right hand was wrapped around the throttle – releasing the gas would cause the Cat to come to a dead halt, which would most likely spell a death sentence.

Losing precious seconds, he released the throttle and reached around his body to pull his useless left arm into his lap. The pain didn't lessen in the least, but at least the limp arm was no longer dangling in the wind. Gritting his teeth in agony, he opened up the throttle again, shooting forward.

North knew he was running for his life. He swallowed hard, his stomach threatening to empty into his throat. He couldn't remember a time when he'd felt pain this intense.

A gunshot cracked behind him. Snow and ice spit just to his right, too close for comfort. He sensed that he was putting some distance between him and the Ski-Doo, but knew he couldn't afford to squander precious seconds by looking back. He doubted that his shattered body would respond anyway. He swore and hunched lower behind the windscreen, hoping to reduce the drag created by his upper body hitting the wind, but knowing it wouldn't really matter much anyway.

He turned the throttle as far as it would go praying that he could squeeze more momentum out of the Arctic Cat, but the machine was already at its maximum running speed. North prayed it would be fast enough to outrun whoever was at his back then swore at instant later when he hit an obscured ridge of ice and became airborne, losing precious speed and forward velocity while the Cat's track spun uselessly in the air.

He fought to keep the heavy snowmobile under control; his nostrils flared in pain and his breaths were reduced to short gasps that fogged the inside of his visor. He felt the warmth of blood seeping down his left arm and knew he needed to apply pressure to the wound but there was no time to stop and administer first aid.

Despite the sub-zero temperature, sweat dripped from North's forehead and down his neck. His vision was impairing by the foggy visor, and he was becoming weaker by the minute. He tried to regulate his breathing and block out the pain. As he sped on through the dull Arctic afternoon, he prayed that he was on the right course to the cabin and that he would live to see another sunrise. But most of all, he prayed that he would live to see Andi again.

Several minutes later he realized that he was barely moving; the snow machine beneath him was meandering over the snow slower than he could walk. His dulled senses slowly registered the fact that he couldn't hear his pursuer either.

Although he was dizzy and fought to keep upright on his seat, he slowly turned his head to scan the trail behind him. Only clear white snow and dull skies were at his back. He moaned in joy and pain and the sudden realization that he might survive his ordeal after all.

North brought the Arctic Cat to a stop and killed the engine. Inside his parka, the flannel shirtsleeve on his left arm was sticky with blood. He tried raising it and was rewarded with a new bout of blinding pain. This time he couldn't keep the vomit down, and barely had enough time to drag his helmet off before the vile, steaming stream shot from his mouth. Leaning over as far as he could he vomited again and again, until only dry heaves wracked his body.

When his stomach finally quit clenching, he slowly dragged his tortured body off the Cat. He scooped up a handful of snow and brought it to his numb lips, shoving a little into his mouth. It quickly melted, allowing a few drops of water to trickle down his parched, aching throat.

Feeling slightly more alert, he scrutinised the surrounding

terrain and detected a familiar rise in the land; he guessed that the cabin would be about two kilometers away. North knew that his only chance of survival was to apply pressure to his wound, call Soap for an immediate pickup and then get to the cabin as fast as he could. He was losing blood and becoming weaker by the minute.

With one hand he fumbled the Arctic Cat's seat-latch open and lifted out his satellite phone. Looking for something to fashion a tourniquet with, he spotted an old scarf at the bottom of the storage area. He shrugged out of his parka and with stiff, frozen fingers and his teeth managed to wrap the scarf around his wounded arm. He tied it as tightly as he could, hoping to staunch the loss of blood. It wasn't great, but it was the best he could do.

Praying that the battery wasn't dead, North turned the phone on. He breathed a sigh of relief when it crackled to life. His addled mind fought to remember Soap's phone number. After two aborted attempts, he managed to reach him.

"North, you don't sound good. What's the problem?"

"I'm about two kilometers southeast of the cabin. Having some trouble but I think I can make it back there. I need to come out right away. Can you pick me up?"

"Roger that. Will be there as soon as I can. Hang tight boy."

North turned off the precious phone and stowed it back under the seat. Firing up his machine with one injured arm wasn't an easy task and he swore repeatedly and viciously, his frustration and pain forcing him to reach deep into his pool of strength.

Finally mobile again, he pointed the snowmobile in the direction of the cabin. Every bump was excruciating torture, and with each minute that passed he found it harder to keep his mind and body focused on the increasingly difficult task of staying astride the moving snowmobile. It seemed like hours before he spotted his dad's cabin in the distance. The sight of it made him want to weep for joy.

"Maybe I'll make it out of here alive after all" were his last

barely coherent words before everything went black.

SIXTEEN

When he regained consciousness North discovered, after a few moments of blurry-eyed disorientation, that he was lying in a hospital bed. A very bright and angry pair of green eyes were only inches from his, staring at him intently.

"Who shot you? What the hell happened out there?" Andi rattled off questions without waiting for answers.

He'd been shot? North closed his eyes and struggled to fit the fragmented pieces of his memory back together. *Snowmobile ... tundra ... Twin Otter ... black, black, black. The guy in black had shot at him!* His throat was parched and raw and he likely couldn't reply even if he could pull a coherent thought together.

"You could have died!" Andi's anger dissolved into tears. She leaned over the bed railing and kissed his cheek tenderly. "Oh, my God, sweetheart, I'm so, so sorry," she murmured. "This is all my fault. I should never have let you go out there."

North reached up and ran his fingers through the veil of dark hair that fell across her cheek. He detected a faint trace of lavender and took a deeper breath, committing her scent to memory. "I'll be okay Babe," he croaked. His voice was rough and scratchy. "My throat hurts more than anything."

"They likely intubated you during surgery." She straightened and slowly sank into the chair beside his bed, leaving one hand resting on his shoulder.

"I had *surgery?*"

"Yes," she nodded. "They had to fix the hole that bullet left in your shoulder. Does it hurt very much?"

"I'm going to be just fine, Babe," he said with a lazy grin. "They must be giving me some wicked drugs cause I'm feeling pretty good right now." Intravenous tubing trailed from his arm as he reached up to cover Andi's hand with his own.

A stout nurse walked briskly into the semi-private room. The frown on her face immediately morphed into a smile when she recognized Andi. "Hey, Andi, I didn't expect to see you here tonight."

Nurse Lisette McKerrel was the wife of one of Tuktu's pilots, and both Andi and North knew her from the various social activities and Margo's TGIF parties. She looked at their hands clasped on the bed, her eyebrows lifting in surprise. "Oh, I didn't know. Well, good for you guys." She smiled warmly.

"Now, let's get you settled down for what's left of the night, North. You need some sleep."

"Naw, let me go home," he mumbled, reaching down to throw the blanket back.

"No way, my dear. You're not going anywhere tonight. Doctor's orders." Nurse Lisette laid a gentle hand on North's chest and eased him back against the bed. She straightened his blankets and tucked them in around him, then adjusted the intravenous drip. "We need to get more fluids and antibiotics into you, young man. You lost a lot of blood today. Andi can probably come pick you up tomorrow morning after rounds, though."

"You're a very lucky fellow, you know," Lisette continued as she checked North's vitals. "That bullet missed all the important stuff in your arm, like your humerus bone and major blood vessels. It just winged you, really. Thanks to the frigid weather out there, you didn't lose as much blood as you could have, either." As she chatted, Lisette efficiently removed North's pressure bandage, checked the wound site and securely reapplied a new sterile dressing.

Andi had backed away from the bed, giving Lisette room to

maneuver around North. She paled at the nurse's comments and when her knees began to shake, she dropped into a chair by the foot of the bed. Both North and Lisette ignored her, their attention focused on his arm.

"You're going to have to leave him now, Andi. I just gave him another shot of Demerol. He needs some rest. Don't worry though, honey, we'll take good care of him." Lisette smiled warmly at Andi.

She rose from the chair and stepped unsteadily to North's side, her eyes brimming with tears. She kissed him gently, barely brushing his parched lips, and ran her fingers over his cheek. "I'll be back first thing in the morning. You get some sleep, okay?" A lone tear ran down her cheek. North reached up and brushed it away with his thumb.

"You too, Babe," he mumbled, smiling groggily. "Give the mutts my love."

Deep within the recess of Andi's slumbering brain, the annoying beep of an alarm finally registered. Groaning, she rolled over and hit the clock, then forced one eye open a crack to look at the time. It didn't feel like 7 am; it felt like she'd just gotten to sleep.

When the memory of the previous night's events jolted her to awareness Andi sat bolt upright in North's warm, soft bed. "Oh, my God," she muttered, "I *did* just barely get to sleep." She dropped back against the pillows and let her mind run through the course of events again, trying to recall each horrific detail.

First, there was the distressing phone call from North's friend, Soap, telling her to get over to the hospital; telling her that North had been shot, but was still alive.

She remembered her reckless race to town, praying every inch of the way to an untrustworthy God. She'd prayed for God to leave North here, on earth, with her. She'd prayed and pleaded with God not to hurt her again, not to break her heart. It was at that moment, speeding recklessly down a black and icy road high above the Arctic Circle that

Andi realized she was desperately in love with North Edward Charles Ruben. In the face of death, she surmised, one finally realizes what's really important in life.

When she arrived at the hospital, Soap was sitting in the waiting room staring at a muted television. North was in surgery, he explained, but a nurse had just come to tell him that he was doing just fine. He'd lost some blood, but the doc was stitching up the wound and said he would be back on his feet in no time.

It took two long hours before Andi had finally been granted her short visit with the man she loved. Soap had long since left, claiming that he was too tuckered from a long day and too much excitement. Before leaving he explained how he'd received the call from North, requesting immediate pick up at the cabin. When he landed he found North barely conscious inside the ice-cold cabin. It had been a hellish trip home for the old bush pilot; North had slipped in and out of consciousness several times, and Soap feared that he'd lost him more than once.

Andi asked Soap if he knew who had shot their friend, and he replied that North had been in no condition to talk.

"Well, did you report it to the RCMP?" she asked.

Soap just looked at her sternly with his rheumy old brown eyes. "If North wants to report it, that's his own business."

"Well, doesn't the hospital report gunshot wounds?"

"Could be. You'll have to ask 'em."

Frustrated with the old man, Andi sought out the duty nurse. She wasn't next of kin, though, and the nurse would tell her nothing. She was extremely lucky that they had finally agreed to let her spend a few minutes with the patient when he had eventually been returned to his room.

After returning to North's place in the wee hours of the morning sleep eluded her, even though she was mentally and physically exhausted. She was past the point of being tired. The last time she glanced at the clock it was 4 am. Even the normally slumbering sled dogs were restless, roaming the compound and muttering, almost as though they could sense Andi's distress. The thought fleetingly passed through her sleep deprived mind that perhaps the dogs had some instinctive or telepathic awareness of their master's unpleasant incident. Did things like that really happen, she wondered?

Now that it was morning she was almost comatose with fatigue. While she waited for North's ancient coffee maker to quit spitting she wandered around his snug cabin wrapped in one of his green plaid flannel shirts and admired the beautiful carvings and artwork displayed in every room. She always felt comfortable and secure in North's home, but sorely missed his presence.

When the coffee was ready, she quickly downed her first mug of the fortifying brew. By the time she was halfway through her second mug she could feel the welcome effects of the caffeine and took a few minutes to relax and enjoy the rest of the cup. Then she threw on the clothes she'd worn the day before and prepared to brave the cold. The mutts had to be fed. Before she did that, though, she needed to know how North was. She dialed the hospital.

"Resting comfortably," was all the ward nurse would tell her. "No other information will be available until after doctor's rounds at 10:00." *Damn nurses*, Andi thought, slamming the phone down.

She walked out into the dark Arctic winter morning. Feeding North's sled dogs took almost an hour; each animal had its own individual bowl, some getting more rations than others. Once the dogs had finished eating the bowls had to be collected and washed. Andi shivered as she stepped into the warm building that housed the indoor kennels. She washed up the metal bowls while young Qannik frolicked at her feet. The small dog had grown a lot since Andi had first met her. Although Qannik still spent her nights indoors, she was now big enough to interact with the older dogs during the day.

Andi loved the pure white pup. She knelt on the floor and Qannik squirmed and wiggled around her, leaving a little yellow puddle of ecstasy for Andi to clean up. Andi laughed and hugged the furry ball of energy, planting a big kiss on her wet black nose.

"Okay, my little snowflake," Andi cooed, "out you go. It's time to go play with your big friends." Qannik raced out into the pen, yipping with glee at her freedom and tumbling over clumsy paws in her excitement to join her mentors. Andi closed and locked the kennel door and gate to the outside pen before returning to the house.

Though dawn was still an hour away the sky was already lightening. Andi slowly retraced her steps to the house, weaving through the high banks of snow bordering the pathway. She tilted her face to the heavens, closed her eyes and let the fresh breeze wash over her face, trailing over her cheeks and teasing the wisps of dark hair that had escaped from her purple qiviut toque.

And then it happened again. First Andi's ears began to burn, then a black shadow slid past her eyes. She dropped to her knees in the snow, eyes pressed shut, heaving from the putrid odor of death and decay that assailed her senses. She tried to stand but was incapable of movement, locked to the ground by an invisible force. Fragments of swirling red and pink ribbons swam before her closed eyes. Long, haunting minutes passed before the invisible assailant released its grip on her.

When she eventually stumbled to her feet again, she lifted her eyes to search the predawn sky for a clue to her distress. Just as the time before, the heavens held no testimony. There was absolutely nothing to explain the premonition of dread and death that enveloped her.

She hurried up the path to the security of North's house and poured another cup of coffee, clutching the hot mug with numb, trembling fingers. It took her nerves longer to settle this time. The event had lasted longer and had been much, much more intense than the first one. When the worst of her shaking had subsided, she stripped and stepped into the shower, letting the soothing power of hot water ease her tense and sore muscles.

Before leaving the house she rummaged through North's closet for a clean shirt to take to the hospital. She picked up her purse and briefcase, locked the cabin door behind her and headed out to the airport, driving as fast as she dared on the snowy roads.

The last thing she wanted was her own company.

SEVENTEEN

Later that morning Andi strode into North's hospital room to find him sitting on the edge of his bed in a faded blue hospital gown. His long black hair, normally secured back by a leather thong, was hanging loose over his broad shoulders. Two pretty, young nurses were fussing over him.

"Hey, Andi!" North grinned. "Good to see you, Babe."

Andi glared at the nurses for a moment before turning her green eyes toward him. "Yeah, good to see you too. How are you feeling?"

"A little worse for wear, but these two angels just changed my bandage and are rigging up a sling for my arm. The doc says I'm not supposed to move it too much for a couple of days." North grinned at the nurses.

"How does that feel, North? Is it comfortable?" Nurse One asked. Nurse Two giggled.

"Feels just fine, Suzy. You're doing a great job."

Andi felt like puking on her shiny black boots. The man was incorrigible. He was almost on his deathbed and still flirting with every pretty girl he came across. "Well, if you're ready to go, *North*, we should get a move on," she interrupted, tossing his clean shirt onto his lap.

The nurses began cleaning up the bandages and equipment scattered on the bedside tray and bed. "We're done now," Nurse Two said. "Don't forget this prescription the doctor gave you." She handed the slip to North, her fingers lingering unnecessarily as he grasped the paper. "You'll need these antibiotics and painkillers at home. And the doc wants to see you again in about five days."

I'll give you painkillers, Andi thought. "Where's your clothes?" she demanded gruffly.

"Oh, right here," Nurse One chirped, reaching into the metal locker. "Can we help you get dressed, North?" she asked, batting long eyelashes.

"I think we can manage on our own." Andi grabbed the clothes from the nurse and glared at North again. North grinned.

The two nurses strolled slowly out of the room, glancing back at North and wishing him well. Andi followed on their heels and tried to slam the door shut. It's hard to slam a pneumatic door with any effect, she discovered.

She stomped back to North's bed and threw his clothes on his lap. "Get dressed," she ordered. She strode to the window and gazed out at the parking lot below, her back to him. She tapped her foot impatiently and crossed her arms over her chest.

"Um, Babe."

"What."

"I kinda need some help here."

Andi turned around to find North semi-nude, his hospital gown draped around his waist, his good arm inside the sleeve of the clean flannel shirt sleeve she'd dropped in his lap. She slipped the sling off the other arm and gently guided the shirt sleeve over his arm and bandaged shoulder. That done, she replaced the sling and buttoned up his shirt, brows pressed together in concentration.

North's eyes followed her every movement, a lopsided grin on his lips. She offered her arm and supported him while he struggled to get on his feet. The hospital gown dropped to the floor.

Relieved to see that he had his boxers on and very aware that her cheeks were on fire, Andi bent down and slipped his feet into the legs of his jeans, then pulled them up and over his slim hips. Though dark brown bloodstains blotted the denim waistband, she couldn't help but notice the fine, black hairs curling on North's taut belly. She couldn't seem to catch her breath; the incorrigible man didn't have an ounce of fat on him.

Her face burned and she struggled to ignore the erratic behavior of her pounding heart. She reached down to zip up his jeans, trying to keep her eyes adverted and fumbling blindly with the button. The man really was useless with only one functioning arm.

With North's pants firmly fastened to his body, Andi finally let out a long breath. She was reaching for his socks when she realized that the subject of her ministrations was being unusually quiet. She glanced up to discover his dark eyes glittering and the man in question struggling to control his mirth. "What's so damn funny?" she snapped.

"You look luscious with pink cheeks, Babe."

"My cheeks are *not* pink!"

"Are too. So are your ears. And your nose." North snickered. "Looks so damn cute."

"You're on drugs. What would you know?" she glowered. "Do you want me to put your socks on or not?"

"Please." He tried to raise his arm in the sling and winced.

"Stay still, then." She struggled with his socks and boots. That done she picked up his parka. Her stomach flipped when she saw the profusion of blood staining the fabric. The bulky old garment was loose, and she was able to drape it around the sling, satisfied that North wouldn't freeze on the drive home. If the parka looked this bad, Andi was glad she hadn't seen the bloody shirt the doctor had cut from his body.

Andi linked her arm through North's good one, and the couple slowly made their way to the hospital exit. She wanted to get him a wheelchair, which he adamantly refused. With the patient safely deposited on a chair near the hospital's front door, Andi ran outside to get the Land Yacht, first warning North that it would take a few minutes to warm up the old station wagon.

When she pulled up to the patient loading zone and before she could even open her car door, North pushed through the glass doors of the hospital and staggered outside, his lips and eyes narrowed with determination. Andi flew out of the car, reaching him only in time to open the door and help ease the injured man into the passenger seat. Burning with anger and not trusting her voice, she silently fastened his seatbelt.

She pulled out of the hospital parking lot and headed toward the pharmacy. "I'll go get your prescriptions filled. Do you have the papers they gave you?"

"Take me home first," North instructed.

Andi glanced at her passenger. His honey-hued skin had taken on a pale tinge. "No," she said calmly. "You need that medication and there is no sense driving all the way out to your place, then right back again. It will only take a few minutes."

Beside her, North stared out the window and mumbled something unintelligible under his breath. Andi didn't care to ask him to repeat himself. The man was quickly becoming an insufferable patient.

She stopped at the pharmacy and was back to the car in ten minutes. One of the perks of small-town living – there was rarely a lineup for anything.

"Since we're in town anyway I may as well stop at the gallery and see how Ruby is making out."

Andi turned incredulous eyes to her charge. "I don't *think* so," she retorted. "How can you possibly be worried about the gallery at a time like this? You were just extolling your sister's knowledge and expertise the other day, or have you already forgotten?"

North had been very proud of the fact that he had recently begun to depend on his youngest sister, Ruby, to occasionally handle the day to day operations of the Qamutik. Ruby had only one more year left before she earned a Bachelor of Commerce degree from the University of Alberta in Edmonton. He claimed she was sharp as a whip, and he loved her dearly.

North grumbled something unintelligible again and fidgeted in his seat. Andi was adamant on getting him home and to bed, though, and since she was behind the wheel North didn't get much say in the matter. He continued to stare moodily out the window for the duration of the ten-minute trip to his cabin, grimacing occasionally.

"You should get Paul to upgrade your wheels," he said when they turned up his long driveway.

Andi looked at him in surprise. "Why? I love this old boat."

"The shocks suck."

"It starts when I need it to. That's all that counts."

"The ride's worse than my Cat."

"You're grumpy, North. Your pain killer's starting to wear off?"

"I'm *not* grumpy. I just think you deserve a better car than this," North mumbled at the window.

Andi tried to hide the smile that tweaked her lips. Typical man, she thought; when in pain, they get grumpy. "Why don't you just lay your head back and try to relax," she said gently. "I'll have you home and into bed in no time."

North's head whipped around, making his unbound hair fly. His dark eyes had a suspiciously lewd glint in them. "Is that a proposition, Babe?" he grinned. "I think I'm feeling better already."

It was exactly noon when Andi and North pulled up to the cabin. Four hours had lapsed since she had fed the dogs and left for the airport that morning.

They could hear the frantic yelping and barking of the mutts even before they opened the car doors. "Sounds like someone is going to be happy to see you." Andi smiled.

"Christ, I've never heard anything like it," North grumbled, as he slowly eased out of the car. "You fed them this morning, didn't you?"

"Of course."

"They're not usually this loud. I wonder what's bugging them."

"They probably just miss you. Let's get you settled inside and then I'll go check on them." Andi held his elbow to steady him when they reached the short flight of porch steps.

"I'm not an invalid," North shrugged her hand off, then immediately reached for her when he saw the hurt in her eyes.

"Sorry, Babe. Guess I'm just a little touchy right now. Come here." He drew her close and wrapped his good arm around her, leaning down to kiss her gently. "Thanks for everything you're doing for me. I really do appreciate it, even if I'm acting like an oaf."

Andi nodded, not trusting herself to speak. Arm in arm they climbed the front steps. Andi handed North his keys and he unlocked the door.

"You go on into the house," she said, handing him his small bag of prescription medications. "I'll go plug the car in."

Thirty seconds later an anguished roar came from inside the house. Andi flew back up the steps and threw the door open. Whatever North had managed to do, there was no doubt in her mind that he was in extreme pain.

"North, what happened?" she shouted, running into the tidy home with her boots on. "Are you all right?"

He stood at the open back door, clutching the doorframe and staring into the yard. In their pen, the sled dogs continued to bark frenetically.

"*No!*" North cried. "Oh, God, no, not my dogs! Not my dogs!" He crumpled to his knees, his harsh, piercing cries dwindling to a mournful keening.

Andi ran across the room and knelt beside him, grasping his arm. "What is it, North?" she cried. "What's the matter with the dogs?"

He shuddered violently and remained silent, either unable, or unwilling, to speak.

Andi rose and looked out the back door, peering over the high snow banks along the path. She gasped, struggling to catch her breath. Her hand flew to her mouth as hot, bitter bile rose in her throat.

Her premonitions of death, danger and mayhem had become brutal reality.

The normally white snow inside the large dog pen was a stained muddle of red and pink. Pandemonium met her eyes as the usually well-mannered Canadian Eskimo Dogs ran in circles, snapping and snarling at each other and at nothing at all, their lips curled in anger and fear. They had become wild beasts, howling and racing in confused, tight circles, tails held low between their legs.

North was on his feet again, swaying unsteadily. He raised a leaden arm and pointed to a dog lying near the front gate, its thick grey fur matted with red blood. It was Juno. He wasn't moving. Andi saw another prone canine further along the fence, blood staining the snow around it.

North lunged from the house and down the stairs, running gracelessly down the path and to the gate of the dog pen, his grief and fury masking the pain he would surely be feeling in his newly stitched up shoulder.

"No, North! Don't go in there," Andi screamed at the top of her lungs, her words reaching North's ears even above the chaos in the pen. "It's too dangerous! Those dogs are going crazy!"

Andi flew down the snow-covered path in his wake. A fleeting sense of *déjà vu* gripped her; she had been warned of this tragedy and done nothing to prevent it. Now it was too late.

She grabbed North's arm when she reached the gate. "You can't go in there! Those dogs will kill you!"

North fumbled with the gate latch, his hands shaking violently. The gate's busted padlock lay nearby on the snow. Andi bent to retrieve it.

"Leave it," North commanded. "It's evidence." His eyes were black and bottomless. Andi knew that look all too well. She'd seen something very similar whenever she'd looked into the mirror after Natalie died.

The clamour of screaming, distressed animals was deafening now, their cries louder since they had spotted their master. Andi could feel their panic and smell their fear. Fear had the smell of blood. She shuddered with the strength of its intensity.

"Stay here," he ordered. "I have to go in and see if I can save them. They won't hurt me."

He opened the gate with one clumsy hand and slipped through, quickly closing it behind himself. There was blood everywhere. The dogs were going wild from the acrid, coppery smell, snarling and circling each other in their distress. They kept their distance from North, but their keening and clamour subsided fractionally.

He knelt on the bloodstained snow beside Juno and laid a gentle hand on the huge sled dog's body, bending close to the prone animal's head. "Juno? Can you hear me boy? Juno?" North entreated the dog to acknowledge him, but the magnificent Canadian Eskimo dog didn't respond. Bright red blood matted his once pristine grey coat. Too much blood.

North reverently closed Juno's beautiful blue eyes for the last time. He stroked his faithful companion's broad neck for a moment, then began searching for the source of the blood. Within seconds his probing fingers found the cause – a bullet hole at the base of the dog's skull. North gently stroked Juno's silky head for a moment, then struggled to his feet. He looked at Andi through the metal fence and shook his head. "He's dead. Shot."

Careful not to make any sudden moves, he slowly walked to the next inert dog. Faithful Eska was dead too, shot in the head.

Still the dogs circled, yipping, growling and mistrustful. Their peaceful world had been torn apart. They didn't know how to react when their instinct to run and hide was barred by a metal fence.

North knelt on the snow and extended his hand to his female lead dog, who paced and panted several feet away. "Easy Kia, come girl. Come, Kia." She wouldn't come, or even allow North to approach her.

North moved slowly through the madness in the pen until he stood next to the long wall of the kennel. He looked up at it for what seemed like a long time before he turned to Andi. "Look at this," he shouted above the steady, high-pitched keening.

She followed his gaze and stared at the white plywood wall. A crude message was scrawled in large, dripping red letters across the wood:

MIND YOUR OWN BUSINESS
NEXT TIME IT WILL BE YOU

Beneath the bloody warning lay another dead animal. Andi thought it looked like Aleeka.

"North, can you see Qannik?" Andi cried, suddenly remembering the pup. "I left Qannik outside this morning. Do you see her?"

North shook his head. "No, I can't see her anywhere. She could be hiding in one of the doghouses. Or ... or she's dead too." His voice was strained, the words reluctant to leave his mouth.

Tears coursed down Andi's frozen cheeks. She grasped the mesh on the metal fence, shaking it in anger and frustration. "You have to find her! Qannik! Come, Qannik," she called, frantically searching the yard for a sign of the fluffy white pup.

"Andi," North said firmly, seemingly once again in command of his emotions. "Go into the building and open the outside door in each kennel. I'm going to try and get the dogs separated and inside." He tossed her a set of keys.

After only a moment's hesitation she nodded and ran to the front door of the kennel building. Despite her trembling hands she quickly had all of the dog doors open.

The clamour outside had noticeably quietened.

"Okay, good work," North called. "Now open the fridge and take out the bowl of caribou meat. Throw a hunk into each kennel, and then bring the bowl out to me."

As Andi dispersed the raw meat North could sense a change in the dogs' demeanor. Black noses twitched and tested the air, detecting the scent of food. The incessant howling and snarling had diminished, and soon Chance took a few tentative steps toward her kennel.

Andi brought the bowl of raw meat outside and handed it to North over the top of the high fence.

"Now go into the house, and close the door," he instructed.

Andi opened her mouth to protest, but one look at the determination and pain in North's eyes changed her mind. Reluctantly she returned to the house and walked slowly up the path and into the house.

She got no further than the open back door though, watching intently as North walked slowly toward the kennel entrances, calling to his dogs in a low, calm voice.

"Come Kia. Come Nanuk. Come Suka. Chance, here girl." He dropped the smallest hunks of caribou meat in the snow, trying to lure the dogs into the safety of their kennels. With Juno gone, Kia would become the pack leader. She was the next Alpha Female. If North could convince her to enter the kennel the rest of the dogs would follow.

"Kia, Duska, Chinook. Come!" North commanded. After another moment's hesitation Kia loped toward him and snatched the small piece of meat from the snow. She swallowed it in one gulp. North reached down to stroke her silky head and was rewarded with a soft whine. The big dog leaned hard against him, looking for security and comfort. "Come, Kia. Let's go inside," North said in a gentle, but firm, voice.

He walked slowly to the first open door, Kia at his side. He threw another piece of meat into the kennel and pointed at it. "Go. Inside," he said firmly. Kia turned, and with her tail low and nose to the ground, slunk slowly into the kennel. North closed the door, securing her from the carnage outside.

Working quickly, he soon had the rest of the sled dogs inside their respective kennels. All but Qannik. There was still no sign of the young pup, but at least the turmoil and confusion had calmed. North left the pen and trudged toward the kennel building.

Andi finally closed the cabin door and turned away from the horror outside. She was numb – not only from the cold, but from grief and despair as well. If she felt this bad, she could only begin to imagine how North felt. Those dogs out there were like family to him.

She kicked off her boots and threw her coat on the floor beside the door. She was shivering, frozen from the inside out. She decided to make a pot of coffee and found the familiar task comforting in its normalcy.

Back in the kennel, North had fed the dogs and turned on the radio. It was tuned to a station featuring calming, relaxing music and he almost always left it playing when the dogs were inside. He was eager to give each surviving animal a thorough examination and check for any further injuries, but he knew that what they needed most right now was calm rest. He was also aware than his own stamina was quickly waning, and was feeling exceedingly lightheaded. Assured that the dogs were settling down and appeared to be recovering from their ordeal, he turned down the lights and walked out the door.

Before he escaped to the warmth and comfort of his home, though, there was one more thing he had to do. He opened the pen door and began searching for the missing Qannik in earnest. There was a multitude of hiding places amongst the high piles of snow, dugouts and doghouses.

"Qannik, here pup," North called softly. "Come, Qannik." North pushed away the pain in his aching arm, concerned only for his pup's safety. If she was still here, he knew she would have retreated as far from the chaos as she could. He searched the entire yard slowly and methodically, kneeling painfully on the ground to check first one doghouse, then the next. But there was no sign of the youngest team member.

He had one more doghouse to check and had almost given up hope when he heard what sounded like a mewling kitten. "Here, Qannik, come on baby. Come, girl." He called to her softly, his voice barely above a whisper, afraid to frighten the young dog even more than she already was.

North knelt down and peered into the doghouse. He spotted the shivering white ball huddled in the farthest corner. Warm tears tracked his cheeks and he smiled in spite of the devastation around him. "Hey, Qannik, it's okay, girl. Come, little snowflake." The pup continued to shiver and shake, mewling pitifully. Despite the small piece of caribou meat North held offered the young dog, it took almost five minutes to convince her to leave the perceived safety of her cold corner.

Once she finally worked up the courage to approach North, her dam of doubt broke. She wiggled and yipped and squirmed, crawling out of the house and right into his lap. She covered his face with puppy kisses, licking the tears from his face.

North hugged the pup close and when the initial frenzy of greeting was over he scooped her up in his good arm and carried her to the gate. She dug her head deep into his open parka, and he encouraged her to hide there.

He fervently wished there was somewhere for him, too, to hide from the blood and carnage that defiled their once safe haven.

EIGHTEEN

When North opened the cabin door clutching his white bundle the fragrance of fresh coffee welcomed him, displacing the coppery scent of blood in his nostrils.

Andi sat at the kitchen table, staring vacantly into space. Her grief-stricken eyes met his, reflecting the anguish he felt in his heart. Then she realized what he was holding in his arms.

"You found her!" she cried, running across the room and throwing her arms around both the man and the pup. Qannik began squirming again and frantically licked Andi's face, lapping up her salty tears just as she had done North's a few minutes before.

"Oh, North, thank God you found her," Andi sobbed. She lifted the pup gently from his grasp and held her tightly in her arms, kissing her head, her face and her cold, wet nose.

North wrapped his free arm around them both, drawing them close and resting his chin on Andi's head. For a few moments time stood still for the small group, and even Qannik relaxed within the warm comfort of their embrace.

A minute later North broke away. "I have to wash," he said, his voice leaden. He had managed to get blood on both hands and removed his sling to soap them at the kitchen sink, grimacing at the effort. He stood at the kitchen sink for a long time, holding his hands under the steaming water until Andi came to his side and closed the faucet. She handed him a towel and gently guided him toward the living room sofa.

"Sit down," she said softly. "I'll help you get your boots and parka off."

North followed her obediently, exhausted and numb from the pain of his loss, and still weak from his ordeal of the day before. Andi set Qannik down on the carpet. The little dog curled into a ball, her back against the sofa, and immediately closed her eyes. She, too, was exhausted.

"Lie down," Andi instructed when North's boots and coat were laying on the floor. She pulled a thick woolen afghan from the back of the sofa, placed a pillow beneath his head and tucked the warm blanket around his shivering body. Then she ripped open the bag of prescription drugs they'd picked up from the drugstore. "It's time for drugs," she said, handing him two Demerol and a dose of antibiotics. "I'll get you a glass of water. Would you like a cup of coffee too?"

"Please."

She delivered the water and lingered until she was sure he had swallowed the pills before she went to pour their coffee. When she returned North had pulled himself upright. He reached for the coffee, warming his hands on the thick pottery. Qannik hadn't moved a muscle.

"I'm so sorry about the dogs, North. I wish I could do something to take away your pain," she said softly, emerald eyes brimming. She dropped to her knees beside the sofa and stroked his dark head.

The bleak emptiness in North's eyes made Andi's stomach clench. She'd looked into those eyes before – eyes reflecting complete and total despair. The eyes she remembered had been her own.

"Just stay with me," North sighed, his voice barely a whisper. "Don't leave me."

"Ten wild horses couldn't drag me away," she said, her sad smile failing to reach her eyes.

North drank from his cup and sighed deeply. "Can you drag the phone over here for me, please? I have to call the vet and the cops. I need them out here ASAP."

"Sure." Andi got up and picked the phone up off the kitchen counter, doling out the long extension cord. "I'll dial for you. RCMP first?"

North nodded. She set the phone on the coffee table and handed him the receiver.

The Royal Canadian Mounted Police emergency line was answered after the first ring. "Yeah, this is North Ruben, out on Low Road."

"Yes, Mr. Ruben. How can we help you?"

"Someone's shot and killed three of my sled dogs," he stated, unusually abrupt.

"When did this happen, Mr. Ruben?"

"Just this morning."

"Are the shooters still there?"

"No, there was nobody around when I got home."

"Are you injured or in danger?"

"Yeah. I mean *no*. My dogs were shot, not me. I'm fine."

"All right, we'll have a patrol car out soon."

"Thanks. Bye."

"Good-bye."

The next call North placed was to the veterinary clinic that cared for his dog team. They promised to send a vet out late that afternoon.

Andi sat on the floor beside him nursing her coffee. "Are you planning on telling the cops you were shot yesterday?"

"Nope."

"And why not?"

"What good will it do? They'll never find the guy, and there's no bullet for forensics."

"But-" Andi began.

"No 'but', Andi," North interrupted. "I'll look after this myself."

Andi stared at him in frustration, but realized it wasn't the time or place to argue with a sick man. Instead, she just smiled and said, "Can I get you anything else?"

North shook his head slowly, and yawned. He laid back against the soft pillow Andi had arranged under his head. "You know this means war." North's words were spoken softly, but with conviction and a more than a hint of menace. "Killing my dogs means war. You realize who's responsible for this, don't you?"

"No." Andi looked at him questioningly. "How could I?"

North merely stared at her. "Think, Andi. Who have I pissed off recently that would stoop to something like this?"

Realization dawned in her eyes about the same time as her face turned ghostly pale. "No! You don't really think this is connected with what happened yesterday, do you? It can't be!"

North's eyes drooped; the Demerol was doing its job. He struggled to open his eyes again. "What do *you* think?" He grumbled. Who else would want to slaughter my dogs and leave a threatening message in their blood? It sure as hell isn't the act of a friendly neighbour."

"Oh my God," Andi moaned. Fresh tears welled in her eyes. "I'm so, so sorry that I got you involved in all of this," she sobbed.

"It's not your fault, Babe. How could we have known that we were up against such ruthless killers? But we have to take this threat seriously, Andi. They obviously mean business."

Andi nodded absently, her free hand stroking Qannik's thick, soft fur. She and North both fell silent, each absorbed in their own private thoughts and grief. Two minutes later North was down for the count, his breaths deep and steady.

She was glad the Demerol had knocked him out and wished there was something she could do to ease her own pain. Her eyes strayed to the open bottle of red wine sitting on the kitchen counter. When she'd first arrived and spotted the bottle the day before she'd had no trouble resisting the urge to have just one quick sip. After what had happened today, though, it was harder to ignore the itch that she knew from experience would only keep getting stronger. She badly needed to go to a meeting, or at least call her sponsor.

Instead, she got up and walked to the kitchen, each step slow and deliberate, her moccasins making not a sound on the pine floor. She set her empty cup next to the bottle of Cabernet Sauvignon and picked it up. The long, cool neck of the dark green bottle felt pleasing and comfortable in her hand. It felt familiar. She pulled out the stopper North had used to reseal the bottle, smiling sadly at the pewter Husky adorning it. The little touch was so very *North*.

She lifted the bottle to her nose and inhaled deeply. It smelled so damn good.

She clutched the bottle to her breast for a moment, her eyelids pressed shut as if that small act of defiance would help to curb the need and desire coursing through her veins. "Just one little sip won't hurt," she whispered. Tears began to trickle from her eyes, which she had yet to open.

She lifted the bottle to her lips, then pulled it away before taking a drink when something warm and solid leaned against her leg. She looked down into Qannik's trusting, loving brown eyes. The young dog seemed to be smiling, her shiny black lips curled up at the corners. Andi set the bottle back on the counter and drove the stopper into the neck. Qannik's fluffy white tail swished back and forth on the floor.

"Thanks, buddy," Andi whispered, her tears falling on the dog's soft white head when Andi leaned down to stroke it. "Let's go have a cuddle, shall we?"

Andi picked up the small dog and eased her exhausted body into North's favourite La-Z-Boy. She kicked up the footrest and settled her small saviour in her lap, the pull of the demons within her quelled, at least for now.

Qannik immediately curled up and closed her eyes, and Andi too quickly dozed off. She started awake half an hour later. When she glanced at the sofa, she was surprised to see North staring at her.

"What are you doing, Babe?" he asked softly, with just a hint of a smile on his tired face.

"I must have fallen asleep," she said groggily. She rose from the chair, returning Qannik to the floor, then knelt down at North's side. She kissed him gently and held her cool hand to his cheek, their eyes locked on each other's, seeking reassurance.

Andi had just leaned in for a more serious kiss when they heard a vehicle approaching the house. Alarm flared in North's eyes.

"Quick, lock the door and pull the blinds," North ordered, disengaging her arms from his neck.

Andi flew to the door and threw the deadbolt home. Before she could close the blind on the large front window a car drove into the yard. "It's only a patrol car, North. The RCMP are here."

"Oh. That was quick." North pushed back the blanket and struggled to a sitting position on the couch.

Andi swung the front door open before the police officer had a chance to knock. Both she and North had met Constable Marc LaPierre before, and the officer's concern seemed genuine when they gave him the details of the devastation they'd found in North's back yard.

When LaPierre had finished questioning them and jotting notes into a small pad Andi offered to take him back to the dog pen.

"No, I'll do it. They're my dogs." North stood up too fast, swaying on his feet a moment before he collapsed back onto the sofa. "Damn it," he groaned.

Andi rushed to his side and laid her hand firmly on his chest, just as Nurse Lisette had done, forcing him back down to the cushions. "No, North. You're not in any shape to go out there again. I'll show Constable LaPierre whatever he needs to see. You need to rest." North glared at her for a moment before his head hit the pillow.

"He had a little snowmobile accident yesterday," she explained to LaPierre at his questioning gaze. "That's why he … why he was at the hospital," she stammered. She'd never been a very good liar.

"Come this way, please." Andi zipped into her parka and shoved her feet into her boots before she opened the back door.

To his credit, the young police officer did a thorough inspection of the dog pen, including photos, a rough sketch and measurements. He pulled on latex gloves and carefully bagged the broken padlock and various evidence samples, including swabs from the bloody snow surrounding each of the deceased dogs. The threat written on the kennel wall was photographed and samples of the bloody writing medium taken for forensic review.

"Was the building broken into?' he asked.

Andi shook her head. "No, just … just this." She gestured to the dog pen."

"There should be no need for me to go inside then," he affirmed.

"No, and its best that you don't. The surviving dogs were all very disturbed by what happened. It will take them a while to recover. North's vet is on his way out to examine them today."

"Understandable," LaPierre nodded sadly. "Understandable."

His last task appeared to be the most difficult for the gentle police officer. He knelt beside each of the three dead dogs, searching for and finding the bullet wounds North claimed were there.

Unfortunately, his search for bullet casings proved futile.

"What a damn shame," LaPierre declared when he had completed his grisly task. He shook his head and stood to take a last look at the once beautiful Canadian Eskimo Dogs. "Those are some mighty fine-looking dogs. They must be worth a lot of money, too. Any thoughts on who may have done this, Ms. Nowak? Or what that message on the wall means?"

"No, not at all. Neither of us do, but you may want to talk to North again when he's more coherent. The pain killers the doctor gave him are pretty strong so he's going to be groggy for the next day or so."

LaPierre nodded solemnly and tugged the dark blue woolen toque he wore lower over his ears, which Andi absently noted were rather large. "Well, I'll file a report and let you know if we come up with anything," he said.

He packed up his gear, and after one more glance around the dog pen Andi walked him out of the compound, once again locking the gate securely behind them.

"Just one more thing before I leave," LaPierre called.

Andi turned and looked at him enquiringly.

"I know you say that the building was not broken into, but I just want to take a quick look around it before I leave."

"Oh. Okay," Andi nodded. "If you want."

LaPierre slowly walked the perimeter of the building, eyes scanning the snow-covered ground and walls intently. Once he stooped and picked something minute up with a pair of tweezers, inserting it into a small glassine bag that he then slid into his parka pocket He spent several minutes examining the windows and front door.

Andi watched him closely throughout his search, occasionally stamping her feet against the cold.

"Right, then. I'm done now." LaPierre stated.

"Did you find anything unusual? Any sign of a break-in we weren't aware of?

"No, nothing. Just a burned match, but it could have been there for a while."

"Neither one of us smoke," Andi confirmed before he asked.

She walked him around the house to his patrol car. "I'll get on this right away. If you have any more trouble, or remember anything else, you let us know immediately, all right?"

Andi nodded mutely.

The RCMP officer scribbled some numbers on the back of a card and handed it to her. "Here's my contact info and your police file number. Call any time," he smiled.

"Thank you," Andi replied. "We really appreciate your help. Can we clean up the yard now? The vet will want to remove the ... the bodies."

"Yes, go ahead. There's nothing left here for us to look at." He opened the trunk of his patrol car and shoved his gear inside.

After the patrol car drove away Andi stood outside, leaning against the railing of the front porch until her fingers tingled. She should have worn her gloves, she thought absently. Once again she craved something to take the edge off. The day had proved to be too much for her; had brought back too many memories of sorrow and pain.

Oblivious of the familiar, soothing act, she twirled the silver AA ring on her cold finger and thought about the bottle of Cab Sav sitting on the kitchen counter. She knew that tonight, more than any other, she needed to go to a meeting. How could she leave North alone, though?

Spurred by the frigid air she opened the door to North's cabin and slipped into its comforting warmth. She needed to thaw out before North's veterinarian arrived.

NINETEEN

"Are you awake?" a familiar voice whispered. Warm breath teased her ear.

"Uh uh. Go 'way."

"Wake up, Andi. I need to talk to you," the voice murmured.

She slowly and languidly drifted to awareness, captured as she was by her dreams.

"Oh!" she gasped, shrinking into the soft pillows after she finally opened her eyes, only to find herself staring into a pair of mesmerizing dark brown ones. "North, what are you ... what's happening?" she stammered, still groggy with sleep.

"Easy, Babe. It's morning. I'm just going out to feed the mutts. Just wanted to see your smiling face before I left." North leaned down and nuzzled the warm, lavender-scented skin below her ear.

"Mmm, good morning to you too, sweetheart," she breathed, letting her eyes drop closed again. Her words had barely been audible to her own ears. Then her heart slammed into her ribs and her eyes snapped open, forcing any threads of lingering sleep from her senses. She hoped to God North had missed her last remark.

She sat bolt upright. "How are *you* feeling this morning?"

North was already on his way to the back door. "I'll live. You stay warm until I get back. I won't be long."

The door slammed shut, but not before letting a stream of frigid air into the house. And rolled off the sofa and stretched languidly. Her back was unusually sore, her shoulder muscles stiff. The last of the fog in her head cleared, allowing the horror of yesterday's slaughter to seep back in. She slumped back onto the sofa, but her heaving stomach soon had her running for the bathroom. When the violent bout of sickness was over she slowly dressed, stopping often to wipe tears from her eyes.

She called the office and left a message on the answering machine that she was taking a sick day. She was pouring her second cup of coffee when North stomped into the house, knocking fresh snow from his boots. It was barely seven o'clock, and still dark and frosty outside.

Andi filled another mug for North and set it on the kitchen table next to hers. She sensed his despair and sorrow, and said nothing. She knew he would talk to her when he was ready.

They drank their coffee in silence – a silence that wasn't uneasy, but rather the comforting silence of two people with mutual, compatible thoughts. She glanced around the tidy kitchen sensing something was different, but having trouble placing what it might be. It took her a few minutes to realize that the open bottle of wine had disappeared. She looked at North with new awareness, and more than a little appreciation.

When he'd finished his coffee North picked up the bottle of antibiotics, flipped the lid up with one hand, and shook two pills into his palm. "Guess I need another dose of these."

"I'll get you a glass of water," Andi offered, rising from her chair. "How's that shoulder feeling?"

North wiggled his left arm, still encased in its sling. "It's stiff but doesn't hurt too bad, really."

"More Demerol?" Andi asked, pushing it toward him.

"Nope. Not taking any more of that shit. It makes me loopy. I think a couple of Tylenol will be good enough." He went to the bathroom where Andi could hear him rummaging in the medicine cabinet and returned with a small bottle of Tylenol. He handed it to Andi. "Damn childproof lids," he grumbled. "Can you open this for me please?"

"You'd better go lie down again," Andi suggested after North had taken the Tylenol. "The best thing you can do right now is rest and sleep."

North picked up his coffee cup and deposited it in the kitchen sink. He braced his hips against the counter and stared out the window a few moments. "I've cleaned up the pen as best I could," he said, his voice rough. "Washed the wall and shovelled up as much of the blood as I could. It's starting to snow pretty good. If we're lucky it'll cover up the rest of that mess."

Andi brought her own empty cup to the sink. She stood next to him in silence, their shoulders barely touching, the electricity between them palpable. There was really nothing more she could say to comfort him – her presence said it all.

"The vet said it's best not to let the dogs back out until most traces of the blood are gone. They'll smell it for a long time anyway, no matter what we do." North's trusted veterinarian had visited late the day before, as promised. She'd checked all of the Eskimo dogs including Qannik for injuries and removed the three corpses. North rubbed a hand roughly over his face; fatigue, pain and sorrow had etched new furrows in his strong, handsome features.

"Have a nap, North, and when you wake up I'll make you a delicious breakfast." Andi grasped his hand and guided him to his bedroom, the only one in the small home. He slipped off his sling before lying down.

"Stay with me for a while, Babe," he entreated. "I could use a little TLC right about now."

Andi hesitated only a moment before easing down next to him, carefully avoiding his injured arm. Then she pulled the thick eiderdown comforter around them both. North let out a deep breath as Andi spooned closer to his broad chest, rejoicing in the warmth and comfort of his body. She closed her eyes and tried her best to clear her mind of yesterday's horrors.

They both fell into a deep sleep, exhaustion taking its toll. Andi woke two hours later, momentarily alarmed and confused by the unfamiliar presence of a body next to hers. Just as quickly she remembered where she was, and who lay next to her.

Daylight had crept in while they slept, and Andi let her eyes wander around the pleasing room, taking in the decidedly male décor. Light brown walls framed the dark brown wooden dresser, nightstands and bed frame. A dark hunter green duvet cover and woven throw rugs of several shades of brown and green added muted colour. It all came together nicely, she decided; rather like sleeping in a forest.

North's discarded clothes lay scattered on the floor, and boots and shoes lined the wall under the window. A few pieces of breathtakingly beautiful Northern artwork adorned the walls. It was a lovely, calming room.

Laying within the security of North's strong arms, Andi felt an unfamiliar awakening in her body and her soul. When North's warm lips brushed that most tender spot beneath her ear she gasped softly. It was the most intimate, exquisite touch she'd ever experienced. A wave of heat coursed through her center, running a line of fire from her neck to the tips of her toes. She moaned, unaware that she had made a sound.

"Good morning again, Babe," North whispered hoarsely.

She carefully rolled over to face the source of her pleasure. North's ruggedly handsome face was only inches from hers. His brown eyes were dark, almost black, and a lazy, sexy smile curved his lips.

Andi grazed his full lips with her own. She saw passion rising in his eyes and her body flushed with pleasure. Their lips met again but this time their kiss was demanding, hot and wet. North's tongue licked her bottom lip, his teeth nibbling gently until she opened to him. He captured her tongue before she had time to resist.

The man took her breath away. Andi groaned and wrapped her arms around his hard body.

He responded with a deep, passionate growl, his pillaging tongue seeking the deepest recesses of her mouth. North threw a leg over Andi's slim body, urging her even closer into his embrace. She felt his hard maleness against her belly and her body responded with a searing bolt of heat. Before long they were both breathless, gasping for air but not ready to stop.

"I've been waiting for this for so long," North breathed. He lifting his lips from hers and covered her jawline in a series of soft, moist kisses. Every touch of his tongue sent small jolts of ecstasy to Andi's brain and her ears tingled with pleasure.

When North's hand lifted the hemline of her sweatshirt to caress her breasts, Andi pressed herself closer to his roving hand. She wanted to feel his hands on her breasts and on every inch of her aching body.

"Take it off," North whispered, drawing his hand away from her burning flesh. Desperate for his touch, Andi grasped the bottom of her sweatshirt with both hands and yanked it over her head. Her arms flew up and her hand slammed into North's bandaged shoulder.

"Ouch! Fuck!" North shouted. He rolled onto his back and clasped his injured shoulder, moaning in pain.

"Oh, my God, I'm so sorry!" Andi cried, rocketing off the bed and unsuccessfully trying to cover her bare breasts with her hands. "Are you okay?"

"I'll live," he gasped, his eyes squeezed tightly closed. "Maybe you'd better get me some of that Demerol after all."

Andi grabbed her sweatshirt and pulled it over her tangled hair. She ran to the kitchen and back again with a glass of water and the bottle of Demerol.

"I'm so sorry, North," she said tearfully.

"It's over, Babe. Don't worry about it." North gave her a crooked smile and downed two Demerol. "You'd make me feel a whole lot better if I got that breakfast you promised," he teased, wiggling his heavy, black eyebrows.

"Of course. Coming right up," she promised and padded out to the kitchen.

North nodded off to sleep again, waking to the delicious aroma of bacon. He loved bacon. Saliva poured into his mouth and he realized that he hadn't eaten a thing since the meager, tasteless hospital breakfast he'd had yesterday morning. Yesterday felt like a lifetime ago.

Andi appeared in the doorway balancing a heavily laden tray. She set it on the bureau and pulled the curtains open. Bright sunshine streamed into the room. "You're awake I see. She smiled shyly. "How's the pain? Can you sit up?"

North nodded. "I'm fine, and I don't need breakfast in bed. Let's go eat in the kitchen."

"Nope," Andi chirped. "Just sit up a little and be a good patient, okay? I don't want to be forced to hurt you again."

North's heavy black eyebrows knit together in determination. He was in more pain that he would admit, as his cautious, slow movements attested. Andi carefully placed another pillow behind his back and smoothed the bedcovers. She set the tray, heavily laden with orange juice, bacon, eggs, hash brown potatoes, toast and coffee on his outstretched legs.

"Have I been asleep all morning?" North chuckled before he dug into the food. He was starving. "This is wonderful. Where's yours?"

"In the kitchen. I'll go get it."

Andi sat cross-legged on North's bed, her own substantially smaller plate of food balanced on her knees. The close proximity to the man who had almost become her lover made her flush – a rosy stain that spread from her chest, up her long neck and ended at the tips of her perfect ears.

"You hot?" North grinned, munching on a piece of toast.

"Um, yeah. It's a bit warm in here, don't you think?" Andi said, pulling at the neckline of her sweatshirt. She knew exactly what the devil meant, but didn't want to admit it.

North chuckled and scraped the last bit of egg yolk from his plate. "That was delicious, but now I feel like I need another nap," he yawned.

"That Demerol is wicked stuff," Andi agreed.

"You going to be here when I wake up, Babe?"

"I should be, but I do need to make a quick trip to town. I need some clothes from home and I should pick up a few groceries too. Do you want anything in particular?"

"A caribou burger and fries from To-Go's?" he asked hopefully.

Andi laughed. "I'll pick up a couple on my way back. We can have them for dinner." She picked up North's tray and gave him a chaste kiss. "You be good while I'm gone. I'll be back later this afternoon."

North's eyes were already closed. "I'll be heartbroken if you aren't," he sighed.

While North slept the day away in a Demerol blur, Andi hurried through her errands in town. North had been right, and fresh snow had continued to fall throughout the day. It was already building up on the roads and she wanted to get back to his place before the driveway became impassable. The Land Yacht had good snow tires, but it wasn't a 4-wheel drive.

On a whim she swung by the RCMP detachment to see if they had looked at her blown tire yet. The results were in: one bullet hole, confirmed; no suspects; case closed. Andi wasn't happy with the decision to close her file, but at least she had her answer.

Her last stop before heading back to North's was To-Go's. The warm, mouth-watering aroma of burgers and fries tormented her all the way to Low Road. She plugged the car in and shuffled through the mounting snowdrifts, needing several trips to haul the bags of groceries, clothes, briefcase and fast food onto the small porch.

She stomped the snow off her boots and let herself into his warm, welcoming cabin. It annoyed her that North still refused to keep his front door locked.

"North, I'm back!"

"I'm in the bedroom."

She quickly transferred her loot into the house and closed the door. The wind had picked up and a light dusting of dry snow had already drifted through the doorway. Andi kicked off her boots and slipped into her comfortable, warm moccasins. She set the fragrant To-Go's bag on the kitchen table and threw her parka, hat and mitts on the sofa. She'd deal with them later.

She went in search of North and headed to his bedroom. At the doorway to his room she stopped short. North stood in front of his dresser, evidently examining his injured shoulder in the mirror. His long black hair looked wet and was tied at the nape of his neck with a leather thong. And he was stark naked.

"Oops, sorry," Andi mumbled, backing away in haste, but not before taking a second to appreciate his very impressive physique.

North turned toward her, apparently unconcerned with his nakedness. "Hey, come back here. I was just checking out my bullet wound." He raised his left arm for her to examine. "Whaddaya think? Pretty impressive, isn't it?" He grinned, one long eye-tooth peeking out, looking like his normal confident self again.

Andi felt her face redden. *Full frontal view*, she thought helplessly. She closed her stunned eyes. *You bet it's pretty impressive, North Ruben.*

"Can you check this out for me, Babe? Does it look like its healing okay to you?" He'd removed the bandage and apparently had had a shower in her absence.

She shuffled into the bedroom, making a valiant effort to keep her eyes on North's face and upper body while her deceitful, cheating pulse did a tango.

"Did you shower?" she asked accusingly, even though she already knew the answer.

"Well, yeah."

"Weren't you told to keep the wound dry?"

"Uh, yeah. But I kept it dry. More or less."

"Geez," Andi said, shaking her head and frowning. "Well, it doesn't look too bad as far as I can see. I'll put another bandage on it after you're dressed." She turned to leave.

"Here," North said, holding out one of the wrapped bandages the sweet hospital nurses had sent home with him. "I've got one already."

Andi sighed and took the package of sterile dressing from North's hand. She ripped it open. She gently taped the gauze over the hole in his arm, stoically keeping her eyes on her task and no lower.

North sniffed deeply and grinned again. "I smell caribou burgers."

"Wow," Andi smiled. "That's an impressive smeller you have there. If you get some clothes on we can eat them before they get any colder than they already are."

"We can nuke them."

"True. Just not the same, though."

Two minutes later, fully dressed and his arm back in the sling, North groaned in delight. He'd managed to dress himself while Andi set the table and deposited two reheated caribou burgers, with cheese and extra bacon, and an extra-large fries on his plate. "He took an immense bite. This sure hits the spot."

"Glad to see you still have an appetite," Andi said as she dug into her own burger and fries, promising herself she would hit her exercise bike the second she made it home again.

When every last morsel of food had disappeared, Andi put a fresh pot of coffee to brew and they retired to the comfort of the sofa. The sat nestled together, North's good arm around flung over her shoulders, her head on his. They were both satiated by the heavy meal and tired after the emotional day. Andi's eyes drifted closed.

After a few minutes of companionable silence North suddenly said, "This whole thing is getting out of hand."

Andi's head shot up and she stared into his indecipherable brown eyes. "What is?" she asked cautiously, afraid that he was talking about their newly intimate relationship.

"My dogs getting killed. This." North pointed to his wounded shoulder. "You know, my chances of qualifying for the Iditarod in '97 are pretty much shot now. I'll never be able to replace those dogs in time, never mind getting a team in shape. My gut tells me this is all connected to that damn diamond mine."

Andi extracted herself from his arms and went to pour their coffee. "It's possible," she said slowly, "but I really doubt it. Who would do this to you?" She handed him a cup and nestled back under his arm. He hadn't moved an inch.

Andi blew away the steam rising from the black brew and took a cautious sip.

"I think it's time we find out what's really going on out there," North scowled. She felt his body tense. He had every right to be angry.

"I'm going to hunt down the bastard who shot my dogs. I'll hunt him down and shoot him like he shot my poor defenseless mutts."

Andi sighed. His words made her uneasy. "Maybe it's time we went to the police, North. I don't think we should deal with this ourselves."

North slammed his mug down on the table, sloshing coffee onto its polished surface. "We don't have any real evidence, Andi! What are you going to tell them? If anyone should go to the cops, it should be Carlos Sante. He's the one who claims he's missing diamonds. *He* must have some evidence. I'm sure his damn diamonds are at the root of this mess. Let's talk to him." North, his burst of anger spent, picked up his mug again and swiped at the spill with his sock.

"I've been hoping to talk to Carlos again," Andi said, frowning at North's attempt at cleaning, "but he hasn't called me back."

"Maybe someone is threatening him, too," North speculated. "You never know."

"I'll give him another call tomorrow."

They finished their coffee in silence, each absorbed in private thoughts. North hugged Andi closer and kissed the top of her dark head. "Well, we'll never get anywhere sitting here like this. It's time to make an action plan."

"What do you mean? What kind of action plan?" Andi wriggled out of his grip and stood in front of him, her eyes flashing. She planted her hands on her denim-clad hips. "I don't like the sound of that. You got shot once already, North Ruben. Isn't that enough?"

North grinned. "The fun is just beginning, Babe. But before I do anything," he added, struggling to his feet, "I'm going out to feed the mutts. And then I'll tell you about my plan."

"Well, I'm coming too," Andi glowered. "I want to visit Qannik. And when we're done with the dogs, you're going right back to bed."

North smiled slyly. "As long as you're coming with me, Babe, I'll go anywhere you want to lead me."

"You're insufferable sometimes."

TWENTY

As soon as Andi pulled up to Tuktu's Dispatch Centre early the next morning her ears started to tingle. She tried to ignore the annoyance, wanting nothing more than to let her thoughts linger on the details of her very memorable awakening. She'd very reluctantly left North's rumpled bed only minutes earlier and still imagined she detected the heady scents of sweat and sex, even after a hasty shower.

Their first union had been nothing short of amazing; it was beyond a doubt the best in her entire life. North was evidently a quick healer.

They'd had a huge argument the night before so maybe the old beliefs were right – make-up sex was the best. North's 'action plan', once he'd reluctantly decided to share it with her, was that he would return to Pivot Lake today and resume his surveillance on O'Neill and the unidentified snowmobile driver in black.

Andi had lost it on him. Only a day out of the hospital, the man was in no condition to resume such strenuous activities. He had no business being alone on the Arctic tundra, and when she announced that she would go with him, he flatly refused.

Their discussion on the matter hadn't ended well, at least not in Andi's opinion. There didn't appear to be any way to change North's mind. He was stubborn to the core. He'd insisted that she shared his bed instead of sleeping on the sofa again, but when they'd eventually retired for the night, after long hours of heated discussion, she'd promptly rolled over and given him the cold shoulder.

The early morning make-up sex had almost been worth the fight.

When she'd pulled up to the office she'd been surprised to see Paul White's car sitting outside. He rarely came to work on a Saturday, and never this early in the morning. She'd just walked through the outer door of the old hangar when Paul strode out of his office. Can I see you for a minute, Andi?" he asked, uncharacteristically gruff.

"Sure. I'll just drop my things off and be right down. Good morning, by the way."

Paul disappeared into his office without a word. The entire interaction mystified her. It was very out of character for the amicable, easygoing man she'd come to know as a friend.

So whatever THIS is all about, it must be why my ears are burning, Andi thought with more than a little trepidation.

When she joined her boss just minutes later, said ears burned and tingled with an intensity she'd seldom experienced before. The sensation was uncomfortable and totally distracting. "So what's up, Paul?"

The compact, suited man rose from his desk and closed the office door. "Sit down, Andi." He indicated the chairs situated in front of his desk. His expression was grim. "I'll come right to the point," he said after he'd taken his chair again and picked up the pen he habitually held. "I hate to tell you this, but I've had a complaint about you. Someone has made some very serious allegations about your conduct with this company. I'm trying very hard to keep an open mind about this but considering the encounter we had with Louis Teto last week, I really don't know what to think any more."

Andi was dumbfounded. Whatever she anticipated, she hadn't expected something like this. She stared at the man before her as her mind raced. "What's this all about? What's been said about me?" she demanded.

A long, pregnant pause filled the room with silence. Finally, his lips pressed in a grim line, Paul replied. "You've been accused of attempting to sabotage Tuktu Aviation, Andi. Of deliberately trying to run us into the ground financially."

Andi gasped, her green eyes indignant. "What? What the hell are they talking about, Paul?" She leapt to her feet, only to find her legs too weak to keep her upright. She collapsed back into the chair.

Paul held up a hand in an attempt to placate her. "Easy now, Andi. I said you've been *accused* of sabotage. I didn't say I *believe* it. I want your side of the story before I make any decisions."

Andi's face was devoid of colour, her voice strangled. "I don't understand! How could you even *think* I'd sabotage Tuktu? You know I love this company as much as you do!"

"There were a couple of things mentioned, either of which could get our licenses lifted or drive away our best customers."

Not trusting herself to speak, Andi stared at Paul with questioning eyes.

"First," he said, tapping his desk blotter with his pen, "I've been told that you're blatantly disregarding the flight crew requirements for the oil companies and the government flights."

Andi opened her mouth but Paul held up a hand to silence her. "Let me finish."

"And second, you're accused of tampering with flight time billings as well. And accepting personal kickbacks for it."

"But it's not true! None of it is true!" Andi protested. She stood up, clutching the side of Paul's desk for support. Her face flushed with indignation and outrage. "How can you believe such crap, Paul? Don't you know me better than that by now? I'd like to know who the hell is feeding you these lies."

"Ah, well, that's the thing, Andi. Considering the source, I have mixed feelings about this whole thing."

"Who is it, Paul? You have to tell me. How can I possibly defend myself if you don't tell me who my enemy is? You at least owe me that much."

Paul deliberated for what seemed like a lifetime, a mixed range of emotions crossing his features.

"It's someone who's been with me for a very long time," he finally said. "Someone I've trusted completely and absolutely in the past." Paul shook his head and peered at Andi intently through his silver-rimmed glasses. "The thing is, unless I'm a total failure at judging people, I just don't think this kind of thing is in your nature, Andi."

"You're damn right it's not in my nature. The day I started working for you was the day Tuktu became my baby, too. I'd do anything for this company, and you should bloody well know that by now."

"Yeah, I do know that, Andi. That's why I'm so fucking confused by all of this." He ran a hand roughly over his face. "My gut feeling is that you're completely innocent of these accusations. But you have to understand – I've poured my whole life and every penny I have into this company, and if there's any chance, even a *remote* chance, of it being in jeopardy, I have to investigate. I won't lose my life's work, Andi."

She nodded, tearful eyes beseeching. "I didn't do it, Paul. None of it. But-" she couldn't bring herself to finish the sentence. She wanted to tell Paul about O'Neill's suspicious escapades. She wanted to talk to him about her suspicions … *needed* to talk to him, in fact. But she just couldn't bring herself to do it. What if she was one hundred percent wrong about everything? She'd not only cause a lot of trouble for many people, but end up looking like a fool in the process. It just wasn't worth it. Not yet.

"But what?"

"Nothing. My mind was just wandering."

"I want to believe you, Andi, but I just have to prove it. So," he said, rising from his chair, "leave it with me for a few days. I'm going to audit the books and hopefully put an end to this crap."

Andi nodded bleakly, and blinked her tears away. "Can you just tell me one thing, Paul? Please tell me who has accused me of these things? Who is it that's trying to ruin my life?"

Paul stood and looked his Operations Manager in the eye. He hesitated only briefly, his eyes lifting to the dispatch center above them.

"It's Jessica, Andi."

The pale pink hues of dawn began to lighten the mid-morning sky, captivating Andi's attention while she nursed her third coffee of the morning. Paul had left the office immediately after dropping his bomb on his Ops Manager, who now sat at her desk pondering not only the bizarre accusations, but also the foolhardy trip North would embark on later in the day. She didn't approve of his plan and refused to wait around and see him off. At the time it seemed like a good opportunity to catch up on her neglected paperwork. She wasn't so sure about that now. She could barely think of anything except him.

The events of the past two weeks needed to be explained, one way or another. And the sooner the better. She wished she could speak to Carlos Sante again, but her calls to his Pivot Lake office continued to go unanswered. She would try to find a home number for him today. He *must* have some explanation.

Andi heard movement on the stairs.

A moment later Princess Jessica Hartman came to an abrupt halt and glared at Andi through the open office door. "Oh. I didn't expect to see *you* here today."

Not trusting herself to speak, Andi merely smiled benignly and shrugged. She had no intentions of letting Jessica know that she was aware of her lying accusations. Andi doubted that Paul had spoken to her yet.

Jessica continued to scowl at Andi beneath furrowed brows, then seemed to come to some sort of decision. She turned her nose up and stomped to her desk.

Almost immediately the havoc of a busy day broke loose and Andi's Saturday sped by. Her thoughts were never far from North, though. She hoped and prayed that this time he would stay safe out on the frozen tundra, and that he would have better success at tracking down his assailant. She knew that if they could only identify the black-clad snowmobile rider they would be one step closer to solving her mystery.

Throughout the day she continued to call Carlos Sante's office. Just as before, nobody answered her calls and no answering machine clicked on for her to leave a message for him. The lack of communication with the mine's Supervisor left her feeling uneasy.

Jim O'Neill wasn't on the day's flying roster; Andi had checked with Ayame the evening before. North had still insisted that he would get Soap to fly him back out to the hunting cabin today anyway. In his haste to save North's life, the old bush pilot had abandoned all of North's gear there. North wanted to restock his food and get his gear organized. He wasn't sure what kind of shape his Arctic Cat was in either, or if it would even start.

At 4:00 Andi closed her office door and said good-bye to Jessica. The two women had barely spoken to each other during the eight hours they'd spent in the close confines of the office. You could cut the tension with a knife, as the old cliché went.

She was back on dog tending duty at North's place while he was on his quest. She loved looking after the dogs, but it troubled her that she would have to miss another AA Meeting that night. Too often in the past few days she'd felt an almost overpowering craving for a drink; she knew that she needed the ongoing support of her group. She decided to call her sponsor as soon as she finished with the dogs. He would help her through her latest mini-crisis.

The mutts were overjoyed to see her, especially Qannik. North had released them back into the big open pen, and they greeted her like a long-lost friend, running and jumping and yelping their welcome. The recent snowfall had erased all signs of the massacre, and North had taken the time to replace the broken padlock and hastily throw a coat of paint on the kennel wall.

Andi loved all the dogs, but definitely had a soft spot for Qannik. North had warned her against continuing to bring the growing, rambunctious pup into the house with her. "She needs to learn how to be a sled dog now, not a pet," he'd admonished.

By 8 pm Andi was seated at North's kitchen table waiting for his call and nibbling on a fried egg and cheese sandwich. Lost in thought, she jumped when the phone rang a few minutes past the hour. "Hello?" she answered cautiously.

Just the sound of North's deep voice made her breathe easier "Hey babe, how are you?"

"We're all good, everything is just fine here. How are you doing?"

"Great, and I got some fabulous photos this afternoon and at sunset. I'm going to try and get some of the Northern Lights later tonight."

"Sounds good. I'm glad to hear you're okay. I have a one o'clock meeting tomorrow, and after that I'll be able to spend the rest of the day with the dogs." Once again, using the code they had previously agreed upon, Andi had relayed the estimated time of arrival for the service flight into Pivot Lake the next day.

"Great, and thanks again for looking after the mutts. I really do appreciate it."

"Well, I love doing it. So we'll talk again in the morning, right? Eight sharp?"

"Will do. Take care, my love. Good night."

Andi's heart jumped. Did she hear him right? Did he just call her "my love"? Butterflies danced on her heart and she had trouble catching her breath. "Um, yeah. Good night, North," she stammered before hanging up the phone.

Andi sat at the kitchen table absorbing the enormity of those two little words. Her full lips twitched into a lopsided, silly grin, and fireworks sparkled in her emerald eyes. "He loves me!" she squealed to the empty cabin.

Only a short time ago, Andi had thought she would never love, nor be loved, again. Her heart hadn't been broken by the tragic death of her sweet Natalie – it had been shredded to pieces and ripped from her body. Even now, Andi wasn't sure she was prepared to commit her heart to love and loss again, but it seemed like the time to make a decision had arrived.

She was too excited to remain indoors, so she bundled into her parka and boots and slipped her hands into her new Otter mitts, a gift from North. The huge felt-lined mitts looked rather silly, hanging around her neck on purple idiot strings, but she loved them.

She stepped onto the back porch, closing the cabin door securely behind her. The dogs had already settled down for the night, some curled into tight balls in the snow, nestled near each other for warmth, and some in the doghouses scattered around their pen. They lifted their heads and sniffed the air when Andi entered their pen, but only a few roused themselves to pad quietly over the fresh, white snow to greet her.

Andi found a hard mound of snow near the centre of the enclosure and sat on it, wiggling around until her butt had made a comfortable depression. Qannik immediately attempted to climb into her lap but was firmly nosed down by Kia, who growled a short warning deep in her throat. Since Juno's death, Kia had established her position as Alpha dog – the leader of the pack.

Although the moon was barely a sliver in the black night sky, the pen and kennel were awash with light. North had insisted that she keep the bright yard lights on at all times. Now, as Andi peered upward at the night sky, she wished that the security lights were off so she could enjoy the light show dancing above.

She sat for almost an hour on the hump of snow, Qannik nestled on top of her boots and Kia curled up beside her. When the frigid night air finally penetrated her insulating layers and she started to shiver, she took comfort in the knowledge that, although her body was cold, her heart was once again warm.

For the first time in over five years Andi felt the icy shroud that had enveloped her heart begin to melt. Warmth and love stirred within her, and long forgotten contentment settled on her soul.

She had come to a decision.

TWENTY-ONE

North sat at the cabin's shaky old table while morning's pale pink glow lightened the landscape. He'd passed a comfortable, though cool night, and had managed to get enough sleep to awaken refreshed and alert. Every movement of his injured shoulder brought a fresh pang of pain. He regretted his hasty decision to embark on this harebrained plan before his body had healed, but it was too late now. He was here to do a job, and he would do it. He tossed down two extra-strength Tylenol with the cold dregs of his breakfast coffee and shoved the small vial of pills into a parka pocket.

He'd checked in with Andi already and was sorting through his camera lenses by the light of a Coleman lantern, trying to decide which one would best serve his purpose. Finally he chose the 1200-millimeter telephoto lens. It had the longest range of any in his collection, but it required either a tripod or an extremely steady hand to produce a clear, focused photo. That might be a problem in his current condition. He cleaned and polished the expensive lens carefully, then stowed it and his Nikon 35 millimeter camera into his backpack.

North glanced at his watch, surprised to see that it was already approaching 11:00. He brewed a fresh pot of coffee, then packed a thermos and the two bacon and egg sandwiches he'd made at breakfast. He glanced at the satellite phone and thought about leaving it behind, but it had likely saved his life a week ago; he stored it under the seat of the Cat.

After double-checking that he'd extinguished the flames on the Coleman stove and the heater North bundled up and slung his rifle across his back.

This time he knew the exact location of his destination and his black Arctic Cat flew over the frozen tundra. As he approached the clandestine meeting site he carefully scanned the region for a new hiding spot, preferably on higher land. He needed to conceal his snowmobile and himself, but wanted to be close enough to get some shots with his zoom lens if another meeting between Jim O'Neill and the snowmobile driver took place again today. He was determined to help Andi find out whom O'Neill was meeting with.

Stopping briefly to check the wind direction with a wetted finger, North was satisfied that the prevailing northwest wind was holding true to course. He'd position himself to the northeast, he decided, to avoid possible detection under the approach path of the Twin Otter on its route from Pivot Lake. After making a wide berth directly north and then due east of the landing site, North raced to get into position before the Twin Otter arrived. *If* it arrived.

After five minutes of reconnoitering, he chose a spot that was marginally passable for his needs. He had hoped to find a higher knoll to provide a better angle for photographing the meeting, but the Arctic tundra was sadly lacking any truly elevated land features.

Ignoring the pain in his shoulder North set to work with the small, collapsible miner's shovel he'd brought along, scooping snow and ice from the northeast face of the knoll to create a snug cave for the Arctic Cat. Then he banked the snowmobile with snow, piling it as high as he could before covering the machine with his white blanket. He stepped back to view his handiwork and was satisfied that only the most intense scrutiny would expose him.

As a final safety measure, he brushed away all trace of his tracks with a gloved hand, beginning a hundred feet from his hideaway. A freshening wind came to his assistance and the ever-present dry, loose snow blew over the land. In places, his tracks were already becoming invisible. He was already exhausted, and grateful for Mother Nature's assistance.

North squirmed into the small space he'd left open for himself and pulled his pack and rifle in behind him. Then he banked up the snow to conceal the entrance. It wasn't perfect, but it was the best he could do. His nostrils flared and beads of sweat dotted his forehead as he fought to control the red-hot pain piercing his shoulder and extending down his arm.

His exertions had created a whole new level of pain, and he once again berated himself for ignoring Andi's pleas that he take more time to recover before he set out on his mission. He was pretty sure he'd opened up his stitches too, but was afraid to look. He fumbled with the zipper of his parka and tossed two more painkillers into his mouth, dry swallowing the horrible tasting tablets with a grimace.

With his long snow knife, he carved a small hole through the west-facing wall of his cave. He needed a space just large enough to aim his long zoom lens through the packed snow. He sat back on his heels and eyeballed the hole. It looked large enough for his purposes. He dug into his pack and attached the zoom lens to his Nikon, then carefully inserted the long, heavy lens through the hole. He breathed a sigh of relief; it fit perfectly.

Resting on its snowy ledge, the lens would be as stable as on a tripod. He withdrew the lens and hung the heavy camera around his neck, zipping his parka up around it. The warmth of his body would ensure the batteries didn't freeze. He just hoped he'd have something to aim at.

It was 12:45 and his preparations were complete. North settled down to wait for his subjects, making himself as comfortable as possible in the cramped, dim ice-blind. He had a raging hunger, and wolfed down both sandwiches and half of his coffee.

Although North wasn't expecting any visitors until at least 1:30, he became restless and anxious as 1:30 and then 2:00 came and went. He was cramped and cold and at 2:30 had given up hope when he heard the distant drone of an approaching aircraft. "Yee ha!" he shouted, glad that his preparations and pain wouldn't be for nothing.

He unzipped his parka and pulled out the camera, then fitted the long zoom lens into its snowy support. Then he hunkered down to wait, eyes glued to the blank, white canvas of snow in his viewfinder. He was by no means a religious man, but he prayed that he'd chosen his viewpoint correctly.

Two minutes later, its engines screaming, the invisible aircraft landed. North listened intently, tracking its movements in his mind's eye. With a surge of power and snarling props the plane taxied nearer. A satisfied smile crossed North's face when the familiar white and blue Tuktu Aviation Twin Otter slid into his camera's viewfinder. A second later it taxied out of view just as quickly.

"Shit," North swore softly, his breath escaping in a white, foggy cloud. He lifted his head above the protection of his shelter, fearing that he'd misjudged the Twin's parking area after all. Relief flooded his pounding heart when he saw the Twin Otter turning around to reposition itself into the wind for takeoff.

He pulled his head back and silently implored O'Neill to stop within the narrow range of his lens. Moments later the aircraft slipped slowly into view, but continued until only the tail section was within his viewfinder.

"God damn it," North breathed. Beads of perspiration trickled down his forehead from beneath the rolled-up rim of the black balaclava he'd worn under his snowmobile helmet. He swiped them away in annoyance, barely noticing them.

Working rapidly, he withdrew the camera and hung it back under his parka, then grabbed his snow knife. With precise movements he carefully chipped away at the side of the hole, thankful that his granddad's old bone knife wouldn't glint in the sun. When North had enlarged the interior side of the hole and angled a new track, he reinserted the lens. It fit perfectly, and the airstair door was directly in his sight. He sighed in relief at his small victory.

Kneeling on the cold, packed snow he peered into the camera intently, blinking seldom and barely breathing. It seemed like hours passed before he detected the distant whine of a snowmobile, but in reality, only ten minutes had lapsed from the aircraft's arrival.

He snapped off a few shots of the aircraft, both long distance and zoomed in to clearly identify it as C-ITTA, and belonging to Tuktu Aviation. His injured shoulder ached; cold and stiffness were setting in.

Eventually the familiar yellow Ski-Doo slid into view. The airstair door of the Twin Otter dropped open when the snowmobile slid to a stop in front of it. North zoomed in again, taking several close shots of the Ski-Doo and its rider dressed from head to foot in black. He zoomed out again and took several more quick shots of the yellow snowmobile parked beside the Twin Otter.

Zoomed in on the aircraft again, he captured images of Captain Jim O'Neill as he descended the airstair door and again as he shook hands with the helmet-clad snowmobiler. The unidentified driver unzipped a pocket on his snowmobile suit and pulled out a small brown envelope. He passed it to O'Neill, North's camera capturing every movement with the continuous shooting feature of his camera.

Then the two men disappeared into the aircraft, pulling the airstair door closed behind them. North took the opportunity to drop a new roll of film into his camera. Then he settled down to wait.

Ten minutes passed. If there was one thing North had learned from his father during the hours and weeks they'd spend hunting on the tundra together, it was how to stalk and wait for your prey. He put those lessons to good use now; he waited patiently, adrenalin warming his limbs and chasing away his aches and pains.

When the aircraft's door popped open again he was ready; his camera didn't miss a thing. When the snowmobiler descended the steep metal stairs North realized that the moment he had been waiting for had arrived, and gave himself a mental pat on the back.

The man in black clutched his helmet under his arm. Jim O'Neill and Hank Brister stood in the open doorway of the aircraft until their guest reached the ground, then Hank pulled up the airstair door.

North didn't recognize the tall, dark blond man who straddled the Ski-Doo before shoving the black helmet back on his head, but he knew someone would. He let out a long breath and grinned, the cold skin of his face stiff and uncooperative.

While North waited for the snowmobile and aircraft to disappear from view he repacked his camera and equipment. He carefully stowed the precious exposed film in a warm inner pocket of his parka.

He was almost woozy with exhaustion and pain but he grinned again despite his discomfort. Andi would finally get her evidence.

North paced, glancing at his watch every few seconds. At 7:50 pm, ten minutes before their agreed upon time, he turned on his sat phone. He was too eager to wait another ten minutes before sharing his good news.

Andi answered his call immediately. "Hello."

"Hi Babe! Hey, just wanted to let you know that I had a great day today. Got lots of photos for the gallery. Some real fabulous shots, too. You're going to love them."

"That's wonderful news North! I'm so excited. When are you coming out?"

"I'll be in Inuvik by noon tomorrow. Can't wait to see you, Babe. Get ready to celebrate."

"I'll be waiting. Can't wait to see you either. How are you feeling?"

"I'll live," North replied. He had no intentions of telling her that he'd popped over half his stitches and his wound had bled copiously. He'd had to replace the dressing and put on clean thermal underwear and a new flannel shirt when he'd returned to the cabin. He didn't want her worrying any more than she already was.

"Well have a good night, and stay warm."

"I'll be hitting my sleeping bag soon. Sleep well, my love. See you tomorrow."

Exhausted from his labors and the exhilaration of capturing O'Neill and his cohort on film, North fell into a deep, dreamless sleep.

Overhead, millions of diamonds twinkled brilliantly against the backdrop of a black Arctic night.

The bedclothes knotted around her thrashing legs, eventually falling to the floor in a heap. Andi twisted and turned, moaning softly in her sleep. The room was cool, but her face, neck and breast glistened with sweat and her dark hair lay in a tangled disarray on North's pillow.

She cried out in her sleep. "Nat! Nat, come back."

Andi awoke from the nightmarish dream in a breathless panic, her heart pounding. It was back. After six glorious, dreamless months, the horrific nightmare had resurrected itself and once again attacked Andi's slumbering psyche.

For almost a year after her young daughter's tragic death, the same nightmare tortured Andi's nights. In the dream she was running down a snowy street after Natalie, calling to her: "Stop! Natalie, come back!"

But Natalie won't stop; she won't come back to her mother. Giggling and laughing, the girl in Andi's dreams keeps running away, always just out of her reach. She turns and throws a mischievous smile over her shoulder, lighting up her chubby baby face.

And then Natalie's fine brown hair flies across her face and her beloved features are hidden from Andi's fearful eyes forever when the white truck races in from nowhere. Natalie screams, and the last thing Andi ever remembers when she awakens is the gut-wrenching, piercing screams of her precious little girl.

And now the horrific nightmare had returned.

Andi huddled on North's bed, arms wrapped around her knees to quell her trembling. Eventually the chilly morning air dried her damp skin and she became chilled. She pulled the down filled comforter from the floor and wrapped it around her shaking shoulders.

And then she put her head to her knees and wept.

She wept for her lost child. She wept for her lost marriage. She wept for her dead mother. She wept for North's dead sled dogs.

And she wept for North, because she knew she could lose him, too.

Finally, exhausted by her tears and the hellish dream, she fell into a deep, dreamless slumber. When she awoke again the sun was shining and the mutts were complaining for their breakfast.

She was drained from her restless sleep, depleted of her usual energy and running on empty. She splashed some cold water on her face and threw on yesterday's clothes. Before she stumbled out the door to feed the dogs, she put a pot of coffee to brew.

She'd need more than one fortifying cups before she could face Paul White's Monday morning management meeting.

TWENTY-TWO

"I think that about wraps it up, people," Paul stated, flipping his notebook closed. "Unless anyone has anything to add, we're done here."

Andi felt like the meeting had gone on forever. She had trouble focusing and her mind constantly wandered away from the discussions and agenda at hand. When she finally escaped to her office at the end of the meeting, grateful to have a few moments to herself, Paul waylaid her.

"Andi, can I see you in my office for a minute?"

"Of course." She followed him downstairs with more than a little trepidation. She knew full well what he wanted to talk about.

"Close the door, please," Paul said, taking a seat behind his cluttered desk.

Andi, her hands cold and clammy, sat in the same chair she'd occupied just days earlier. Her breathing was ragged and her fortitude weak. The night and its unpleasant interruption had taken its toll on her.

A little voice in her head told her that now was the time to share her findings with her boss. North had proof now. She'd neglected to share her thoughts and suspicions with Paul during their last meeting, but she *had* to tell him. She opened her mouth, trying to find the right words to simplify a rather complex situation. Her head felt like it was stuffed with wool, her thoughts a jumble of knit one, pearl two.

"I spent a few hours looking through records and air bills this weekend," Paul began, interrupting her reverie. His expression was sober, which was not a good sign. Then his face broke into a wide, toothy grin. "I found absolutely nothing to support Jessica's accusations, Andi. Everything seems to be in perfect order, just as I suspected it would be."

"Oh, thank god," Andi breathed. She sat back and closed her eyes for a moment. "You don't know what a relief that is. I was afraid that she may have tampered with the records."

"I don't think Jessica would take time away from her busy social life to spend any extra time in the office," Paul chuckled.

"Why do we even keep her around, Paul? Maybe it's time we did an evaluation on her so we have something in her record if we ever decide to let her go."

"I agree. She used to be a great employee, and a much more conscientious dispatcher. Lately her performance really seems to be slipping. And now *this*." He lifted his hands in the air, palms up, at the word *this*, accentuating the single word.

"I'm so sorry for putting you through whatever this is really all about, Andi. I'll never trust Jessica again."

"Not your fault," Andi shook her head and smiled sadly. "You just did whatever you thought you had to do to save your company. I get that, but I'm just glad it's over. I have to admit, though – you had me worried."

Paul peered at her through thoughtfully. "You'd better keep your eyes open around here, Andi. It seems like trouble has been following you lately."

Do it now! Tell him! The nagging voice in her head was back, but it was too late. She'd missed the window of opportunity again. Revealing all to Paul would have to wait until she had concrete evidence in her hands. And North was bringing it to her.

Andi trudged up the stairs. Paul was right, of course. She'd had more than her fair share of trouble lately. And she suspected she hadn't seen the end of it.

The rest of the management team had dispersed to their offices. Andi filled her cup from the bottom of the coffee pot and walked into dispatch. Ayame was manning the desk. "Don't you ever take a day off, Ayame?" she teased. "Pretty soon we're going to have to set up a bunk in here for you."

"Well, I don't make the schedule, and the Prin ... I mean *Jessica*, evidently needed to go to Vancouver again this week." Ayame rolled her eyes.

"Huh. She's been going to Vancouver a lot lately."

"Yeah, at least twice a month I'd say. What a waste of time and money."

"Does she ever say what she's doing in Vancouver?"

"No, and I don't ask because I don't really care."

"I know what you mean. Sometimes it's best not to get Jessica going about what she does. Maybe she has a new man down there. But then again, we would have likely heard about him by now. It's strange though, isn't it? She never even mentions going to visit her family, and I know her mom and dad are there. And at least one sister."

The phone rang, ending their discussion. Andi slipped into her office, intending to catch up on the mountain of paperwork accumulating on her desk. After fifteen fruitless minutes of shuffling paper from one side of her desk to the other, she gave up. There was no way she could concentrate on mundane tasks when too many questions rolled around in her head: why were Jim O'Neill's flights to the mine returning late; why were diamonds missing from the Pivot Lake mine inventory; why couldn't she reach Carlos Sante, and who had shot North and his Canadian Eskimo Dogs? Too many questions with no answers.

She leaned back in her chair, staring out the small office window at the bustling airport beyond. Her eyes fell on the ugly yellow Twin Otter sitting like a stranded duckling on the tarmac in front of Tuktu's maintenance hangar.

Suddenly Andi knew *exactly* what she needed to do. She ran into the dispatch office and searched the booking schedule. *Yes!* The ugly duckling was scheduled for a 10 am departure to Pivot Lake the next day. Andi waited impatiently for Ayame to hang up the phone. "Are there any passengers on tomorrow morning's Pivot Lake run?"

"Nope, cargo only."

"And who's flying?"

"Dan and Tom."

"Perfect. I think I'll tag along. I need to talk to someone out at the mine. Can you get hold of Dan and let him know I'm going with them, please and thanks?"

"Sure thing, boss. But are you sure you should be going out there again after what happened last-" Ayame's voice trailed off when she saw the thunderous look on Andi's face. "I'll call Dan right now," she whispered.

Andi went back to her office and began working out the fine details of her plan. She was revitalized, her fatigue and morose vanishing in the path of new purpose.

Andi shrugged off her parka, wondering what her fridge might produce for dinner, when her phone rang.

"Hi, Babe."

"North, you're back!"

"Yeah, and I'm starving. Got any dinner plans?"

"No, but I'm starving too."

"Why don't you meet me at the Finto in thirty? I have a lot to tell you, and I think you're gonna like the news."

Twenty minutes later Andi was seated in a quiet corner of the Finto restaurant, toying with the silverware laid out on the table's white cloth. She checked her watch impatiently.

By the time North arrived she'd drained her water glass and was strumming the table with impatient fingers. "Finally," she muttered when his tall figure approached the table. He leaned down and kissed her cheek, squeezing her shoulder gently before sitting in the chair across the table from her.

"Well? Tell me what happened," Andi demanded. Her green eyes were wide and a pale blush tinted her cheeks. No signs of her earlier exhaustion remained.

"Not before we order. I'm famished."

"Jesus," she muttered, "where's the waitress? What do you want, anyway?"

North grinned, enjoying the suspense. "I'll settle on a menu, to start."

After they'd ordered their meals – Andi was secretly pleased to find that their waitress was a sixty-something grey haired grandmotherly type named Martha who had no interest in flirting with North – and North had quenched the worst of his thirst with a long pull of cold beer, he recounted his adventure, leaving out no detail.

Andi hung onto his every word, occasionally interrupting with a question or comment. When he was done, he set a large manila envelope on the table. "Here. You'll want to take a look at these."

Andi pulled a thick wad of glossy colour photos from the envelope. "How did you get these developed so soon?" she asked, her hushed voice and eyes filled with awe. She was only vaguely aware of her rapidly warming ears.

"I have a dark room at the gallery. I do all of my own developing and enlarging," North replied.

"I should have guessed."

Martha unceremoniously deposited their appetizers on the table. North dug into his sizzling escargot.

Andi ignored her own dish of garlicky snails, pushing the hot dish to one side. She flipped through the photos quickly and then went through them again slowly, studying each one. She looked up at North, a crooked smile on her lips. Her ears were definitely tingling now.

"Bingo," she whispered. "You got 'em, sweetheart."

North grinned. "I knew you'd be thrilled."

Andi pulled her cooling escargot closer and gulped them down, oblivious of their savoury flavor and uninterested in soaking up the gelling garlic butter with the soft bread on her dish. She finished just as Martha brought their entrees.

As soon as the waitress marched away Andi leaned across the white expanse of table and said softly, "So you know what *I* think?"

"What do you think?"

"I think," she said, tapping a slender finger on the figure of the blond man with Jim O'Neill, "that Carlos' missing diamonds definitely have something to do with *this* guy, whoever he is."

"I have no idea who he is," North mumbled through a mouthful of rare prime rib.

"Well, we need to find out, and I've already made a plan," Andi announced smugly.

"I thought you didn't like plans."

Andi glowered at him and took a dainty bite of her perfectly cooked Arctic Char. While they ate their meals, she laid out her agenda for the next day.

"I don't think that's a very good idea, Babe," North commented when she was done. "I mean, after what happened last time."

"Ugh, not you, too! Ayame said exactly the same thing. What's wrong with you guys? Don't you think I can look after myself?"

"Well-"

"I'll be careful," she interrupted. "What could possibly go wrong?"

North pleaded and cajoled with her for the next hour, but there was no way he could change her mind. Andi had a mission, and there wasn't a thing he could do or say to dissuade her.

TWENTY-THREE

At 9:45 the next morning Andi climbed into the ugly yellow duckling and pulled the airstair door closed behind her. The Twin Otter's cargo was loaded and Dan and Tom were already doing their pre-flight check. Andi locked the door and picked her way through the loaded cabin to the front of the aircraft. The crew had left a single seat down for her. She fastened her seat belt and settled back to enjoy the flight. Within minutes they were taxiing away from the hangar.

She loved to fly, and smiled in spite of her worries. The pristine white snow sparkled and glinted beneath them as they winged northeastward toward Pivot Lake. Andi searched for caribou, hoping to catch a glimpse of the elusive northern creature. All too soon though, they started their descent to the ice strip at the diamond mine, and Andi's thoughts returned to her mission.

The Pivot Lake crew was waiting for them when they taxied up to the makeshift terminal. The day was warmer than normal for this time of year and most of the men were hatless, their parkas unzipped. Andi left the aircraft before they started to unload the cargo. She studied each face carefully, but failed to spot anyone who even slightly resembled the dirty blond snowmobiler in North's photos.

"Hey, Jacques, how are you?" Andi greeted the only mine employee she recognized. After they exchanged brief pleasantries, she pointed to a late model yellow snowmobile parked nearby and asked, "Do you think I could use that machine for a bit? I just need to run up to the office. Be back in twenty minutes or so."

"Sure, 'elp yourself," the agreeable French Canadian smiled.

To the Tuktu Captain she called, "I'll be back in half an hour, Dan." He acknowledged her with a wave of his hand and she hopped onto the snow machine. Moments later she was roaring up the path to the office complex.

Her goal was to find Carlos Sante and show him the photos. She was positive that the unidentified man worked at the mine. If so, Carlos would be able to identify him. She pulled up to the main door of the complex in a flurry of snow, hit the kill switch and pocketed the key. She didn't want anyone running away with her ride before she was done with it.

An amicable young woman sat at the reception desk. Andi knew her from previous visits, and she waved Andi through the inner doors to the offices, never missing a word of her telephone conversation. Andi smiled her thanks and entered the heart of the complex.

She deliberately slowed her pace and plastered a relaxed, open smile on her face when she walked into the huge 24-hour cafeteria. Helping herself to a cup of coffee as cover, she casually glanced at each face in the room, hoping to find someone who resembled her mystery man. Disappointed, she nodded at the four men seated at a nearby table enjoying mounded plates of spaghetti and meatballs, then casually strolled down the hallway leading to the offices.

When she reached Carlos Sante's office she knocked on the door. Getting no response, she glanced up and down the deserted hallway, then opened the door, mildly alarmed to find it unlocked. Carlos *always* locked his door.

She peered into the dim room. The band of light seeping in from the hallway told her all she needed to know; Carlos's desk was bare. Its surface, every square inch of which was normally stacked with files and papers, was clear.

She flipped the overhead light on and stepped into the quiet room, closing the door behind her. She set her nearly full coffee cup on the corner of the desk and gazed around the small office in bewilderment. Carlos had evidently moved out, leaving no trace of his former presence behind. She reached for the black phone on the desk and lifted the receiver to her ear. She punched line after line, but heard no dial tone.

Cognizant of her limited time, she checked her watch. She still had about fifteen minutes before she had to get back to the Twin Otter. She opened the office door and peeked out, then slipped into the hallway. Just as she was closing the office door two athletic-looking men, similarly dressed in khakis and white dress shirts, turned the corner and strode down the carpeted hallway toward her. The taller of the two looked to be younger by several years. His blonde head was bent, his hands clasped behind his back. He appeared to be intently listening to what the older man was saying. Andi's heart sped up. Was this the man she was looking for? The hair colour was about right, but she couldn't see his face clearly.

The older, shorter man was looking straight ahead, speaking rapidly and gesturing emphatically with his hands. He spotted Andi immediately, her hand still on the doorknob. His long face was heavily lined, his dark grey hair fashionably cut and brushed back from his face. The man's features darkened when he spotted Andi and he stared at her intently, obviously displeased by her presence.

He muttered something and the blond man looked up. Andi's breath caught in her throat, but he wasn't the person she was searching for.

Both men picked up their pace and stopped in front of Carlos's office. Andi didn't recognize either of them.

"Can we help you with something?" the shorter man asked without preamble. He was clearly the superior of the duo. When Andi looked into his eyes her stomach flipped. They were the palest, coldest eyes she had ever seen. Icy silver, they emitted evil.

She swallowed convulsively, then embarked on a fit of coughing and sneezing. The two men stepped back a foot. "Oh, yes, please," Andi said when she had composed herself and gathered her thoughts. "I'm having some trouble," she said, flashing the men what she hoped was a beguiling and sexy smile. "I'm looking for Carlos but he's not answering his door."

Andi turned and knocked on the door again, confirming her words. "I don't have the wrong office again, do I? I'm *always* doing that!" She giggled and tossed her hair over her shoulder, then peered at them through the dark veil. She tried her best to look lost and confused.

"These darn doors all look the same," she gushed sweetly.

"Carlos doesn't work here anymore," intoned the taller man, clearly unimpressed with her attempt at feminine charm. "Do you have some business with him?"

The two men had stepped apart, effectively blocking Andi's path. She felt trapped, caught in the act of trespassing. The tingling in her ears reached an alarming level, unlike she'd ever felt before.

"Oh, no, not really," she cooed, trying her best to imitate Princess Jessica's flippant mannerisms. She toyed with a lock of dark hair, tilted her head and bestowed a toothy smile on each man. "I'm just paying a little visit to another friend who works here and Carlos is an old family friend. I haven't seen in just years! Thought I'd surprise him with a quick visit. A surprise-like visit, you know what I mean? I didn't know he didn't work here anymore." Andi opened her eyes as wide as she could and fluttered her long eyelashes. "But I'd be *so* happy if you could point me in the direction of the little girls room, hon," she winked at the blonde.

The two men exchanged a clearly disgusted look and shorty pointed back down the hallway toward the cafeteria. "Down to the end of the hall, then take a right. Washrooms are just off the cafeteria."

"Well, I thank you ever so much. And if you ever see Carlos again, please tell him Betsy says hi and sends her love!"

Andi glided around the men and sauntered down the hallway, swinging her hips as best she could in her heavy winter boots. As soon as she was around the corner she let out a long, shaky breath and wiped her burning forehead. On weak legs she hurried toward the cafeteria. At least that much of her story had been true; she did need the ladies room.

Disappointed by the failure of her mission she headed to the exit. When she spotted the young receptionist still seated at her desk, a thought occurred to her. Who knows more about everyone and everything than a receptionist? Smiling warmly, Andi walked up to the desk, noting the nameplate sitting to one side beside a sickly pale dieffenbachia. "Hi, Rita, how are you today? Nice plant."

Rita smiled back at Andi, her perfect teeth startling white in her dark face. She was dressed according to the code of the North; blue jeans and a man's red-checked flannel shirt. Her long, black hair hung in a lustrous braid over her left shoulder. "I'm good, thanks. How 'bout you?"

"Oh, just fine. Better after coffee and that delicious apple pie. You have some awesome cooks here," Andi laughed, rubbing her stomach. "I guess you don't get many visitors dropping by this god-forsaken place, though, do you?"

"No, we sure don't. But it has gotten a *lot* busier since they hit that new kimberlite pipe. There's actually been a fair amount of action around here the past few weeks," the friendly young woman replied, clearly enjoying the impromptu visit.

Stretching her back and stifling a fake yawn, Andi asked casually, "I was surprised to hear that Carlos Sante quit. When did that happen?"

Rita leaned forward conspiratorially, now that the ice was broken. "Well, Carlos didn't quit, I can tell you that right now. He *loved* this place. He lived for his job. Nobody's saying for sure what happened. One day he was here, and the next day his office was cleaned out. Nobody ever saw him again." Perhaps suddenly realizing that she'd said too much, Rita glanced around nervously before asking, "Do you know Carlos well?"

"We were just business acquaintances, really. But I always liked him. He seemed like a great guy," replied Andi sincerely. "So when did this all happen?"

"Uh, I guess about a week ago or so."

"You wouldn't happen to have a phone number for him, or a forwarding address?" Andi asked.

"I can't help you there. You'd have to go to Human Resources." She pointed back the way Andi had just come from.

"I'm in kind of a hurry, my plane is waiting. I'll just give them a call later. But, hey, it was nice talking to you, Rita. You take care, and don't work too hard!" Andi waved and hurried out the door before the two creepy goons decided to check up on her.

She fired up the snowmobile and was half way back to the ice strip before she remembered the mug of coffee she'd left on Carlos's desk. Groaning, she realized her mistake and said a silent prayer that the two unfriendly men hadn't checked the office after she left. The warm cup would be a dead giveaway. They'd know she'd actually been inside Carlos's office. More anxious than ever to escape, Andi glanced back at the mine complex and gunned the throttle.

The Twin Otter was ready to depart. The crew was waiting for her by the makeshift terminal talking to Jacques.

"Glad you made it back," Dan laughed. "We were getting worried about you. Thought we'd have to form a search party."

"Sorry for being late guys. Are you ready to go?"

"Yup, ready to roll." The two pilots bid farewell to Jacques and began preparing the Twin Otter for departure.

When they were safely out of earshot, Andi pulled the photo of the mystery man out of her pocket. "Hey, Jacques, do you by any chance have any idea who this guy is?" She handed him the picture, a fairly clear shot of the blond man standing next to his Ski-Doo.

"Oh, yeah. That be Henrik Bruller. And dat der is his mean machine," he nodded, pointing to the shiny yellow snowmobile. He frowned. "Where you get dis picture?" he asked in broken English.

"Oh, one of the flight crew must have taken it I guess. I found it sitting in the coffee room at work and I thought I recognized this guy from the mine, but I wasn't sure."

Andi's ears were burning big time now. Not one to tell lies, she had suddenly found herself lying at every turn. She was turning into a regular pro at deceit. "What does Henrik do around here?"

"Oh, he be a real big wig, Jacques said in a condescending tone, twirling both forefingers in the air. "That guy be da Project Manager, but he jus' really a big pain in da ass! You ask any of da guys, dey tell you that Bruller is a bully too. One mean sum-na-bitch! You stay away from 'im, eh? He's no good."

"Okay, I certainly will! Thanks heaps, Jacques. I'd better get on that plane before they leave me here." Andi laughed weakly and reached for Jacque's hand. "See you again soon, Jacques. You take good care."

The props were already turning when Andi ran up the airstair and pulled the door closed. As she settled in for the trip home and the pounding in her heart eased, she couldn't prevent the grin that spread from ear to ear.

Her mission had been a success after all. She finally had a name for their mystery man. Wouldn't North be pleased!

TWENTY-FOUR

An hour later the Twin Otter landed at the Inuvik Airport. After checking in at dispatch and retrieving her briefcase Andi decided to head straight to the RCMP detachment. She finally had a name, and she had photos. She had all the evidence she needed. Regardless of what North said, she didn't think the two of them could handle the situation by themselves any longer.

She pulled up to the detachment, bolstering her courage as she walked in the front door and requested an interview with the Constable on duty. She was escorted to a small interview room deep within the detachment, where she patiently waited to talk to an officer.

"Good afternoon. I'm Constable Gordon. What can I do for you this morning, Miss, uh, Miss Nowak?" The young Constable peered at the receptionist's note to confirm her name. His pink, hairless cheeks and smooth chin made Andi wonder if he was even old enough to shave. Beneath heavy black eyebrows, smallish eyes of a non-descript colour stared at her as if she were a suspect, not a complainant.

Andi drew the photos out of their envelope, along with a detailed account she had written earlier in the day of the recent events and her suspicions. She briefly explained the reason for her visit before handing them over to the young officer. He took the sheets from her, glanced at them briefly and lay them on the table.

"Can you tell me again what this is all about?" he requested, tugging on his left earlobe.

Andi gave him a slightly longer but still condensed version, including her visit to Pivot Lake that morning. She closed her summary by nudging the photos toward him – photos he had so far totally ignored. "These photos are the hard evidence you need to do something about this!" she said earnestly.

Constable Gordon flipped through the photos and pulled on his ear again. "Do you know this man?" he asked, pointing at a clear picture of Jim O'Neill.

"Yes. That's Captain Jim O'Neill. He's a pilot for Tuktu Aviation, the company I work for."

"And who is this guy?" he asked, this time pointing to the partially obscured features of Bruller.

"I don't know him myself, but someone else identified him as Henrik Bruller, the Project Manager at Pivot Lake Diamond Mine."

"So let me get this straight," the officer drawled, tapping a finger on Bruller's face. "You think this guy is stealing diamonds from the Pivot Lake Mine and passing them on to this pilot of yours?"

Andi nodded.

"And you don't know exactly how long this has been going on, or what O'Neill's doing with these supposed smuggled diamonds. Is that correct?"

Andi nodded again, more slowly this time.

"And your boyfriend, uh, North Ruben, got shot at by some guy on a snowmobile, and then someone took some pot-shots at his dogs too. Is that about correct so far?"

Andi began to seethe. The condescending mannerism of the young RCMP officer told all she needed to know. North was right; the police were just going to make a mockery of her accusations. "Yes, that's correct," she said through clenched teeth.

Constable Gordon picked up a photo of Jim O'Neill standing on the airstair of the Twin Otter, a helmeted, unidentifiable Henrik Bruller handing an envelope to him.

"So," the officer continued, his expression smug, "can you tell me exactly what you see in this photograph that is an unlawful act?"

"Nothing. You can't see it, but there are stolen diamonds in that envelope. I'm sure of it."

"Right. I see nothing illegal either. All I see, Miss Nowak, is a pretty picture of an airplane parked in the snow, and a couple of friends having a visit. And last I heard, there's absolutely nothing illegal about that." The Officer dropped the photos onto the table and leaned back in his chair, hooking his thumbs through his belt loops.

"So what you're telling me," Andi said, her voice shrill even to her own ears, "is that you're not going to investigate this? You're not going to do anything at all about it?"

"Yeah, I guess that's about right Miss Nowak," Constable Gordon said, rising from his chair. "Unless you have some concrete evidence that diamond smuggling is going on here you're just wasting our time. We haven't had any complaints from the mine about any missing diamonds, stolen or otherwise."

Andi remained seated at the table, dumfounded. She couldn't believe what she was hearing. The RCMP wouldn't even consider an investigation. She tossed the photos and summary back into her briefcase. Constable Gordon opened the door of the interview room and Andi brushed by him without a word. She was pissed off and had no time for civilities.

The Land Yacht lurched away from the parking lot a little faster than necessary. Still fuming, she realized she had a brutal headache. A glance at her wristwatch told her why; it was almost 5:00 pm and she'd missed lunch. She stopped at To-Go's for her favourite fast food. There was no way she was going to cook after the day she'd had, and a big, juicy burger and fries would hit the spot. She needed to be alone and didn't feel like company, North's included.

Twenty minutes later she was nibbling on her caribou burger while she examined North's photos again. She'd thought about it a long time, and finally formulated a workable theory: Henrik Bruller was somehow smuggling diamonds out of the mine and handing them over to O'Neill, who passed them on to Jessica. Jessica then transported the stones to Vancouver and sold them there. Andi's Sixth Sense told her she wasn't wrong, and that she'd be able to bust open their little diamond smuggling ring. But how to prove her theory?

She racked her brains for a solution. She needed to find a way to prove that Jim O'Neill, Hank Brister, Jessica Hartman and Henrik Bruller were all involved in diamond smuggling. She also needed to locate Carlos Sante; she was convinced that the conscientious mine employee hadn't suddenly quit. He'd been fired, or worse.

She pulled out a legal pad and pen and began to make some notes. Putting a name to the face behind the snowmobile helmet was a windfall. It proved beyond a doubt that there was a connection between Jim O'Neill and Henrik Bruller. And it also proved that the flight delays were connected to Carlos Sante's missing diamonds. There could be no other explanation, and she was determined to prove it.

By the time she dragged her weary body to bed she'd formulated another plan and knew exactly what she was going to do. She just hoped she could produce the evidence she so desperately needed to confirm her theory.

She closed her eyes and prayed that, if she actually did pull it off, she'd be able to get someone to believe her.

"Hi, Jessica, welcome back," Andi said cheerfully, deliberately putting more warmth into her voice than she felt. "I hope you enjoyed your week? I hear you went to beautiful Vancouver again. I love that place."

Three days had passed since Andi's foray to Pivot Lake, and Jessica was once again seated at the dispatch desk when she walked into the office on Friday morning. She turned to Andi and shot her a moody, suspicious look. "Yeah, I was in Vancouver." After glaring at Andi a moment longer, she turned back to her desk.

Andi dumped her belongings in her office, got a cup of coffee and strolled back into dispatch. She picked up the charter schedule and flipped through the pages, but there was only one trip she was really interested in – the next service flight Jim O'Neill was flying to Pivot Lake. Captain O'Neill and First Officer Brister were due to depart Inuvik at noon.

Andi devoted her morning to the most pressing of her duties and at 12:05 heard radio chatter announcing the departure of C-ITTA for Pivot Lake. O'Neill and Brister were on their way, and right on schedule.

Two hours later it was time for Andi to put her latest plan into action. She walked into Jessica's office, where the sullen blond sat sipping a cappuccino. "Jessica, I have Operations Manual amendments to do today, so I'll be out of my office for the rest of the afternoon." She hefted a stack of paper in hand. "I'm going over to the terminal to do the photocopying first, so I'll be there for a while if you need me."

Required by Transport Canada, the Operations Manual was like a company bible; the thick volume contained details of company operations and safety procedures. Up-to-date copies were required to be held by each company officer and located in each aircraft, and updating the manuals was a tedious, boring task. Once the photocopying was done, Andi stacked the amendments into a box and drove over to her next stop – the maintenance hangar.

There was still no sign of C-ITTA as Andi hauled the bulky box into the hangar, plopping it on a chair near the entrance door. She extracted a copy of the amendment and made her way to Ken's office, noticing that Liz, the maintenance secretary, was nowhere around. Ken's office was at the end of a short hallway, and Andi found him seated at his desk. "Knock, knock," she called, rapping her knuckles on the open door.

Ken looked up from the huge maintenance manual he was reading and smiled when he saw her. "Hi, Andi. Come in."

"How are you?" she asked, dropping into an empty chair. Ken had more or less taken her under his wing when she'd arrived at Tuktu Aviation a year ago, and she'd always be grateful to him.

"Swamped, as usual," he laughed, indicating the towering mass of maintenance manuals and binders littering his desk.

"I'm just here to update your Ops Manual," Andi said, waving the sheaf of papers in her hand. Ken swiveled in his office chair and reached to the huge bookcase lining the entire back wall of his office. He plucked his copy of the Operations Manual from the top shelf and passed it to her.

"I'll have it back for you shortly," she said.

"No problem. I was just leaving to make a run into town. Just leave it on my desk when you're done."

Andi suppressed a grin. Pieces of her plan were starting to fall into place. "Okay. Hey, it's pretty quiet around here today. Where are Liz and everyone else?"

"Well, Liz has a bad cold, so she went home at noon, and some of the guys were in really early this morning so they've already taken off for the day."

"I see. Well, I'll let you go then. I have to go upstairs and sort through some things anyway." Clutching Ken's manual, Andi ran up the wooden stairs to the mezzanine level of the hangar where the roughly equipped pilots' lounge was located. Large, grimy windows looked out over the hangar floor and one small window at the end of the room overlooked the parking lot. A long plastic table surrounded by stackable plastic chairs, a telephone, a cabinet for flight crew mail and an ancient coffee pot were provided for flight crew use.

From her vantage point in the lounge Andi would be able to hear and see O'Neill's arrival. She wiped the sweat from her hands and opened Ken's Operations Manual. It took only a few minutes to insert the updated pages and record the entry in the book's log. That done, she checked her watch. The Pivot Lake run was already forty-five minutes late returning, which could only mean that O'Neill and Brister had had another clandestine meeting with Bruller.

With Ken's Operations Manual in hand, she trotted down the stairs to the hangar floor and back to the Chief Engineer's office. She knocked once and when there was no response opened the door and placed the manual on his desk. She was on her way back to the pilots' lounge when she remembered the heavy box of amendments she'd lugged into the hangar. Backtracking to the front door, she picked up the box and carted it back to her car. The parking lot was empty; Andi seemed to have the hangar to herself.

Back upstairs she fidgeted and paced as the minutes dragged by. She picked up a copy of *Wing's* magazine but couldn't concentrate long enough to read through an article. It was after four o'clock when she heard the snarl of propellers from an approaching aircraft. Her stomach lurched and she jumped from her chair like a nervous deer.

She sped down the stairs. Since the maintenance staff had left for the day, the cavernous hangar was dim and eerily silent. Heading to the far side of the building where a small pedestrian door opened airside, she wove her way around several small aircraft. With the exception of the medevac-dedicated Piper T-1040, which had a permanent parking spot in the heated hangar, all of the other aircraft inside the shop were in various stages of repair or inspection. Engine cowlings hung open and various wires hung from service areas and power units. Immense red toolboxes dotted the pristine cement floor.

After reaching the small door she cracked it open far enough to confirm that Tuktu's Twin Otter was taxiing up to the hangar. She pulled the door closed and melded into the shadows crowding the hangar walls. It would take several minutes for the crew to park the aircraft and prepare it for the night.

Patience was not one of Andi's better qualities and after only two or three minutes she chanced another peek out the door. O'Neill was climbing down from the cockpit, his bulky black map bag in hand.

Hank Brister was already outside the Twin Otter, securing the wheels with chocks. There appeared to be no passengers and since the cargo doors were still closed Andi guessed there was no cargo to unload either.

O'Neill's rough voice boomed across the tarmac when he advised Hank that he was on his way to the Brass Rail for a Friday TGIF drink. The First Officer promised to join him there when he'd put the aircraft to bed for the night.

Andi pulled her head back into the hangar, blood coursing through her veins and her heart pounding. It was time to put her plan into action. O'Neill would walk through the hangar, she knew, entering through the pedestrian door. If he followed his regular routine, he would climb up to the mezzanine level and pilots' lounge to check his mail slot before leaving the building.

She dashed to the front offices on the main floor. A moment later she heard the heavy metal pedestrian door at the back of the hangar slam shut. Andi stepped into Ken's empty office and closed the door. She picked up the phone and punched a button to reach an empty line, then dialed the phone number for the hangar. Immediately, a loud jangling ring pierced the silence. After letting it ring three times, she put the line on hold and then counted to three before punching the intercom button. The paging system crackled to life.

Muffling her voice, Andi spoke gruffly into the receiver, "Jim O'Neill, line two. Jim O'Neill, line two please." She slammed the receiver down, her heart fluttering wildly, and then crept out of Ken's office and down the short hallway. She peered around the corner. O'Neill was, as per her plan, trudging up the stairs to the pilots' lounge to answer the page.

To Andi's joy, he'd left his big black ace case at the bottom of the staircase.

When the pilot disappeared from sight Andi ran to the mezzanine stairs. She could hear O'Neill shouting, "O'Neill here. Hello? Hello? What the hell!"

Jim O'Neill's temper was legendary and Andi had already had a taste of it; she didn't want another. She grasped the pilot's heavy flight bag and ran for the front door.

She slipped from the maintenance building into the dimness of late afternoon, closing the door quietly behind her. Seconds later she sped away from the airport, her old brown Land Yacht heading for town.

Step one of her plan was complete.

TWENTY-FIVE

Only when she was safely home and behind locked doors did Andi take a steady breath again. Her heart still raced, but at least it was no longer pounding within her chest.

She set the stolen flight bag on her kitchen table and stared at it for a few minutes, her ears burning in anticipation and fear. She prayed that whatever she found within the case would be worth the huge risk she'd just taken. Now that she had it in her possession, though, she was afraid to open it. She had just committed a criminal offense; she'd compromised her normally high moral standards and turned into a common thief.

Andi realized her hands were shaking and that she craved something to calm her nerves. At that moment she would gladly trade her soul for a bottle of gin, and it took a supreme effort to push the tempting thoughts aside. She reached for the metal closure on the front of O'Neill's flight bag, snapped it open and lifted the flap to expose the bulging contents within.

She carefully lifted out each item and inspected it closely. The bag was packed with various maps and charts, an out-of-date Canada Flight Supplement, Instrument Flight Rule approach plates and various magazines. A whiz-wheel, calculator, Leatherman and expensive looking sunglasses were pushed into pockets lining the interior of the bag, and the bottom was littered with pens, a small Mag-Lite and an open roll of Rolaids.

She turned her attention to the two large pockets and unzipped the first one, revealing O'Neill's company I.D., ramp pass and license.

As soon as she touched the zipper on the last pocket, her ears flamed. She instantly knew that whatever she was looking for was at her fingertips.

Inside the pocket was a brown manila envelope. She pulled it out, surprised by its considerable weight.

Andi pushed aside the books and papers spread on her kitchen table, ripped open the envelope and poured out its contents. The dull rocks that lay before her did not resemble diamonds in any way, but she knew that the grey stones were in fact rough diamonds. She'd spent hours reading everything she could get her hands on about the diamond mining industry, and Carlos Sante had also been a wealth of knowledge. She thought of him again and made a mental note to renew her efforts to locate the mine's former supervisor.

Carlos had once given her a rapid, somewhat unsanctioned tour of the entire Pivot Lake Diamond Mine facility, which was the largest of its kind in Canada. She'd been awed by the immense earth-movers, each machine the size of a two-storey house. They slowly wound down almost eight hundred feet to reach the bottom of the kimberlite pipes, and then scooped up thousands of tons of frozen granite and kimberlite volcanic rock.

The rock was then taken to an on-site processing plant and run through a series of crushers to separate the rock from the diamonds, resulting in sand-to-golf-ball sized stones. Once separated, the diamonds zoomed along on a conveyor belt, to be deposited in locked bins. The entire process was, of course, automated and secure. Workers were not allowed to pick up any debris from the floor or touch any stones by hand.

How these stones came to be sitting before her was an amazing feat in itself. Only someone with the highest security clearance at the mine could possibly have access to them.

Before her were over a dozen rough diamonds of various sizes. Cautiously, she picked up the largest of them. It was a big one – about an inch in diameter. Her fist wrapped around the rough diamond and she sat down, suddenly too exhausted to stand. Her thoughts and feelings ran rampant. One moment she was elated that she'd finally found the evidence needed to link Jim O'Neill to the missing diamonds, and the next moment fear clenched her throat, making it almost impossible to breathe.

She didn't have any idea what these rough, uncut and unpolished diamonds were worth, but she knew O'Neill would be out of his mind with rage at having lost them. She no longer felt safe, even behind her own locked door.

The early evening light faded quickly, leaving Andi sitting in darkness, clutching the stone. It had absorbed heat from her hand, and no longer felt cool. Suddenly, her hand began to tingle and a low vibration began to emanate from the warm rock. It was almost too faint to be noticed, but Andi's senses were more acute than most peoples were. Her heart filled with dread, yet she couldn't release the diamond from her clasp. It seemed like her hand had a mind of its own, independent from the rest of her body.

What she needed more than anything was a drink to steady her nerves. Still clutching the warm diamond, Andi threw the stairwell door open and ran down the steps. Coco had liquor. Coco always had liquor, and she'd be only too glad to share it.

The harsh ringing of her telephone stopped her cold, one foot on the last step and one on the foyer floor. She turned and raced back up the stairs to her suite. She hadn't turned on any lights and now she stared at her phone in the dim living room, too afraid to answer it.

After the fourth shrill, demanding ring, she picked up the receiver. "Hello?" After a few silent seconds she heard a soft click when the caller hung up.

The call unsettled her. On heavy feet, she walked to the stairwell door and locked it. Her physical, violent need for alcohol had abated.

She twirled the silver AA ring on her finger; the close call left her with a heavy and guilty heart.

Minutes later, the phone rang again. Andi's hand hovered over the receiver and her nerves jangled with every demanding chime. She picked up the receiver. "Hello?" she whispered.

"Hey, what are you doing at home? I thought you were coming over after work." Garth Brooks wailed in the background about thunder rolling at 3:30 in the morning.

"Oh, Margo!" Andi gasped, "I'm so sorry. I forgot all about TGIF. My day was just nuts. All I want to do is go to bed and curl up with a book."

Margo laughed, and Andi could hear her best friend take a drag from her cigarette. "Well get your ass over here! I'm on my third beer already."

"I really can't. I wouldn't be good company tonight."

"Don't be such a party-pooper, Nowak! Get your ass over here," Margo demanded.

"Next Friday. I promise."

"Okay, but you're missing a good one," Margo admonished, shouting to be heard over the music someone had just cranked up again.

"Thanks, Margo. You guys have a great time."

"Oh don't worry! We will," Margo chortled before the phone went dead.

Andi rubbed a hand over tired eyes and decided that a hot bath might ease her tension. She'd taken three steps toward the bathroom when the phone rang again. She snatched it up. "Margo, I told you I'm NOT coming!" she laughed.

But there was no loud music in the background, and Margo's gravelly voice didn't cajole her. Heavy breathing backed by silence assaulted her nerves. Andi's ears burned and she struggled to breathe.

"Hello? Who is this?" She listened intently and sensed, more than heard, deep, menacing laughter flirting over the airwaves. A moment later the line went dead, but the eerie call was long enough to instill terror in her heart.

Andi slammed the receiver down. She knew these were no ordinary prank calls and contemplated calling the police, but quickly dismissed the idea. They would only laugh at her. She'd call the only man who seemed to really care about her. North.

She dialed his number with a shaky hand, willing him to pick up. The phone rang until North's answering machine clicked on. She disconnected, and tried again. There was still no answer. Andi glanced at the clock on her kitchen wall, surprised to see that it was already past seven. North should have fed the dogs by now, she thought, but maybe he's still outside with them.

Her mind raced over her options. Her first impulse was to throw the flight bag back in her car and race to North's place. But what if he wasn't home? And what if whoever was playing phone games with her was outside her door, waiting for her? Her nerves were raw and she couldn't seem to think straight.

With trembling hands, she dialed North's number again, and once more there was no answer. This time she left a message. "Hi North. It's me. Um, can you call me as soon as you get in? Doesn't matter what time. I really need to talk to you. Bye."

Evening dragged into night and Andi paced, jumping at every small sound. She repacked O'Neill's flight bag, attempting to return each item to its proper spot. Dinner was out of the question; her stomach was in knots. Several times she picked up the phone to call North, each time replacing the receiver without dialing. She knew North would phone her back when he could.

Finally, looking for a distraction, she turned the television on. She sat perched on the edge of the sofa, staring at the small screen without really seeing it, and glancing periodically at the menacing black bag still sitting on her kitchen table. When her phone finally rang two hours later she jumped, barely suppressing a scream. She answered it cautiously. "Hello?"

"Hey, Babe. Did I wake you?"

"No," Andi sighed in relief. "No, I was up. I've been hoping you'd call."

"Well I would've called earlier, but it's been a hell of a night." Andi's exhausted brain finally registered the fatigue in North's voice. Her senses flared.

"Why? What happened?"

"Well, you won't believe this."

"I'd believe just about anything today. What happened?" she asked again, her heart in her throat. "Are you okay?"

"Yeah, I'm fine. I'd like to know just what the hell happened myself," North complained. "I was late getting home from the gallery, and I'd just come up to the house after feeding the dogs when a vehicle pulled into the yard. It was dark out already, so I went to the front door and turned on the porch light. Before I could open the door some asshole started taking pot shots at my house!"

"Oh, my god, North! Are you sure you're all right?" Andi cried. "And what about the dogs? Are they okay?"

"Yeah, yeah. We're all fine. The bastard just sprayed up the front of the house with a shotgun. He cracked my picture window and shot out the porch light, and then he took off."

"And you didn't see who it was? Could you identify the vehicle?"

"Andi!" North shouted in exasperation. "When he started shooting I ran as far as I could from the front of the fucking house!"

At the other end of the connection, she blinked rapidly. "Right. I'm sorry," she apologized. "Stupid question."

"Awe, Babe, I'm sorry too. I didn't mean to snap at you. I'm just tired and fucking mad."

"I know. And just for the record, it *was* a stupid question. So did you call the police?"

"Yeah, some young cop named Gordon came out and looked around. He didn't seem too interested. He just asked who I'd pissed off lately. Prick."

"That was the same one I talked to on Tuesday!" Andi exclaimed. "He wasn't interested in the photos I showed him or what I had to say either."

"I'm not surprised," North grumbled, "and I'm still kind of pissed off that you went to the cops before telling me first, but I think I have a pretty damn good idea who's behind this and I'll be damned if I'm going to let him get to me."

Andi sighed. "Well, that's why I was trying to reach you tonight. I did something again today that was probably pretty stupid."

"What?"

"Oh, God. I still can't believe I did it," Andi lamented. "I met Jim O'Neill's flight when it returned from Pivot Lake this afternoon and I stole his flight bag. And you'll never believe what I found inside!" Before North could respond, she whispered, "I found a big bag of diamonds in his bag!"

"Are you serious? He'll kill you if he finds out!" North shouted.

"Hey, I'm already scared shitless right now, so please don't yell at me."

"Sorry, Babe. I just don't want you getting hurt."

"I've already had two hang-up phone calls tonight. The first time they didn't say anything, but the second time I could hear a man laughing. It was an evil, mean laugh. And then he just hung up. It scared the shit out of me."

"I'm coming over. Don't answer the phone again and do *not* open the door to anyone until I get there."

"There's no need for you to come over, North," Andi started to argue before she realized she was talking to a dial tone. But she was glad he was coming. She didn't need her inherited Sixth Sense to warn her that her life, as well as North's, was in danger. And she knew the reason why, too – 'the stone without a name'.

She thought about the Inuvialuit people and wished that she, too, knew nothing about the diamonds that were buried far below the Arctic land she loved so much.

'The stone without a name' had brought nothing but trouble into her life. Whoever said that 'diamonds were a girl's best friend' had to have his head examined.

TWENTY-SIX

Andi drifted slowly from the depths of a deep, untroubled sleep. She stretched languidly, sliding her foot over the long, hard leg next to her own. She opened her eyes and, in the dim glow of a night-light, feasted on the masculine figure next to her. His very presence and the heady, male smell of him made desire bloom in her belly.

With slow, deliberate movements, she traced the lines of his strong, smooth face, his skin singeing the tips of her fingers. Her hand moved unwaveringly downward, her fingers lightly stroking his chest, then teasing his small, brown nipples.

With feather-light touches her hand moved lower, tracing the soft line of hair running down his taut abdomen to meet the tight curls at his groin. Her smile was more of a sigh when her hand brushed lower. She gasped in surprise when a firm hand encircled her own.

"Don't start anything you don't intend to finish, Babe," he murmured, his voice husky.

"I intend to finish," Andi whispered, covering his mouth with her own, her tongue darting through his pliable lips. Arousal hit with a strength that left her breathless. She pushed North onto his back, and with the grace of a tigress straddled his groin. She was wet and ready, frantic for the feel of North inside her. She guided him to her centre, taking him in one smooth movement.

"Andi, oh Babe," North groaned, "you're gonna kill me."

Later, after their need was quenched and their bodies slick with sweat, Andi leaned down and brushed North's lips with hers. The eyes that gazed at her, still black with passion, were tender and questioning.

She lay on his chest and nuzzled his neck, their bodies still intimately entwined.

North stroked her long back, his large hands eventually trailing down to encompass her soft, round buttocks. He pulled her closer to his body, unwilling to lose their connection. Only when the sweat had dried and their breathing had slowed did he murmur, "What time do you have to leave?"

"There's a 10:15 flight," Andi said, glancing at the bedside clock. Her nose caught a tantalizing aroma; North's coffee maker was doing its morning thing. "Coffee?" she asked, reluctantly disengaging from his arms.

"Absolutely."

Andi turned on the reading light beside his bed and pulled on the robe she'd brought to North's place late Friday night. She padded into the kitchen, her slippers silent on the wood floor. While the spurting machine pushed out the last drops of caffeine-laced brew she stared into the early morning darkness and thought about the past thirty hours.

Upon arriving at her place late Friday night North had insisted that she pack an overnight bag and spend the weekend with him. Not wanting to leave Jim O'Neill's flight bag behind, Andi had carted it along too.

They'd talked for hours, huddled together in North's warm bed, until exhaustion took its toll on them both. The next morning North packed his qamutik, Andi packed a lunch and a thermos of coffee, and they spent hours traversing the tundra with a team of six Canadian Eskimo Dogs. Andi had her turn at the helm, practicing her mushing. It was an idyllic, carefree day, and they agreed not to talk about the recent shootings while they were out on the land. They wanted nothing to mar their time together.

Now, through the cracked picture window North had covered with 4-mil poly, a quick fix until the glass could be replaced, Andi could still feel a chill seeping into the room. She shivered when the cool air brushed her skin, still warm from North's bed.

She filled two mugs and carefully manoeuvred back to the bedroom. She set the brimming cups on the nightstand before crawling back into the warmth of North's bed. "Are you asleep again?" she asked, nudging his shoulder.

"Nuh. Maybe." His words were muffled under the heavy down duvet.

"Well get up. Here's your coffee," Andi said, playfully poking him in the side, her finger colliding with rock hard muscle.

North responded by dragging her back under the covers where their short skirmish ended in a long kiss. When Andi finally broke from his embrace, she handed him his cup and they reviewed the plans they'd formulated over the weekend. Too soon she flipped back the covers and kissed him again before she murmured, "It's getting late. I have to get ready to go."

"I'll make us some breakfast. Bacon and eggs good for you?"

"Yeah, definitely. I'll go shower and pack."

An hour later, cruising to the airport in the weak pre-dawn light, Andi's eyes wandered to the briefcase sitting on the seat beside her. The diamonds were safely concealed within an inner pocket of her leather case, but their very presence made her horribly uncomfortable.

It was approaching 8:30 am when Andi pulled up to Tuktu's maintenance hangar. On Sundays the skeleton staff normally didn't trickle in until close to noon; she shouldn't be interrupted. Andi flipped through her key ring until she found the one for the front door of the hangar, then unlocked it and lugged Jim O'Neill's heavy flight bag, less its treasure trove of diamonds, to the foot of the mezzanine stairs.

For lack of a better plan, she'd decided to replace the bag in the approximate vicinity from where she'd taken it from. A large rubber trash can sat in the corner just below the staircase; she shoved the bag behind it. Although it was hidden from sight, Andi knew it would be discovered the next time someone emptied the trash. In time, the flight bag would be returned to Jim O'Neill, minus its very valuable and incriminating contents.

After locking up behind herself Andi headed directly to the main terminal building and parked her car in one of the spots reserved for Tuktu Aviation employees. She grabbed her small suitcase, slung her briefcase and purse over her shoulder, and hurried into the terminal. The building was still quiet at this hour. Canadian North ran scheduled service from Inuvik to Yellowknife and Edmonton daily, but their ticket agent wouldn't arrive for another few minutes.

Andi unlocked the door to Tuktu's ticket office and brewed a pot of coffee, comforted by the normalcy of the familiar motions. She drank coffee and waited impatiently.

The terminal came to life slowly; janitorial staff, airport operations staff, and the first early passengers staggered in with suitcases, wooden crates and boxes. Andi knew that Ayame was scheduled for the morning shift and dialed the office. "Good morning, Ayame," she said.

"Hey, good morning to you too. You're up early for a Sunday, aren't you?"

"You don't know the half of it," she muttered under her breath.

"Sorry?"

"Uh, nothing. Hey, I'm over at the terminal, Ayame. Something's come up and I have to make a quick trip to Toronto. I'm going to try and get on the 10:15 flight, but I don't want anyone to know where I've gone, okay?"

"Ohhh-kay," Ayame drawled slowly. "But why the mystery? What's up?"

"The less you know the better. If anyone asks where I am, just tell them I went to Yellowknife for a few days. To visit an old boyfriend," Andi said. "No," she added, "come to think of it, you'd better make that Edmonton. There could be too many people I know on the flight from Yellowknife to Edmonton."

"I don't like the sound of this. What are you doing? Does it have anything to do with this Pivot Lake thing?"

"As I said, the less you know the better. Just remember that, Ayame."

"Well, jeez. Does North at least know where you'll be?"

"Yes, he knows all about it. I'll be keeping in touch with him."

"Good."

"Oh, shit," Andi muttered under her breath.

"What's the matter?"

"I'm going to miss the management meeting tomorrow. Damn. Ayame, can you do a huge favour for me? I hate to ask, but I'm kind of in a bind."

"Don't worry," Ayame interrupted. "I'll tell Paul that you called in sick on Monday morning. Maybe you've picked up the same flu that Coco had?" she suggested. "You'll be off for a few days; it's a bad flu."

"Yeah, that might work, as long as nobody tells him they saw me on this flight. I hate lying to him."

"Paul never goes over to the terminal."

"True. Hey, Ayame, did Jessica say anything about what she did on her last trip to Vancouver?"

"Not really. Just the regular ranting and raving about all the wonderful clothes, shopping, restaurants and that kind of thing. Oh, and she was bragging about visiting some really upscale jewellery store. I can't remember the name of it, but it was one of those where they keep the front door locked and you have to be buzzed in. Why?"

"If she starts talking about that jewellery store again, can you see if you can find out which one it is? And maybe where, too? But don't let her know that you're really asking, okay?"

"I'll try, but what's going on? Why do you want to know that?"

"Trust me, Ayame. I have to run now. Hey, don't take any shit from Jessica while I'm gone, okay?"

Ayame laughed, "Don't you worry about me. I know how to handle Princess Jessica. But promise me you'll take care of *yourself*."

"I will, and I'll see you on Tuesday sometime. Oh, and one more thing. Could you try and visit Coco? I didn't get to see her the last few days, and I think she's still not feeling too great. Could you check up on her, please?"

"No problem. I'll take her another batch of Grandma's healing tea. Coco and I get along just fine when she's not bar hopping."

"I don't think she'll be doing much more of that anymore," Andi chuckled, "and I know she'd love some more of your tea. Thanks so much, Ayame."

"No problem. Have a good trip."

"I will. Goodbye."

Through the office's large plate glass windows Andi could see the Canadian North ticket agent at her counter. She turned off the coffee pot, picked up her bags, locked the office door and said a silent prayer that there would be an empty seat on the flight.

For once, luck was on her side and twenty minutes later, clutching her boarding cards, purse and briefcase, Andi passed uneventfully through security screening.

She settled down in the departures lounge to await the boarding call for flight 845 to Yellowknife and on to Edmonton. She was on her way to putting step two of her plan into motion, and she prayed that the small bag of diamonds hidden deeply within her briefcase would be all the evidence she needed to convince Sam Tavernese that he had a problem.

A big problem.

TWENTY-SEVEN

The next twenty-four hours passed in a blur, leaving Andi exhausted. Her emotions ran rampant, wavering between fear, anger, and remorse. The ticket agent in Inuvik had warned her that the connecting Canadian North flight from Yellowknife to Edmonton was fully booked, and Andi spent hours waiting in Yellowknife for the next flight.

When she finally arrived in Alberta's capital city, she claimed her luggage and rushed to the nearest departures board, searching for the next flight to Toronto, Ontario. She finally got a seat on a cramped red-eye, departing at midnight.

From Toronto's Pearson Airport, Andi splurged on a taxi to The Fairmont Royal York, one of the oldest hotels in the city. The cab driver battled with early rush-hour traffic through the city's bustling business and financial region, and it was nearly 9 am before the cab deposited her at the hotel's grand entrance. She checked in, threw her wrinkled clothes onto a chair and collapsed on the bed for an hour of much needed sleep.

At 11:00 sharp, Andi walked purposefully into the luxuriously appointed fifteenth floor head office of Pivot Lake Mines. She was revitalized from her short nap and a long, hot shower. She looked professional in a navy-blue suit, its short, fitted skirt ending just above her shapely knees. She had applied her make-up carefully and wound her shining dark hair into a classic French roll. Her mother's cherished pearls nestled around her neck, their creamy luster lending a shimmering light to her flawless skin.

Andi clutched her briefcase as she strode from the elevator to the reception desk, her shiny black high heels tapping a determined rhythm on the tiled floor. She turned on a 1000-watt smile for the perfectly coifed young woman behind the desk and asked to see the mine's Chief Executive Officer, Sam Tavernese.

The dark-haired, buxom receptionist, identified as Angela Ruso by the gold-toned nameplate on her desk, raised one well-plucked brow and stared at Andi with the most vivid cobalt blue eyes Andi had ever seen. "Do you have an appointment, Madam?"

"No, Angela. I'm afraid I don't. But if you would tell Mr. Tavernese that Andrea Nowak from Tuktu Aviation is here, I'm sure he'll see me," Andi replied confidently.

"Mr. Tavernese has a very busy schedule, and does not see *anyone* unless they have an appointment," the woman stated firmly. "May I ask your business with Mr. Tavernese?"

"It's a private matter," replied Andi, a faint blush rising opportunely on her pale cheeks.

The beautiful young receptionist pursed her crimson lips. "I would be happy to consult with Mr. Tavernese about an appointment later this week if you will state your business with him," she said icily, flipping through the appointment book before her.

"No, I'm afraid I need to see him *now*, please. I only need a few minutes of his time," Andi replied, her voice soft, but equally icy, her jaw set in a determined line. "And Angela, my business with him is of a sensitive, very private nature."

The receptionist lifted her sharp blue eyes to Andi's, exasperation and disapproval tugging at the corners of her pleasingly lush lips. She opened her mouth, but snapped it shut a second later as Andi's icy emerald eyes bore into hers.

"*Very* private," Andi whispered, raising her eyebrows slightly.

With a resolute sigh Angela waved toward the extravagantly appointed waiting area. "Please have a seat, Miss Nowak. I'll see if Mr. Tavernese has a moment to see you."

Three creamy ecru, leather sofas, each flanked by two cherry-wood end tables, were arranged facing the glass wall of the office. An immense, matching square coffee table sat perfectly centered before the sofas. From any seat in the reception area, one could enjoy the breath-taking view of downtown Toronto. It would be stunning at night, Andi thought.

Fifteen minutes later Andi set down the Canadian Diamond Mining book she was browsing through and followed Angela into the CEO's office. Sam Tavernese sat behind a dark wooden desk the size of a lake. Andi crossed a vast expanse of thick mocha carpet and stopped before him. She extended her hand to grip the large paw offered by the tanned, ruggedly handsome man.

"Miss Nowak, it's a pleasure to see you again," Tavernese said easily, smiling as they shook hands. "You're a long way from Inuvik. What brings you to our fair city?" He gestured for Andi to sit in one of the two expansive maroon leather chairs situated before his desk.

"Thanks so much for seeing me Mr. Tavernese. I do apologize for coming in without an appointment," Andi said. "I'm afraid I don't have good news. I, uh, I don't know where to start." She unconsciously pressed the fingertips of her left hand to her throbbing temple. Her right hand still clutched the handle of her briefcase where it rested in her lap.

"Whoa, this doesn't sound good. Before you say anything more, let me offer you a coffee. I know I could use one." While Tavernese rang for coffee Andi opened her briefcase and extracted the envelopes she'd so carefully stored a day earlier. She laid them on the desk before her.

"Now," Tavernese said after he'd hung up the phone. "Let's start by you calling me Sam. And may I call you Andrea?"

Andi relaxed a little and managed a small smile. "Please call me Andi."

"Sounds good. Andi it is. Now, what can I do for you, Andi?" he asked curiously, eyeing the envelopes sitting on his desk.

She opened her mouth to launch into her carefully prepared speech, but was interrupted by a discreet knock announcing the arrival of their coffee. Miss Angela-icy-blue-eyes set the tray on a sideboard and slipped out of the office without saying a word. Sam served their coffee in blue fine-bone china cups bearing the logo and name of his company. "Cream and sugar?" he asked politely.

"No, just black, thanks."

"Sorry for the interruption," he said, handing a cup and saucer to Andi and regaining his seat. "Go ahead."

Andi's hand shook noticeably as she set her cup down on Sam's desk. She took a deep, steadying breath and then, without preamble, launched into a recounting of the events that had brought her to his door, starting with the fateful day, over three weeks ago, when she noticed the late return of the Pivot Lake supply trips.

Throughout her discourse, Sam Tavernese sat silent and attentive to her every word. His eyes never left hers, and his face was completely devoid of any expression. Even his hands remained motionless, folded neatly on the desk before him until he reached up to loosen the perfect Windsor knot of his red tie. Their coffees sat untouched and cooling.

When she had finished recounting her story Sam continued to gaze at her in silence, an unfathomable look in his stormy grey eyes. A frown etched his unlined face, drawing his eyebrows together. Undeterred, Andi picked up the larger envelope and said, "I have some photos to support what I've told you." One by one, she spread out the pictures before Tavernese. First, the gruesome photos of North's murdered sled dogs, the bloody compound, and the warning on the kennel wall. Next, the shots of Tuktu Aviation's Twin Otter parked on the barren, white tundra, with Captain James O'Neill, Henrik Bruller and his yellow Ski-Doo.

Sam Tavernese took his time sifting through the photos, his face paling at the carnage of the bloody dog pen. He paused for several long, hushed minutes and stared intently at the unmistakable face of one of his most trusted employees.

The air in the office was heavy with tension, and it grew even thicker when Andi spilled the rough grey stones onto Tavernese's thick desk pad.

Andi took a deep breath, willed her shaking hands to still, and picked up her tepid cup of coffee. Sam Tavernese had not uttered a word; he sat in silence, staring at the photos and rough diamonds strewn on his desk.

Andi's guts churned and fear dotted her forehead with beads of sweat. She wondered if she was mistaken in his reaction, and that his silence was one of disbelief instead of shock. She set her coffee back down, still untouched.

The tension in the room was a tangible thing. After an unbearably long silence, Sam smiled wryly and picked up the largest of the uncut diamonds. He rubbed a large, manicured thumb over its rough surface. After a few moments, he reached for the telephone and depressed the intercom button. "Angela, please cancel all of my appointments for the rest of the day and get DeMaria and Maniero in here right away. And then call Bertram's Deli. Have them bring up some sandwiches and salads as soon as possible." Sam slumped back into his large executive-style chair, threw the stone on his desk and rubbed his face roughly with the palms of his hands.

After several seconds, he looked up, his eyes seeking Andi's. "Thank you for coming directly to me with this," he said quietly. "If I didn't have these pictures and stones in front of me, I would have insisted that you were terribly mistaken. I've called my corporate lawyer and Chief Financial Officer in. I think they both need to hear your story first-hand."

"I'm sorry to be the bearer of such bad news," Andi said softly, letting out a sigh of relief, "but I'm so very glad that you believe me. I was afraid that you wouldn't."

A few minutes later, after Andi's introductions to the elderly, grey-haired lawyer and dark, stunningly handsome CFO, she recounted the entire story again, but not before the lawyer, DeMaria, had obtained Andi's permission to tape their conversation. The men had just finished examining the photos and diamonds when there was a light knock on the office door.

Lunch had arrived, and the small group moved to a plush conversation area in the corner of the immense office. The men dove into their thick deli sandwiches with gusto, while Andi picked at a green salad. Although fresh and appetizing, she had no appetite.

After Angela cleared away the remains of their lunch and deposited a large carafe of coffee on the low table, they returned to their discussions. DeMaria and Maniero peppered Andi with questions. For the most part, Sam Tavernese sat back and let his two executives lead the interrogation, because that's what it was.

The questioning dragged on into mid-afternoon. When it was finally over, Andi had a few inquiries of her own. "Where is Carlos Sante?" she asked. "What happened to him?"

"Bruller fired him," Maniero, the CFO replied. "He advised us that he found Carlos falsifying inventory records, padding his expense account, and bootlegging at the mine."

Andi's eyes flashed green fire. "And you believed Bruller?" she gasped.

"Henrik Bruller has been our Project Manager since the mine's inception. We do not question his decisions regarding mine site personnel or procedures," Maniero replied crisply.

"Where is Carlos now?" Andi asked.

"We have no idea, but we will find him. We need to talk with him regarding Bruller's accusations."

"And will you give Carlos Sante his job back?

"We will conduct an investigation into the matter you've brought before us," DeMaria said blithely

"And what about North's dead sled dogs?" Andi asked crisply, her annoyance with the lawyer's attitude growing. "They are valuable animals. And what about the shots fired at North? And at his house? And what about his broken window? If it wasn't Bruller himself who killed three innocent sled dogs and shot up the house, then he had someone else do it! What do you intend to do about that?"

The three men exchanged glances, and then the lawyer replied, "You say your friend North Ruben reported the incidents to the RCMP. If they haven't been able to prove who shot those dogs or his window, there is no way you can hold Pivot Lake Mines, or any of our employees, responsible."

"Right," Andi said coldly. "And I suppose the bullet hole in North's arm isn't your responsibility either."

"Have you considered that it may be your pilot, this O'Neill fellow, who may be responsible for the shootings?"

Andi glared at the lawyer for a moment, and then turned to stare moodily at the expanse of blue sky beyond the window. The fact was, she hadn't for one moment considered that Jim O'Neill was responsible, or Hank Brister for that matter.

"We will be questioning Henrik Bruller and conducting an investigation," DeMaria continued. After a moment he added, "Please rest assured that, at this point in time, we do not anticipate pressing charges against Tuktu Aviation."

Andi stared at the lawyer speechlessly for a long moment until she found her voice. "What?" she finally gasped.

"Should the information you've brought before us prove accurate," DeMaria continued, "we will be laying charges against all

217

parties involved in the theft of raw diamonds from our mine, including their transportation and disposal. At this time, I am of the opinion that Tuktu Aviation *may* not have knowingly supplied the method of transportation. Our investigation will either confirm or deny that."

Andi was stunned. She had never anticipated that Tuktu Aviation might be accused of actively and knowingly taking part in the diamond thefts. She turned beseeching eyes to the CEO, "Sam, you have to believe me, Tuktu is NOT involved in this!"

"Antonio, back off," Tavernese snapped, glaring at his lawyer. Turning to Andi, he said quietly, "Andi, we will be investigating this matter in detail, but I feel confident that you, Paul White and Tuktu Aviation will not be implicated in any way. And rest assured that we will make restitution for any damages you and your friend North have suffered." Glaring at the lawyer again, he said in a stony voice, "Mr. DeMaria jumped the gun a little here.

"All right gentlemen," he stated, rising from the soft leather sofa, "I think this meeting is over. Andi, I'd like to have a word with you in private, please."

"Sure," Andi muttered, still in a minor state of shock.

After DeMaria and Maniero filed out of his office, Sam seated himself at Andi's side. He picked up her cold, limp hand, and held it gently between both of his own. "I'm so sorry about that Andi. It was not Antonio's place to say something like that to you."

"It was quite a shock," Andi admitted. "I never, I mean, I didn't anticipate something like that."

"That's a lawyer for you," Sam said with a warm, reassuring smile, "always looking out for *numero uno*."

Suddenly Andi became aware of her hand still nestled between Sam's. She gently extracted it, and reached up to her suit collar, nervously smoothing the material.

"So, how long are you in town for?" Sam asked.

"Just tonight. I'll be heading back to Inuvik first thing in the morning."

"If you don't have other plans, I'd be honored if you'd let me buy you dinner."

"Oh!" Andi's eyes widened in surprise. "Um, no, I don't really have any plans," she stammered.

"It's a date, then. I'll pick you up at your hotel at 7:00. Leave your details with my secretary."

By the time Andi walked out of the prestigious corporate office of Pivot Lake Mines late that afternoon, she was mentally and physically exhausted.

She'd rid herself of the burden of the illicit diamonds, but another weight, something she couldn't quite put her finger on, lay heavily on her heart.

She had just accomplished step two of her plan, so why didn't she feel like she'd done the right thing?

Had she just made a terrible mistake?

TWENTY-EIGHT

The minute Andi walked into her room at the Fairmont Hotel she kicked off her extremely uncomfortable high heels and called North.

"Hi, it's me," she said when he answered the phone.

"Hey, Babe. I've been waiting for your call. How did you make out today?"

"Well, I'm not so sure," Andi said, holding the phone in one hand and kneading her aching neck with the other.

"Did you get in to see the CEO?"

"Yeah, I saw him. *And* his corporate lawyer, *and* his CFO," Andi said, unable to hide her irritation.

"Uh oh. Do you think they believed you?"

"I think Sam does, but I don't know about that lawyer. Do you know what he said?" Andi asked, her voice tight with anger. "That asshole had the gall to say, and I quote, 'Please rest assured that, at this point in time, we do not anticipate pressing charges against Tuktu Aviation'."

"Shit. I didn't see that coming."

"Yeah, you and me both."

"They kept the diamonds, I assume?"

"Yeah, and the photos too. You have copies, don't you?"

"Of course. And negatives."

Andi and North talked for several more minutes, and she recounted every detail of her meeting leaving nothing out, except that Sam Tavernese had held her hand. And had asked her to dinner.

"So you're still coming home tomorrow?" North asked, his voice undeniably hopeful.

"Yes. I haven't booked yet but I'll do that right now. I don't think I'll have any trouble getting a flight."

"Hurry home, Babe. I miss you."

"I miss you too. See you tomorrow."

Andi peeled off her suit and ran a bath, submerging herself in the water's restorative heat. Gradually the tense muscles in her shoulders and back relaxed, but the soothing water had little effect on the knot in her stomach, or the unease in her mind. She knew exactly what she needed to calm her nerves.

She soaked until the water in the tub cooled, toying with the silver ring on her hand – the triangle in a circle. Her mind wandered to the comforting feeling of Sam's warm hand on her own, and the memory drove a needle of guilt through her heart. She knew she should have told North about her dinner plans, so what had stopped her? Was it her guilty conscience, or something else? A single tear trailed down her damp cheek.

She rose from the tub and wrapped an immense, fluffy white towel around her slim body, then marched purposefully to the room's mini-bar. Before she could change her mind, she unscrewed the cap from a small bottle of ice-cold white wine and lifted it to her parched lips.

Andi's green eyes glinted like emeralds in the candlelight, and a wide, slightly lop-sided grin curved her ruby lips. Flickering flames reflected in the gleaming silver and sparkling crystal strewn across the white table cloth of the intimate, and very expensive, Italian restaurant.

Sam Tavernese refilled their tall champagne flutes and with a flourish turned the empty bottle upside down into the ice bucket. Andi giggled, and took a generous sip of the bubbly wine.

"And so that's when I said, 'Papa, I'm going to buy a diamond mine!'" Sam and Andi both laughed a little too loudly at the conclusion of Sam's life story. "And I've never looked back," he added with a smile.

"Oh, Sam! You've led such a charmed life. And I've had so much fun tonight," Andi drawled, her words slightly slurred. "I haven't done this in *ages*."

"Me neither, beautiful. But what about you? How did you end up in that godforsaken Inuvik?" Sam's magnetic eyes reached across the table, drawing her into their mysterious depths.

"Well," Andi hesitated, then softly said, "let's just say that I'm a wild northern girl at heart, and while I've often been drunk, I'm still thirsty." With a flourish, she held her glass high in a silent toast, and downed its contents in one gulp

Tavernese reached across the small table and held one of Andi's hands in his own, rubbing his thumb over her soft skin. He seemed to sense her sadness. "I'm so glad you came for dinner with me. And the night's not over yet." Signaling for the waiter, he ordered coffee and grappa for both of them.

Soft music played in the background, and Andi swayed slowly to a familiar melody, melancholy tugging at her heart. She'd worn her hair down, and her dark tresses rippled over the silk of her thin, creamy chemise. A strand of damp hair caught at the base of her throat, and Sam released Andi's hand to twine it around his finger, giving it a gentle tug before smoothing it over her shoulder. "Why don't you stay in town for a few more days?" he asked, the deep grey of his eyes darkening as they bore into hers. "You don't really have to leave tomorrow, do you my dear?"

"Nope. Can't," Andi replied with a lop-sided grin "I'll be AWOL from the officer again tomorrow as it is."

"And there's nothing I can say to change your mind?" Tavernese coaxed, squeezing her hand.

Andi shook her head and grimaced slightly. "Nope."

Their coffee and liqueur arrived. Sam lifted a delicate crystal snifter to Andi and toasted, "At least we have tonight, my beautiful and wild Northern Girl. At least we have tonight."

The harsh and demanding peal of a telephone jarred her into semi-consciousness. Andi rolled over and flung out an arm, knocking the offending instrument from its cradle and silencing her wake-up call. Her stomach heaved, and hot, sour bile rose up her parched throat. Cold, sticky sweat covered her body like a second layer of skin.

She lay naked on the rumpled bed, too weak to move. Too sick to even think about moving. Her muddled brain fought to knit together disjointed, blurry memories from the previous night.

After several minutes she moaned and forced her scratchy eyes open. The room was not totally dark; the bathroom door was ajar, and a thin streak of light escaped from behind it. She had only the vaguest memory of returning to her hotel room the night before, and even now, she couldn't remember if she'd been alone. She was afraid to find out the truth; afraid to find out if Sam Tavernese had shared her bed last night. Tears welled in her swollen eyes.

She cautiously turned her head. When she saw the empty expanse of bed beside her, she sobbed with relief, and tears trickled down her feverish cheeks. Whatever had, or hadn't, happened last night, at least she didn't have to face him this morning.

Andi slowly sat up and dragged her legs over the edge of the bed. Her stomach's reaction was immediate and violent, and she stumbled to the bathroom. Five minutes later she had retched up the contents of her stomach, but dry heaves continued to plague her. She wished she were dead.

Clutching a glass of cold water in a shaky hand, she returned to the bedroom and replaced the telephone receiver on its cradle. She turned on the lights and rummaged in her purse for headache tablets.

When she caught a glimpse of herself in the full-length mirror beside the dresser, she stared in disgust at her naked reflection. The mirror captured the self-hatred in her eyes, and she despised herself for her weakness.

She spotted her beautiful blue suit lying in a crumpled pile on the carpeted floor, and reached down to pick it up. The fabric smelled heavily of cigarette smoke, and a vivid image of a smoky bar raced through her head. Had Sam been at a bar with her, she wondered, or had she stopped alone somewhere for a nightcap? Her muddled mind couldn't produce the answer.

Andi struggled through a shower, dressed herself in blue jeans and a loose, brown cowl-necked sweater, and repacked her suitcase. Breakfast wasn't an option. When a taxi deposited her at the Pearson International airport, it was less than an hour before her 9 am flight was due to depart for Edmonton.

The long flight and even longer hours spent on-route to Inuvik gave Andi plenty of time to lament her fall from grace – her disastrous fall from the abstinence wagon. She wiggled and tugged on her AA ring, pulling it from her finger for the first time in over two years. The silver symbol of her sobriety felt heavy in the palm of her hand, just as her heart felt heavy in her chest. She had failed herself, just as she had failed her daughter. She had failed to keep her beautiful, darling Natalie alive and would pay the price for that the rest of her life.

Andi leaned her head against the icy window of the Boeing 737 while tears ran unchecked from her swollen, red eyes. She gripped her cherished AA ring, and vowed she would never place it back on her finger. She didn't deserve to wear the beautiful silver 12-Step symbol of hope and healing ever again. She had, once again, proved herself unworthy.

TWENTY-NINE

North was waiting for Andi when her flight landed in Inuvik the next morning. She'd been unable to make connecting flights to the Arctic city in one day and had spent the night in the Nisku Inn, near the Edmonton International airport.

Her stomach had settled by the time she got to her hotel, and she forced herself to have dinner. A good meal and ten hours of sleep had gone a long way toward curing Andi's hangover, but her heart still ached. When North wrapped her in his arms and held her close, her eyes brimmed with tears. She took a deep breath and forced a faint smile to her lips.

"I've missed you so much, Babe," North whispered, pulling her hair aside to kiss her neck. Several passengers, milling expectantly around the baggage carousel, smiled and gave them a wide berth.

"I've missed you too, North," she replied. "More than you will ever know."

North stepped back to take a good look at the woman in his arms. "You don't look too well. Are you feeling okay?"

"I'm just exhausted. These past few days have been hard on my nerves."

"I bet. You'll feel better tomorrow."

"I wouldn't count on it," Andi muttered glumly as a blaring siren preceded the arrival of baggage on the slowly revolving belt.

The days that followed Andi's fateful trip to Toronto did little to improve her mental wellbeing. She got up every morning, drank her coffee, went to work, and let the normalcy of her everyday duties as the Operations Manager of a thriving aviation company get her through the day.

It was the nights that nearly drove her insane.

For the first week after her return she'd been able to convince North that she was exhausted, and he'd kept his distance. It was fortunate for her that he was focused on his sled dogs, spending hours on end on practice runs before the approaching spring weather ruined his training arena. Qannik, too, was getting her share of puppy lessons. Now, more than ever, North was devoted to his sled dogs, though he still mourned the loss of his three devoted canine friends.

After a week of keeping her new lover at arm's distance Andi knew that the time to make a decision about her future with him was swiftly approaching. North's patience was bound to wear thin very soon, and he was becoming increasingly insistent that they spend more time together. Only the Lord above knew more than Andi how much she longed for the comforting security of his arms, but she knew she didn't deserve his love.

She tried in vain to convince herself that she'd done nothing wrong in Toronto. She didn't have the courage to tell the man she loved that she'd fallen off the wagon, and she sure as hell didn't know what to tell him about Sam Tavernese. Her memory of the hours between after-dinner grappa and awakening naked in a tousled hotel bed continued to evade her. And the lost hours – what may have transpired during those lost hours – continued to haunt her every waking moment, and often her dreams.

Andi's reluctance to spend more time with North resulted in her spending more time with Coco Montague, and their friendship deepened over multiple cups of evening tea. True to her promise, Coco no longer frequented Inuvik's rowdy bars. It was during one of their visits that she dropped another bombshell.

"I'm pregnant," Coco blurted out as she sat on Andi's worn, legless sofa, warming her hands on a mug of peppermint tea.

Andi, curled up on the other end of the sofa, choked on the sip of tea she'd just swallowed. The hot liquid sloshed over the side of the cup when she slammed it down on the coffee table. "Oh, no!" she cried in dismay. "Oh, my God, Coco, I'm so sorry." She reached out to grasp the redhead's hand. "When did you find out?"

"Yesterday. I was suspicious, and then I missed my period so I went to the clinic. It's confirmed," she sobbed softly, trying to blink back the tears that threatened to spill from her eyes.

"So," Andi began, then hesitated, "is it-?" she couldn't bring herself to finish her question.

"Yes," Coco answered with a short nod. "It's from my, uh, the assault. I haven't been with anyone else for a few months."

"Coco, did you tell your doctor about the assault?" Andi asked gently.

Coco pulled her hand from Andi's and shrank into the corner of the couch, clutching her tea. "Yes. And that I threw up a lot that night and the next day. She said that's likely why the pill didn't work." She looked up and stared at Andi defiantly, then said, "And she told me that if I want an abortion I can have one, so I'm going to."

If she'd been expecting Andi's disapproval, she got it. "Coco, don't rush into this. You're only a month or so along. You need to think this through carefully before you make a decision that will affect the rest of your life, and that of your unborn child."

"I've made my decision," Coco snapped. "There's no way in hell I'm going to carry the child of that rapist, let alone raise it!"

Andi's better judgment told her not to engage in an argument with Coco about something that was such a private, personal matter. But she couldn't help herself. The loss of a child, even an unborn child, was something she felt strongly about. She knew the trauma of loss first-hand.

"Coco, nobody can tell you what to do. And you don't have to say anything, but just listen to me for a minute, please. The child growing within you is *your* child. He or she doesn't belong to that guy, she doesn't *know* that guy, and she *never* needs to know him. The child is yours; please trust me when I tell you that if you have an abortion, you will regret it one day. One day, maybe five or ten or twenty years from now, you will regret it."

Coco stared silently at Andi, who was crying herself now, unchecked tears rolling from her green eyes. "You'll be sitting somewhere quietly one day, and all of a sudden you will think 'if I had kept my child, he or she would be here beside me'. Or maybe you'd think 'my little girl might be saying "I love you Mommy"'. And then you'll realize that you'll never have a chance to hear your child's first words, or see her first smile. And you will regret the day you ended her life. You will regret it until the day you die."

Andi reached into her pocket for a tissue to wipe away her tears. She blew her nose loudly.

Coco looked down at the cup in her hands, and after several minutes said, "I'll think about it." And then, without another word got up and left Andi's suite, closing the stairwell door softly behind her.

Coco's news left Andi feeling empty and downcast for days. It didn't help her mood that she hadn't heard a word from Tavernese or his colleagues; as the days of early spring grew longer, she became more and more doubtful that she would. The supply runs to Pivot Lake continued to return to base late when Captain O'Neill was at the controls; nothing had changed there either. It seemed that it was business as usual in the diamond stealing and smuggling business.

But, as her wise old Father had often told her, 'If you fall off the horse, you'd better get right back up on its back again', so after a week of berating herself and imposing self-exile Andi attended a long overdue Alcoholics Anonymous meeting. She admitted to everyone present that 'my name is Andi, and I'm an alcoholic', and proceeded to alleviate her guilty conscience.

But even within the tightknit, closed fellowship of the AA group, she couldn't confess her worst fear – that she may have spent the last hours of a drunken night in Toronto in bed with a stranger.

When she got home from the meeting that night Andi went straight to her bedroom dresser where she'd thrown her AA ring. She picked up the ring and studied its familiar triangle in a circle pattern, garnering strength and forgiveness from its gleaming silver symbolism. She pushed it back on her finger, its rightful place, and headed to the bathroom, hoping to restore the equilibrium of her body and soul with a long lavender-infused bath.

One bright Monday afternoon in late March Ayame stuck her head into Andi's office. "Line one, Andi. It's Sam Tavernese from Pivot Lake Mines."

Andi's heart skipped a beat. She'd had no communication with Sam since that fateful night in Toronto, almost two weeks previous. "Oh! Umm, thanks, Ayame. Would you mind closing the door, please?"

Andi sat frozen at her desk for a few moments, steeling herself for the ordeal ahead. "Andrea Nowak speaking."

"Andi, Hi! It's Sam Tavernese. I hope you haven't thought I'd forgotten about you?"

"Not at all, Sam. How are you?"

"Well, we've been busy as hell since you were here. I'm sorry that I didn't call you sooner, but we just completed our initial investigation yesterday."

"No problem. I've been busy myself," she replied evenly, trying to ignore her pounding heart.

"Andi, what I'm about to tell you is strictly confidential, but since you are the one who brought this whole mess to our attention, I have no qualms about sharing our results with you."

"Okay."

"We're absolutely certain that Bruller is responsible for the theft of diamonds from our mine."

"How can you be so sure?"

"We sent a technician in to install another set of security cameras at the mine site. A set Bruller doesn't know about."

"And you caught him red-handed?"

"Yes. The tapes clearly show Bruller making undocumented visits to the restricted area."

"I see."

"Don't get me wrong. We have the best security available, or at least we thought we did. And most of the processes are automated and padlocked."

"I'm sure they are."

There was a long, pregnant pause before Tavernese replied, "You sound skeptical."

"Well, I don't know much about your operation, but if Henrik Bruller is able to access your secure areas at will, then I don't see how you can claim that you have the best security available."

"We think we know how he's doing it. Bruller has been our Project Manager from the mine's inception. He was there when we drove the first stake and erected the first building, but only one person has access to the secured areas and the diamonds. It's not Bruller, but somehow he obtained the codes and a set of keys. We just don't know how yet."

"So much for your security."

"Yeah. Well, now we're paying the price."

"And you're not the only one," Andi sniped.

"Look, Andi. I know you're upset about your boyfriend and his dogs, but I promised that we'd compensate you for the loss, and we will. Just give us some time to sort things out."

Andi sighed. "I'm sorry, Sam. I've just been so *frustrated*. It didn't seem like you were taking any action."

"Well, that's where you come in now. We have a plan and we need your help."

"Sure, whatever I can do."

"We have the evidence linking Bruller to the thefts, but in order to implicate your Jim O'Neill and his co-pilot – uh, what's his name again?"

"Hank Brister."

"Right, we want O'Neill and Brister too. We're going to set up surveillance at the rendezvous point and get all three of them at once."

"Isn't this really a matter for the police?" Andi asked.

"Not as far as we're concerned. We have people who take care of these kinds of things for us so there's no need to involve law enforcement. We'll be handling the matter ourselves. From start to finish," he added ominously.

"Sounds like something the Mafia would do," Andi said with a short, nervous laugh.

"Well, let's just say we know how to get the job done. But, like I said, we need your help."

"What can I do?"

"I have a crew of men flying into Inuvik this week on Canadian North. These guys, along with their gear and snowmobiles, will have to be transported to the rendezvous point without O'Neill and Brister's knowledge."

"When?"

"Friday or Saturday would be ideal. Can you make sure O'Neill and Brister are scheduled for a supply run to Pivot Lake on one of those days?"

"No problem."

"Great. Now, what we've decided to do is have our men waiting under cover at the rendezvous site. With any luck, Bruller will meet your pilots to deliver the diamonds. I'd like to charter one of your Twin Otters to fly our crew out and then pick them up again after the rendezvous."

"I see. I'll check the bookings and confirm we have an aircraft available."

"Great. Now for one more favour, and this is a big one."

"Yes?"

"We need your friend North's assistance. He's the only one aside from O'Neill, Brister and Bruller who know where this rendezvous point is. Do you think you can convince him to accompany us on this expedition?"

"Oh. Well, I can ask him," Andi said cautiously. "How about he just gives you the co-ordinates for the site?"

"I'd really like him to be with us, Andi. He knows the lay of the land. He's scouted it out already and it could mean the difference between success and failure for our mission."

"I see. Well, I'll ask him. If I can't get hold of him right now, I'll have to call you back tomorrow morning."

"And tell him we'll make it worth his while."

"I'll let you discuss that with him yourself," Andi said. "I take it you *are* going to be here for all of this?"

"Yes. I'll fly up to Inuvik on our corporate jet. We have a helicopter stationed there, and I'll take it out to the rendezvous site when your Twin Otter positions the rest of the crew. Our plan is to situate the chopper somewhere near the site, and our ground crew will radio us when the exchange has taken place. That way we have both land and air pursuit covered. And I want to be there when we nail those bastards."

"Look, Sam. It sounds like you've put a lot of thought into this plan, but if you're putting North into any danger whatsoever, I'm not so sure I want to go along with this."

"I understand completely Andi. And I can assure you that we won't harm a hair on his head. And by the way, I want to apologize for my rude behavior."

Andi's heart dropped. She closed her eyes, dreading the worst. "Oh?"

"I'm so sorry that I had to rush off after dinner, but something came up. I trust the taxi driver got you back to your hotel in one piece?"

Her eyes flew open. "Uh, yeah. No problem at all."

"I enjoyed our evening immensely, Andi, and all I can say is that your friend North is one very lucky guy. I'm really looking forward to meeting the man who captured your heart."

Andi's heart fluttered, and for the first time in two weeks, a smile lit up her face. "Thanks so much, Sam. And I'm sure North will enjoy meeting you too."

When she hung up the phone a few minutes later, she felt like the weight of the world had just been lifted from her shoulders.

THIRTY

Sam's team, including North, and their snowmobiles had been dropped off at the rendezvous area at 10 am. Tuktu's Twin Otter, piloted by Captain Dan and First Officer Tom, was on its way to Paulatuk to await pick-up instructions. As far as dispatch and the two pilots were concerned, North had chartered the aircraft and was hosting a one-day Arctic photography session for a couple of well-to-do enthusiasts. They were to be on the land for several hours, and the heavy bags they carried contained tripods and expensive camera equipment. It was as good a cover story as any.

Sam Tavernese, designated code name 'Alpha One', and his private Bell 206 Jet Ranger had touched down two kilometers north of the rendezvous point, just minutes away.

"Hell, ya!" North had exclaimed when Andi called him Monday night to relay Sam's request. It was North who had come up with the diversionary story. It was one that anyone in the small community would believe as he had organized tundra photo shoots for rich tourists before. Another one would arouse no suspicions.

Now it was Friday morning, the last day of March, and the scene was set for Sam Tavernese's trap. Between Sam and North, they had discussed and reviewed every possible scenario and were satisfied that the mission would be completed without a hitch.

There was only one part of their plan over which they had no control: would a meet between Bruller and O'Neill take place today? If not, then Sam had already stated that he was prepared to charter the Twin Otter again.

As the hour approached for Captain James O'Neill's and First Officer Hank Brister's departure to Pivot Lake Diamond Mine – quite possibly their last departure – Andi grew increasingly nervous. She wished that instead of sitting in her warm office overlooking the Inuvik airport and wondering what in the hell was going on 280 kilometers away, she was buried in a snow bank and was part of the surprise reception committee. She'd voiced her desire to accompany the men, but neither North nor Sam would have anything to do with her request.

Therefore, again her wishes, she sat at her desk the entire, long day, drinking too much coffee, shuffling papers and listening to Jessica Hartman conduct the familiar, everyday business of an aircraft dispatch office.

She stared out her office window and tried not to worry about whether or not the man she loved would survive the not-so-ordinary event that was taking place near a diamond mine high above the Arctic Circle.

"Romeo Two, this is Romeo One. How do you copy? Over."

North adjusted the built-in volume control in his snowmobile helmet. "Romeo One, you're coming in five square," he responded. The state-of-the art equipment Tavernese's crew had brought with them from Toronto was peaking his jealousy. In addition to built-in speakers, the snowmobile helmet North wore also had a built-in, voice activated microphone. He wanted one. Make that two.

The three men, deposited on the windswept tundra northwest of Pivot Lake by Tuktu Aviation's Twin Otter that morning, were well-equipped. Each man, along with his snow machine, was concealed beneath ultralight, military issue winter camouflage blankets, making the crew virtually impossible to spot from the air or ground. Careful measures had been taken to remove all signs of their presence in the area; even a highly trained eye would not detect a track nor a footstep.

The waiting seemed endless. North had drifted off to sleep when a deep, clipped voice spoke in his ear with military precision, "Heads up everyone. We have company." North's eyes snapped open and a rush of adrenalin supercharged his muscles. He detected the faint drone of a turbo-prop aircraft, which grew louder by the second. The radio in his helmet crackled to life again as their team leader, Romeo One, did a final, quick review of their plan.

Through the small surveillance slits cut through the camo blanket, North spotted Tuktu's familiar white and blue Twin Otter, C-ITTA. It lined up with the faintly visible landing strip and skimmed on wheel-skis over the windswept snow, stopping precisely where North had indicated it would. The two Pratt and Whitney PT6-A engines shut down, the props continuing to circle lazily for a few seconds before silence ensued.

The small reception committee, each man on heightened alert, waited motionlessly for the next part of the act to arrive – Henrik Bruller. The sun was high in the sky and the temperature of the balmy spring day had peaked at zero Celsius. North was starting to feel too warm beneath his heavy insulated underwear and snowmobile suit.

Ten minutes later the unmistakable buzz of a snowmobile's two-stroke engine invaded the absolute silence of the Arctic. North tensed, his breathing quickening as his 'fight or flight' response kicked in.

A gleaming yellow Ski-Doo roared into view, skidding to a stop directly in front of TTA's airstair door. Moments later the aircraft's door clanged open and the snowmobile rider removed his black helmet, setting it atop the seat of his machine. Henrik Bruller mounted the stairs.

James O'Neill, who had appeared at the top of the stairway, extended a hand in greeting. The two men disappeared into the aircraft and the door lifted shut behind them. So far, everything was going according to North's and Sam's plan.

Ten minutes passed, and then fifteen. North began to sweat.

Thirty minutes passed with no sign of activity. North's eyes burned from staring at the unrelenting whiteness beyond the camo blanket. The wind was blowing from the northwest, causing dry, fine snow to sweep across the hard packed surface beneath it.

Some days, things just don't go according to plan. When North heard the twin turbo-prop engines start to spool up, he knew today was going to be one of those days. The Twin Otter was preparing for departure, with Bruller still on board. Either the man had decided to wind up his clandestine activities at the diamond mine and make his escape with O'Neill, or the surveillance team had been 'made' and Bruller was abandoning his precious Ski-Doo.

"Romeo Two, Romeo One."

"Go ahead Romeo One," North replied.

"Is this the way it went down last time?" the team leader snapped.

"Negative. The engines didn't start until Bruller had exited the aircraft."

"Roger that. Alfa One, this in Romeo One, do you copy? Over?"

"Romeo One, this is Alfa," replied Sam Tavernese from his helicopter, "we copy. What's your status?"

"It looks like our guests are leaving the party."

"Roger that, Romeo One. We'll join you in two minutes. Take action to detain the aircraft. We don't want them getting away. Over and out."

One minute stretched into two, and still Tango Tango Alfa sat motionless, props turning steadily. Suddenly the engines screamed with a short burst of power as the aircraft broke inertia and surged forward, releasing its skis from their tenuous grip on the ice beneath them. Loose snow billowed up around the slowly taxiing plane, creating an effective white screen.

"All teams listen up! Romeo Three," shouted the team leader, "you will position yourself well in front of the aircraft. Do not, and I repeat, do not, let the aircraft take off. Romeo Two, flank the target portside. Romeo One will cover starboard. On my command – NOW!"

The three men burst simultaneously from beneath their white camouflage blankets, already astride snow machines. Tavernese's men had high-powered long-range automatic weapons strapped across their backs. North had only his trusty rifle; evidently, he'd thought wryly when the guns were being distributed, he wasn't trusted with the more accurate, deadlier weapon.

The white and blue Twin Otter taxied over hard packed snow and ice, its propellers snarling as it strained to reach takeoff speed. The snowmobiles were in place within seconds, surrounding the aircraft on three sides.

From his position at the left side of the aircraft, North could see Captain Jim O'Neill's bone-white face through the side window of the cockpit. O'Neill's eyes were as round as saucers.

North felt a moment of pity for the soon-to-be retired and exiled pilot.

The Twin Otter's groundspeed continued to increase, but the two powerful snowmobiles easily kept pace on either side of it. Romeo Three had sprinted ahead of the aircraft and had stopped broadside about 100 meters in front of it.

The cluster of racing machines had narrowed the distance to Romeo Three before North spotted Sam's helicopter rapidly approaching, skimming low over the frozen ground. The Twin Otter's groundspeed was still increasing; North knew that the Twin's cargo load, if it had any at all, would be light and that the aircraft had excellent short takeoff and landing capabilities. He wasn't an expert, but he figured that a desperate pilot just might be able to coax the airplane off the ground before it reached the snowmobile.

The only sure way to stop it would be with the helicopter – or a strategically placed bullet. Possibly many bullets.

North glanced up and noted with relief that Sam's chopper was closing in fast. All of a sudden he glimpsed movement in his peripheral vision. At exactly the same moment the radio in his helmet crackled to life. "All ground units, this is Alfa One. Looks like you've left someone behind. Romeo Two, fall back and find out what the hell's going on, over."

"Roger that, Alfa One." North slowed and turned sharply to his left, throwing up a rooster tail of snow from his spinning tracks. It was virtually impossible to see a thing through the swirling white veil kicked up by the racing snowmobiles and aircraft. He cautiously backtracked, widening the gap between himself and the rest of the crew.

After a few blind seconds he drove out of the thickest part of the billowing snow and saw a dark form twenty or thirty meters in front of him. A quick glance over his shoulder confirmed that the helicopter was hovering directly in front of the now-stationary Twin Otter.

North opened up the Cat's throttle and closed in on his prey. The form materialized into a running figure. He suspected it was Henrik Bruller; who else would be desperate enough to slip from a moving Twin Otter in the middle of an armed pursuit?

Whoever it was, the man was running for his life and reached Bruller's machine before North was able to close in on him. Within seconds, the bright yellow Ski-Doo was racing over the bumpy terrain while its passenger attempted to slide the helmet onto his head. It *has* to be Bruller, North thought again.

"Alfa One, this is Romeo Two," North called into his microphone. "Am in pursuit of a man I believe to be Bruller. Request assistance whenever you're ready. Over."

"Romeo Two, keep him in sight. We'll join you when we get this situation under control. Over."

"Roger that," North acknowledged, his eyes still glued on the black and yellow figure ahead of him. When North saw his quarry reach for a rifle strapped to the side of his Ski-Doo, he had a sense of *déjà-vu;*

only a month ago this very scenario had played out before, and it had ended very badly for North. He didn't want a repeat performance, but neither did he want to disappoint Sam.

North eased off on his throttle slightly, letting a little more distance slip between himself and the other man while he rapidly assessed his situation. A backward glance told him that the Jet Ranger was still hovering in front of the Twin Otter. He couldn't spot the other snow machines, and grimly acknowledged that help wouldn't be arriving any time soon.

Every hunter knows that each second of indecision can spell failure. North pulled his old rifle over his shoulder and released the safety. I'll be damned if I let you shoot me a second time, he vowed silently. Then he opened up the Cat's throttle, determined to close the widening gap.

Bruller disappeared, his route taking him around the same low range of hills that had previously spelled disaster for North. But North wasn't about to fall prey to Henrik Bruller's rifle again. When he rocketed around the corner of the hill and into Bruller's sight, his rifle was already aimed toward the fleeing criminal. North fired a shot, but he was too far away. It fell short of its mark. Bruller sped on, slowing only momentarily to return fire. Luckily for North, it too missed its mark.

North pressed on, and still there was no sight of his team-mates or the helicopter. He was slowly closing in on Bruller, which wasn't necessarily a good thing. North knew that the range of Bruller's rifle far exceeded his. He steadied his aim as best he could on the bouncing machine and fired another shot at the yellow Ski-Doo.

Bruller's body twisted slightly as he glanced back. It was at that precise moment that the God's of Fate were on North's side. Bruller's momentary distraction, the two seconds of time it cost him to look back, was long enough to end the man's getaway.

The Ski-Doo flew into the air, then tipped sideways as it crashed back to earth. It landed briefly on its side, giving North a short glimpse of spinning track and black undercarriage before it executed a quick series of rolls. Henrik Bruller was thrown from the machine before it came to rest back on its side. The man lay belly down in a crumpled heap. His black helmet skidded across the snow and spun slowly ten meters away.

North was on the scene short seconds later and hit the kill switch on his Cat. He didn't sense a trap, but still kept his gun aimed at the downed man. Bruller's Ski-Doo had stalled, and in the sudden silence, North detected the chopper's blades beating the air somewhere over the hill.

He walked cautiously toward the figure lying motionless on the pristine, sparkling snow. The man's rifle was nowhere in sight, but North wasn't about to take any chances.

He flipped up the clear acrylic visor on his helmet and shouted, "Bruller, can you hear me?" There was no response.

Keeping his rifle aimed at the prostrate figure, North edged closer and nudged the downed man with the toe of his boot. He remained motionless.

North could see the man's face clearly now, and recognized him from his photo. He knelt down and pulled off a glove, then checked for a pulse, finding a very faint one.

Henrik Bruller was out cold, but he was still alive.

THIRTY-ONE

Andi resorted to pacing the office floor and twisting the AA ring around her cold finger. She had been craving a drink – just one drink – to steady her nerves, but had settled for too many cups of coffee. Now her stomach burned from the acidic brew. More than seven hours had lapsed since she'd seen the Twin Otter and its cargo of snowmobiles and men away that morning. The waiting seemed endless.

In the next office, Princess Jessica Hartman had no idea that her illicit lover may be making the last flight of his career. For the indolent dispatcher, her day had progressed as usual, and it would soon be quitting time.

It was close to 5 pm when the VHF radio in Jessica's office crackled to life. "Tuktu base, this is helicopter Sierra Tango Uniform, do you copy? Over."

Andi's heart quickened; the call was from Sam's helicopter.

Jessica picked up the handheld microphone and keyed it. "STU this is Tuktu base," she crooned. "Go ahead."

"We're inbound Inuvik, estimating ten minutes. We have an injured man on board and will be landing at the helipad at Stanton General. Over."

Jessica wrinkled her nose and stared at the radio with a confused expression on her pretty face. "Roger that, STU, but I think you have the wrong-"

Before Jessica could finish her sentence Andi ripped the mic from her grasp. "STU this is Andrea Nowak," she said, forcing her voice to remain calm. "We copy that. Please advise identity of the injured man. Over."

"Stand by one."

Andi forgot to breathe. Her heart hammered, beating against her ribcage like a wild animal. Jessica glared at her, then flounced out of the office and proceeded to slam cups around in the coffee room.

The radio crackled to life. "Tuktu base, are you by?"

"Yes, go ahead."

"His name is Henrik Bruller."

Tears of joy trailed from Andi's eyes. "We copy that, STU. Thank you," she said, forcing the words through lips that refused to cooperate.

"And Tuktu, we're supposed to advise that your Twin Otter TTA should be arriving Inuvik in about forty-five minutes. Over."

"Roger that. Thank you. Tuktu base out."

Total silence ensued within Tuktu Aviation's dispatch center. Andi, still gripping the VHF microphone, stood motionless, frozen. A moment later, she realized that Jessica was no longer clinking cups together in the coffee room.

She hung the mic back on its hook and slowly walked toward the coffee room, stopping at the open doorway. Jessica Hartman stood beside her beloved espresso machine, gaping at Andi with naked terror in her blue eyes. Her normally lustrous complexion had paled, and the condescending smirk that usually graced her features was absent.

The two women locked eyes, and Andi was sure she could smell the other woman's fear. In that instant, she knew that Jessica Hartman realized that her life was about to change forever. But instead of feeling delight and satisfaction, Andi was surprised that she felt only sadness for the lost and forlorn figure standing before her.

"I'll stick around until they're back," Andi said calmly. "You can go home now if you want."

Jessica continued to stare at Andi for a few moments, an unasked, and unanswered, question in her eyes. When Andi offered nothing further the Chief Dispatcher darted into her office, picked up her purse and coat and fled down the stairs without a backward glance at her boss.

Andi sat down heavily at the cluttered desk. She was glad that the perilous adventure she and North had stumbled into would soon be drawing to a close. She vowed that when it was over, she would set aside some time to make an important decision; a decision that would affect the rest of her life, and that of the kind, intelligent, handsome and overwhelmingly romantic man who had stolen her heart.

Andi was waiting on the tarmac near the maintenance hangar when the Twin Otter carrying North, Sam and his team returned. She watched in silence as Captain O'Neill and First Officer Brister, after being allowed to secure their aircraft for the night, were immediately escorted by Tavernese's men to a black cargo van parked just outside the security gate. Although she didn't see any hand-cuffs, the two pilots willingly complied with their captor's wishes – possibly due to the rifles slung across their escort's backs.

When Jim O'Neill, encircled by Sam's men, walked by Andi, the look he gave her was one of pure hatred. Little did Andi know that that those few seconds would stay imprinted on her mind for months to come.

While the pilots were being ushered into the waiting van, Sam stopped to talk to Andi and North. "I guess we got lucky today, and I have you two to thank for that."

"No problem," North replied with a tired smile. "I'm glad to be of help. And it felt good to nail that bastard, Bruller."

Andi, however, couldn't muster the words to respond to Tavernese's praise. For some time now she'd been wrestling with the feeling that there was more than met the eye when it came to Sam

Tavernese and his business acquaintances. She still wondered if she'd done the right thing by going to him with her information and the diamonds. Even now, after what had transpired today, she had the uneasy feeling that she should have made another attempt to enlist the help of the RCMP.

"I couldn't have done this without you both," Sam continued. "I can't tell you how much I appreciate your help, but I have to ask you to keep this entire matter confidential. The diamond mine can't afford to let our losses become public knowledge. I'll look after the matter myself."

"We won't say a word to anyone," North agreed readily, hoisting his heavy pack to the other shoulder.

Andi just nodded mutely, not trusting herself to speak.

"What about the pilots in the other Twin Otter?" Sam asked, referring to Dan and Tom, who were still inbound from Paulatuk. "How much do they know?"

"As far as they're concerned," Andi said, finding her voice, "North chartered the plane for his day of photography."

"Excellent," Tavernese nodded. "I instructed my chopper pilot to contact Tuktu's agent at the Paulatuk airport. They were going to let your pilots know that the Twin Otter returning from Pivot Lake had spotted North and his photography crew in the middle of nowhere, and had landed to see if they needed help. And that they ended up bringing them back to Inuvik since they were ready to call it a day. Do you think that will sit right with your guys?"

"I don't see why not. If they question the story, I'll look after it," Andi assured him.

"Thank you both again," Sam said, extending a hand to Andi first, and then North. "Send your bill directly to my attention," he said to Andi with a smile. "Someone will be by tomorrow to pick up the snowmobiles."

Tavernese had already started walking away when Andi called after him. "Sam! Can I ask what you intend to do with Jim and Hank? Where are you taking them?" Her ears were tingling, and she felt an overwhelming sense of fear for the two pilots.

Sam turned to Andi in the fading light, and gazed at her speculatively for a moment before he shook his head slightly. Then he raised a hand in farewell and turned to the waiting van. A few seconds later, he and his unwilling companions were whisked away.

Later that evening, after feeding the sled dogs and spending some time with them, North and Andi wolfed down their own dinner of piping hot pizza. Andi had found a frozen pie in North's cavernous freezer and thrown it in the oven to bake.

Her host was downing a cold beer with his dinner and it made her mouth water. She'd lost her grip on sobriety, but was fighting hard to get it back; trying to focus on North instead of his beer took every ounce of her concentration. "So tell me exactly what happened today," she said, taking a gulp of cold water.

North recounted the day's events, sparing no detail. Andi hung onto every word.

"And what happened when Jim finally shut TTA down?" she asked.

"Sam told me that as soon as the engines stopped, they opened the airstair door and stormed it. I guess they had their weapons pointed at Jim and Hank before the poor guys could blink an eye."

"So they didn't put up a fight?"

"Nah. All Sam had to do is point a gun at O'Neill's head and ask where his diamonds were. I guess they were stashed in his flight bag. Sam said they would amount to quite a few carats. He showed them to me on the way home. They just look like dirty old rocks if you ask me."

"Rough diamonds look like that," Andi said, nodding sagely.

"I guess after that O'Neill realized that his luck had run out," North continued. He burped, took another swig of beer and looked at Andi apologetically over his napkin. "Sorry."

"No worries."

"Then O'Neill just started spilling his guts. He told Sam that he'd been transporting the goods for Bruller for a few years. They'd started out slow, only one or two shipments a year. But in the past few months Bruller had been picking up the pace. Maybe he was getting ready to pull the pin," North speculated, his dark eyebrows knitted together in concentration. "Anyway, O'Neill said that he passed the rocks on to Jessica. She took them to Vancouver and sold them somewhere."

"Ah, so Jessica *is* wrapped up in it too," Andi groaned, genuinely disappointed. "No wonder she makes so many trips to the coast."

"Coffee, Babe?" North asked. His eyes were puffy and he looked exhausted.

"Sure, sounds good." Andi cleared the table and rinsed off their plates while North made coffee. She was struck by the feeling of harmony in the small cabin; they seemed to belong in it together.

"Oh!" Andi exclaimed suddenly. "I just remembered that I have some good news to tell you."

"I could use some good news," North yawned. "What is it?"

"Coco came up for tea last night. She's decided to keep the baby!" Andi's smile was wide, her emerald eyes sparkling. "I'm so happy she's not having an abortion. I think it's the right choice."

"Well, perhaps. But she's got a hard road ahead of her," North said with a shake of his head. "It can't be easy being a single mother."

"I know. I told her that I'd help her out as much as I can if she decides to stay in Inuvik. She's thinking about moving back to B.C., closer to her family."

"I'm sure she'll appreciate your help."

"So did Jim say what happened to the money after Jessica sold the diamonds?"

"Only that they all got a cut. Bruller took 50%; O'Neill got 25%; Jessica 15%; and Hank 10%. It sounds like Hank was a pretty minor player. He was only in on the scheme for a few months. They gave him 10% just to shut him up."

"But I suppose it all amounted to quite a lot of money over the years. I'm surprised the mine didn't notice anything sooner."

"Yeah, me too."

"So, you missed all the action while you were trying to murder Bruller?" Andi asked, batting her eyelashes.

"Ha! I tell you, I've seen enough action to last a life time. I hope we've seen the last of your buddies."

"They're not *my* buddies."

"Well, old Sam Tavernese seems pretty taken with you," North grumbled.

"He's not *old*," Andi snapped, getting up to pour their coffee. She could feel North's eyes boring into her back.

"Is there anything you'd like to tell me?"

Andi's hand froze on the handle of the coffee pot. "No. Why do you ask?" she said calmly, which was difficult with pizza turning to a lump of dough in her stomach.

"Well, he just mentioned a few things that made it sound like he'd spent some time with you. More than just an office meeting."

"We went for dinner. It wasn't important so I didn't bother mentioning it," Andi replied smoothly, depositing two mugs on the coffee table. North lay sprawled on the sofa, his long legs dangling over one end. He sat up and reached for his cup.

"So an extremely wealthy Mafia guy takes you for a fancy dinner in Toronto, and you don't think it's worth mentioning to me?" North asked coolly, black eyebrows raised.

Andi's downcast eyes flew up to meet his. "What do you mean, 'Mafia guy'? Wherever did you get that stupid idea?" she snapped.

"Babe, put the pieces together. All you have to do is take a look at the guy and his men. They have Mafia written all over them. Tavernese? You've seriously never heard that name before?"

"Not all of us have spent time in the east," she retorted. "I suppose you're going to tell me that as a hot-shot lawyer in *Toronto* you had legal dealings with the Mafia?"

"Whatever. You're right, it's not important." North stifled a yawn.

"And absolutely nothing happened between Sam and me in Toronto, just in case you're interested."

"I believe you. I'm just happy this is all over and things can get back to normal around here."

Andi had curled up in North's big La-Z-Boy. "Me, too, but I can't help worrying about what's going to happen to Jessica. And Jim and Hank, too. I can't believe they were all willing to risk their freedom for the sake of some stupid diamonds."

"Well, I personally don't give a shit what happens to them," North said, pulling himself off the sofa. "If they were stupid enough to do what they did, then they deserve whatever they get. I'm tired, Babe. Let's go to bed and forget about this for a while, okay?" He reached for Andi's hand.

She put her empty cup on the coffee table and followed him to his bedroom.

THIRTY-TWO

"You'll never believe this Andi!" Paul exclaimed as he stormed into her office three days later. It was just before 8 am and their Monday morning management meeting would begin in a few minutes. "O'Neill and Brister both handed in letters of resignation this weekend. They left their notices on Steve's desk and didn't have the guts to talk to either one of us," he continued, dark eyes indignant.

"You're kidding!" Andi exclaimed, feigning surprise. "Did they say why?"

"No, they gave absolutely no reason. The letters were identical. They both say that they resign immediately and that's it." Paul looked flummoxed by the uncharacteristic behavior of his ace pilot and his cohort.

"My god," Andi said, shaking her head. "Does the rest of the crew know yet?"

"No. But just between you and me, I don't think anyone will be too sad to see Jim go. He's made a few enemies around here the past year or two. But Steve and I are damn confused by the whole thing. He's going to schedule a flight crew meeting today. You want to join us?"

"Ah, no, thanks. I'm pretty much tied up here," Andi replied. "So you don't have any idea why they resigned?" she probed.

Nope. They just quit right out of the blue. And I haven't told you the rest of it," Paul was restless, pacing the floor of Andi's small office.

"What?"

"I called Jim's place just now, and Sally answered the phone. She's just as confused as we are. Evidently Jim packed a few suitcases and left town in a hurry yesterday. Sally was at the hospital, and when she got home from work there was a letter on the kitchen table saying the kids were next door and that he needed a change and had quit his job. He's gone! He walked out on her and the kids, can you believe it? Poor Sally." Paul had quit his nervous pacing and stood before her small office window, staring into the dim morning light.

"Oh, my god!" Andi cried, truly surprised. "How's she doing?"

"Well, you know Sally. She's a pretty tough girl. Personally, I think she'll be much better off without Jim. He was a great pilot, but a pretty shitty husband."

"I agree. What about Hank? Has anyone seen him?" Andi asked.

"I don't know. He was living at the Captain's House, wasn't he?" Paul asked, referring to the large, ten-bedroom staff house that Tuktu Aviation provided for their unmarried or temporary flight crew.

"Yes, as far as I know."

"I'll ask Steve to check and see if he's still there." Paul said. "But maybe he's left town, too. He and Jim seemed pretty tight."

"So are we still having our meeting this morning?"

"Yes, the others should be here any minute. I'll break the news to everyone when they get here." Paul opened the connecting door into the dispatch office and strode through the doorway. "Ayame, do you have anything on for Jim O'Neill or Hank Brister today?"

A few seconds later Andi heard Ayame reply, "No, they both have a day off."

"Good," Paul said. "I'd like you to listen in to as much of our meeting as you can this morning. It's going to be an interesting one."

"Okay."

Andi sat guiltily through the somewhat irregular management meeting. She bit her tongue several times as the team she had grown to know and respect speculated about the reason for Captain O'Neill and First Office Hank Brister's sudden and perplexing exodus.

Jessica Hartman didn't show up for work either, and when Ayame called her apartment, she didn't answer. It appeared that perhaps The Princess might have gone AWOL as well.

Among all those present, only Andi knew the truth, and she couldn't share it. Sam Tavernese had made it very clear that he expected her and North's silence, and that he would 'take care of the problem' himself.

She sat through the longest meeting she'd ever had to endure, with the knowledge of the truth tugging at her guilty conscience.

"Good morning, Tuktu Aviation. Andi speaking." A week had passed since Sam and North had put an end to Henrik Bruller's diamond smuggling ring, and Andi was spending more time than she wanted filling in for her missing Chief Dispatcher.

"Andi, this is Carlos. How are you?"

"Carlos! My god, it's good to hear from you. I've been so worried. Where are you?"

"Just where I'm supposed to be; sitting at my desk out at the mine."

"Really? But I ... you – uh, where have you been?"

"Well, I had a hell of a run-in with our Project Manager a few weeks ago, and he fired me," Carlos laughed. "I was so damn mad that I flew home to Saskatchewan, picked up my old Mercury and hit the road. Made it all the way down to the Mexican border before I cooled off."

"Really? Well I was getting kind of concerned when I couldn't get hold of you anymore. And nobody seemed to know where to find you."

"Yeah, I know. When I finally got back home there were about half a dozen urgent messages asking me to call the office. Evidently the head honcho was looking for me too."

Andi didn't know how much Carlos knew about the whole situation, but given her promise to Sam, she decided to play it safe and keep her lips sealed. "Well, I'm very glad you're back safe and sound."

"Sorry for worrying you," Carlos sounded sincere. "I had a long phone conversation with Sam Tavernese yesterday."

"Oh?"

"Yeah, he filled me in on what happened out here last week. About Bruller and your crew and all that."

"Oh, okay. I didn't know if you knew all about it, so I didn't want to say anything. You must be relieved that it's all over, eh? You were right about the missing diamond inventory."

"For sure I'm relieved. I just wish I would have caught it sooner. God knows how much we lost at Bruller's hands."

"You can't blame yourself for that, Carlos. That security system Sam installed was supposed to be foolproof, wasn't it?"

"Yeah, but I still feel bad."

"I'm just so glad it's over. You've heard about Bruller?" Andi asked, lowering her voice. "He died in the hospital two days ago."

"Yeah, I heard."

"According to the nurses, the doctor said he was doing really well. Henrik had had a bit of a concussion from the snowmobile accident, but he was on the mend and was almost ready to be released. I guess there's going to be an autopsy."

After a pregnant pause Carlos said, "Can't say anyone here is going to particularly miss him. I know it's not right to speak ill of the dead, but Bruller was an asshole."

"I didn't know him personally," Andi replied, "but, yeah I heard he wasn't the nicest person. I just think it strange that he died so suddenly after having recovered. Almost like, I don't know, maybe someone helped him along to meet his maker."

Carlos let out a gusty breath. "If you want my advice, Ms. Andrea Nowak, I wouldn't be looking into Henrik Bruller's death too closely. You might learn more than you can handle."

It was Andi's turn to remain silent for a moment; she really had no clue what he could be talking about. "Well," she said finally, "I'm glad that you're back and that you're safe, Carlos. Next time you're in town, let me know and we'll go for lunch."

"Okay, my dear, you have a deal. And how are things with you?"

"Too busy. I seem to have lost my Chief Dispatcher, along with the two pilots who were involved in Bruller's scam," Andi grumbled. "All three of them have disappeared into thin air and I'd sure as hell like to know where they are."

"Leave it alone, Andi," Carlos said sternly. "The less you know the better off you are. Promise me you won't go looking for them?"

"Well, I just-" Andi began but was cut off by Carlos's stern warning.

"*No*, Andi. Sam Tavernese has connections you *don't* want to get involved with. Trust me – just leave this alone."

Another line began ringing on Andi's phone. "Okay, okay. I have to go Carlos," she said. "I'm alone up here in the office. Do you want me to call you back?"

"No, it's okay. I just wanted to say hi."

"All right, then. Thanks again for letting me know you're back."

"No problem. Oh, and Andi?" he chuckled. "Next time you come out to the mine, look for the door that says 'Carlos Sante, Project Manager'."

A few hours later Ayame ran up the stairs. She had agreed to take the afternoon shifts, while Andi preferred to work the mornings. With no word from Jessica since her disappearance, Andi had already begun grooming Ayame to take over the position of Chief Dispatcher, and was also training another dispatcher, Chris Bedford. Chris was a promising candidate, having dispatched in Yellowknife for a few months before moving to Inuvik. So far he seemed dependable, self-motivated and bright. And he loved Inuvik, so there was little risk of him decamping any time soon. For now, life in Andi's world seemed to be flowing harmoniously.

She was packing her briefcase with weekend paperwork when a UPS van pulled up outside. A moment later heavy footsteps trudged up the old stairs. Andi walked out of her office in time to see a familiar head poke above the banister. "Hi, David. How are you?" she smiled at the handsome young courier. He was holding a small box.

"Just great, Ms. Nowak," he said. "I'm glad it's the end of my day though. "Got something for you. Sign here, please."

Andi signed for the delivery, bid David goodbye, and walked slowly back into her office. She was mystified. The package, from Pivot Lake Mines in Toronto, was addressed to her, personally, but she was expecting nothing from them. She carefully slit the box open and dug through the Styrofoam popcorn, spilling bits onto her desk.

She pulled two items from the box: a thick, letter size envelope with her name on it and bearing the Pivot Lake Mines logo, and a long blue velvet, jeweller's case.

Her lips twitched with a ghost of a smile. Had Sam Tavernese sent her a gift?

She set the velvet case on her desk and slit open the envelope. It held a beautifully bound, midnight blue folio, emblazoned in gold with the mine's logo. Inside was a letter from Sam Tavernese, and she skimmed it quickly. What it said left her speechless. She read it a second time more slowly, but still could barely comprehend its meaning.

The letter informed her that Sam Tavernese, on behalf of the Pivot Lake Diamond Mine, was extending his great gratitude by bestowing her with a gift – a 'sampling' of diamonds from their mine. Also enclosed, the letter said, was an appraisal for the stones, and a Certificate of Authenticity for each gem.

Andi's face flushed in immediate response to her racing pulse as, with a shaky hand, she leafed through the letter's attachments. First was an appraisal for a quantity of cut and polished Canadian diamonds. Her eyes flew over the document, coming to rest at a value figure that made her gasp; almost one hundred thousand dollars!

The Certificates of Authenticity for each diamond were attached as well, which she flipped through without really reading. She knew from her research on the Canadian diamond industry that each diamond mined, cut and polished in Canada bore a symbol, such as the Canadian flag or a polar bear, as well as a serial number microscopically laser etched into its girdle. The history of each stone could be traced from beginning to end.

Turning back to the cover letter, Andi noticed that it was signed not only by Sam Tavernese, but also by the two corporate officers she had met in Sam's office – Antonio DeMaria and James Maniero. It was also embossed with the company's corporate seal. It all looked legitimate.

She dropped the folio on her desk and with trembling hands picked up the blue case. She opened its hinged lid cautiously. Glittering, sparkling diamonds of various sizes nestled on a bed of black silk. Each gem rested in its own small pocket, separated from the others. She stared mutely at the breathtaking display.

There were four rows of ten gems each. Reverently, Andi picked up one of the two largest stones, which she estimated to be about five carats each. When she held the large diamond to the light of her window, its mystic beauty took her breath away. She gazed at it in awe for several long moments before carefully returning it to the case.

Her fingertips danced over the remaining diamonds. The late day sun struck them, releasing their cold inner beauty from multi-faceted surfaces with jolts of vivid blue, green and red light

A smile spread across Andi's flushed features. She picked up one of the largest stones again and held it between thumb and forefinger.

From somewhere deep in her memory a phrase surfaced unbidden: 'Each diamond is unique – a gemological marvel formed millions of years ago under extraordinary heat and pressure.' They *were* a marvel, she agreed, as her fist closed around the precious gem.

Her smile broadened into a grin. It was a hell of a way to end a work week.

THIRTY-THREE

An annoying jingle intruded on her dream. Andi opened her eyes and saw daylight peeking through the blinds, but a glance at her bedside clock told her it was only 7 am. It was much too early to rise on a Saturday morning.

She reached for the annoying telephone. "G'morning."

"Are you up?"

"No, I'm sound asleep," she retorted hoarsely.

"Uh, sorry to wake you. I just thought I'd see if you want to spend the day with me doing some training. It's okay though, if you're still in bed-." North's sentence trailed off.

Andi flung the bedcovers back and sat up. "No! I mean, yes, I'll come. What time are you leaving?"

"I thought around 9:30 or 10:00. Maybe we could pack some sandwiches and coffee and have another picnic?"

Andi knew North well enough by now to read between the lines. "Sure, I'll bring lunch and you make coffee," she said, smiling in spite of her early morning grumpiness.

"I've missed you, Babe. Haven't seen you for days."

"I've missed you too. See you in a couple of hours."

It was nearing 10:00 when Andi parked in front of North's cabin. Even from the car, she could hear the excited yipping of the sled dogs. She grabbed her small cooler and skirted around the house to the backyard dog pen.

Eight dogs were already in harness and North was bent over the front of the qamutik, adjusting the towline. Concentrating on his task, he didn't notice her approach.

The beauty of the scene stopped her dead in her tracks. It was a fairy-tale picture: eight bright-eyed, panting sled dogs, squirming in anticipation of their outing, were harnessed to an old-fashioned wooden sled. A bright Hudson's Bay blanket was draped over the back of the qamutik, its vivid green, white, red, yellow and blue stripes lending colour and vibrancy to the picture.

Kneeling on the snow beside the sled was her handsome prince, dressed in the traditional hooded, fur-trimmed sealskin anorak and mukluks his ancestors wore hundreds of years ago. Andi was struck anew at the air of calm strength and virility exuding from her lover. His shiny black hair was pulled back and secured with a leather thong, and his full lips curved in a contented smile.

The magic lasted only a moment, and then a change in the dog's united voice alerted North to her presence. "Hey," he shouted above the cacophony, "you made it!"

"Hi, sorry I took so long," Andi called as she carted her cooler to the sled and deposited it beside North. She leaned down and planted a kiss on his lips. "Almost ready?"

"Yup, will be in a minute. Just a sec." North whistled at the dogs, and when he had their attention put them all down in a lying 'stay' position. Their voices quieted to a discontented murmur. So what have you been doing all week?"

Little did the unsuspecting man know that that was a loaded question.

"Thinking about you and me," Andi answered without a moment's hesitation. And it was true; she had spent the better part of the past week examining her innermost hopes and fears. As far as she was concerned, she carried more baggage than most people and had finally forced herself to examine her past, present and future in minute detail.

She got through the difficult task the way she did things best, by writing it all down. She knew that her sorrow, addiction, anger and road to self-destruction all stemmed from one thing – the loss of her child. But she also realized that after six long, miserable years it was time to think about herself and her own life and future.

She would never forget her darling daughter; Natalie would be a huge part of Andi's life forever, but today it was time for Nat's ghost to move over and make room for new beginnings. To make room for love and happiness. Andi knew that the key to her bright and happy future knelt on the snow before her, gazing up at her inquisitively.

North stood up, and brushed the snow from his knees. "And what did you decide about you and me?" he asked soberly, his dark eyes boring into hers.

"I decided that maybe you're worth the risk," Andi replied, a ghost of a smile tugging her rosy lips.

North unzipped his parka and dug into an inner pocket, pulling out a small bundle wrapped in soft suede leather. He handed the package to Andi. She tugged her otter mitts off, letting them swing by their purple idiot strings, and held the package in both hands, transfixed by the possibilities it held.

"Go ahead, open it. It's for you," North urged.

She slowly unfolded the bundle of leather to reveal the wonder within, and gasped in delight. She held in her hands the beautiful soapstone carving she had so admired at North's gallery – 'Mother with Child'.

"I should have told you this before, but I'll tell you now, Andi. I love you, Babe. I want you to be a part of my life forever. We can work through your grief and whatever it is you need to work through, and we'll do it together."

Then, to Andi's shock, he dropped back down to his knees and took her hand in his. "I won't ask you to marry me today, Andi, but I'll ask you one day soon, and I hope you'll say 'yes'."

Emotionally overwhelmed, Andi's voice refused to cooperate, and she could only nod her head. Her eyes said it all, though. Her emerald eyes were luminous, and they were saying 'yes.'

North rose and folded her into his arms, infusing her with his strength and warmth.

A few minutes passed before she stepped back and swept a tear from her cheek. She smiled up at North and handed the beautiful carving back to him as she said, "And I have something to show you too." From the inner pocket of her parka, she withdrew the blue velvet jeweller's case. "It's a present," she said. "For both of us."

North looked at the case curiously. "What is it? A watch?"

"It's not what you think it is," Andi teased as she slowly lifted the lid to reveal the sparkling treasure within.

North's sharp intake of breath was audible even above the restless moaning of the dogs. "Where the hell did you get those?" he asked slowly, his eyes glued to the gems.

Andi carefully lifted out a large diamond, and closed the lid. The brilliant Arctic spring sun struck the precious gem lying in the palm of her hand, reflecting fire from its depths.

"It's just a little thank you gift from Sam Tavernese and Pivot Lake Mines," Andi smiled broadly. "They're worth about a hundred grand! I figure that's enough to buy at least a dozen more Canadian Eskimo Dogs and to outfit a certain someone for the Silver Anniversary running of the Iditarod coming up in two years."

North stared speechlessly at the diamond, a bemused expression on his face. Then Andi added shyly, "And maybe there'll even be a little one left over for an engagement ring."

"Babe, I love you," North said, sweeping her into his arms. He kissed her tenderly, sending delicious shivers up and down her spine.

"I love you too, North. Forever and always."

"Maybe my old Eskimo ancestors were wrong," he said, pulling her closer.

Andi looked up at him, a question in her bright green eyes.

"Our Arctic diamonds shouldn't be called 'the stones that sparkle like stars in the sky'," he said softly. "They are almost as lovely as you are. They're almost as bright as your eyes. They should be called 'the stones that sparkle like Andi's eyes'."

Andi laughed and hugged him fiercely. "Let's go mushing!" she grinned, carefully depositing the precious stone back into its protective velvet case.

Late that night Andi slipped from the warmth of North's arms and out of his bed. On silent feet she padded to the window and pulled the curtain aside to peer at the clear night sky. The Arctic stars shone brightly, glimmering as only stars and diamonds can.

One heavenly body shone brighter than the others – Andi decided it was Natalie's star. "I love you, Natalie, and I'll love you forever," she whispered, gazing wistfully at the brilliant, sparkling sphere. "I'll never forget you, my sweet baby girl." She stood by the window for a long minute, then smiled and crept through the dark cabin to North's bedroom.

She slipped back into her lover's bed and snuggled close to the man who had healed her heart and reawakened her will to live.

ACKNOWLEDGEMENTS

I'd like to start by thanking each and every friend and co-worker who passed through my life during my foray into the amazing world of Canadian aviation. You know who you are – each and every one of you has made my world a more interesting place.

A special thanks to Captain Dan Jones, Hercules skipper, for your patience and enlightening answers to my endless questions regarding Twin Otters and all things aviation. Any errors or omissions on the subject are solely the fault of this author.

My sister, Pat Goshko, deserves a big thank you for her encouraging reviews of my writing, and always being there for me.

My endless appreciation to my husband, Heinz, for your encouragement and proofreading. Your feedback and suggestions didn't go unheeded.

I HOPE YOU ENJOYED

DIAMONDS IN AN ARCTIC SKY

PLEASE READ ON FOR A
SNEAK PREVIEW OF

NORTH: The Last Great Race
(Andi & North, Book 2)

NORTH: *The Last Great Race*

PROLOGUE

I start awake, my heart thudding painfully as I struggle to distinguish reality from nightmare. In my mind's eye, strands of hot scarlet dance and swirl with pristine, cold white, rising and falling and finally pooling in a shimmering pink, wet pool. Voices cried, a high-pitched keening. Were they human, or beast?

It all came back in a rush. I was in Anchorage, Alaska, laying alone on a strange bed, in a stranger's home. My lover and best friend had left days ago, determined to challenge himself and his dreams, intent on conquering a sometimes cruel and forbidding Mother Nature. Somewhere over Alaska's frozen, isolated expanse of land, ocean and mountain between Anchorage and Nome, the man I loved more than life itself was mushing in the Iditarod – The Last Great Race.

I had been blessed not only with my mother's green eyes, but her keenly intuitive nature, as well. Some called our gift the 'Sixth Sense'. This so-called 'gift' had been entertaining when I was younger – waking up and 'knowing' where my father's missing lighter was (between the sofa cushions), or walking to the telephone to call my mother, only to have it ring in my hands (my mother on the other end, of course). Always chalked up to coincidence, these events had once been entertaining. But as I grew and developed, so did my gift. I was now blessed with horribly accurate, uncanny dreams and insights into the future. It wouldn't be so bad if they were insights to joyful, happy events, but they weren't. I prayed that this time my nightmares were only just that – nightmares.

ONE

"COME HAW! COME HAW!" The musher guided his eight powerful sled dogs into a sharp left turn, each furry beast's lolling, pink tongue in sharp contrast to winter's monochromatic white palette. Snow and ice hissed beneath the skis of the light racing sled as it skimmed across the frozen ribbon of northern Canada's McKenzie River. Astride two runners protruding from the back of the sled's small cargo basket, the man's easy, relaxed stance could easily give a bystander the mistaken impression that mushing required little effort on the part of the dogs' human counterpart. His body moved in a continuous, yet seemingly effortless dance, perfectly synchronized with each bump and sway of the sled.

This particular musher was clad from head to foot in traditional Inuit winter garments: fur-trimmed caribou skin anorak, pants and kamiks. His hands gripped the sled's arched, wooden handle bar to maintain his balance and were sheathed in heavy animal skin mitts that extended to the crook of his elbow and were decorated with intricate beadwork. On anyone else, the time-honoured apparel, although warm and practical, would be deemed eccentric. On North Edward Charles Ruben, it looked regal.

North's team of spirited Canadian Eskimo dogs hurdled up the McKenzie River's gently sloping bank, effortlessly towing the sled and its passenger up and over the edge. The muscular, sleek dogs, their coats a rainbow of grey, black, brown and white, sensed they were near the end of their journey and began to yelp. The intensity and volume of their song strengthened as they dashed toward a small group of racing

2

enthusiasts clustered near the finish line. Although the race was merely an impromptu, Saturday afternoon sporting event between friendly rivals, North's victorious shout resounded across the barren tundra when he slid over the finish line, capturing first place. His opponents may have entered today's contest merely for fun, but North Ruben had an agenda. These days, he took every sled dog race and each win seriously; each brought him another step closer to his lifelong dream of conquering the most grueling dog sled race in the world – The Iditarod.

Today's event was a relatively short two-hour run and many of the spectators chose to wait at the staging area since the race's slightly disorganized noon start. In an effort to ward off the inevitable chill of a January afternoon high above the Arctic Circle, they'd built smoking fires inside two 45-gallon steel barrels. The fires crackled and flared inside the lidless, rusted drums, releasing curls of dark grey, acrid smoke into the azure blue sky. Mitten-clad hands warmed over the smoldering fires, while mukluks and heavy, insulated boots stomped the hard-packed snow in an attempt to restore circulation to numb feet. Only the sturdiest of souls, many of whom warmed themselves from thermoses of hot coffee laced with whisky or Southern Comfort, braved a chilly minus 20-degree Celsius day for a bit of afternoon entertainment.

Once across the finish line North applied pressure to the sled brake, slowing his team's pace to a fast trot, then glanced back to check on the position of his closest competitor. His eyes grew wide and a slow smile spread on his cold, chapped lips. His closest opponent had already rounded the river's bend and was heading toward its bank. A cacophony of excited canine voices grew steadily louder, ringing through the otherwise tranquil, icy air. Shrouded inside the deep hood of a bright red Arctic parka, the musher's facial features were obscured in shadow. North laughed at the racer's determined, focused posture, his warm breath expelling a foggy cloud into the air. He knew those dogs, and he knew that musher. Intimately.

Still chuckling, North hopped off the sled's runners and trotted beside it for a few seconds before calling the dogs to a stop. He set the snow hook to prevent his team from wandering away with the sled, pulled off his heavy mitts and tossed his hood back. Heavy black eyebrows drew one's gaze from a square jaw to thickly lashed, chocolate brown eyes. He scrubbed at his chilled face, restoring circulation to skin the colour of dark honey. The dogs, panting lightly from their exertion, were content to sit on their haunches or lie in the snow, waiting for their master's next move.

The second-place musher crossed the finish line with a jubilant cry and slid to a stop next to North. The dogs greeted each other with high whines and sharp yips, their feathered tails sending white flurries of snow swirling into the still air. Judging by the size of his grin, North was pleased to see the slight figure in red as she flew into his waiting arms. "I almost did it, North! I just about had you this time!" Andrea Ruben, North's bride of exactly seventeen days, pulled off her mitts and goggles and tossed the wolf-trimmed hood from her head, releasing a wave of gleaming, dark brown curls. Brilliant emerald green eyes sparkled over high cheekbones and a straight nose complemented by a subtle, upturned tip. She beamed at her new husband and raised rosy lips to his kiss.

Hoots and whistles erupted from the spectators when the newlyweds embraced; North hugged his bride tightly for a moment longer before releasing her. He took a step back and grasped her hand in a firm and formal shake. "Congratulations on running a spectacular race, Mrs. Ruben. You've become one hell of a good musher."

The spectators, led by a familiar voice, began to chant: "Go Andi! Go Andi! Go Andi!" Andrea Ruben, more often than not called 'Andi' by her family and friends, knew the instigator's voice well and would recognize it anywhere. She scanned the crowd and spotted Margo Thomas immediately; her best friend would have been hard to miss, standing at the front of the group in her red-trimmed bright blue parka, grinning from ear to ear and waving both arms in the air. They locked eyes, and Margo gave her a two-thumbs-up salute.

Arm in arm, the Rubens turned their attention back to the race, cheering enthusiastically when two more teams soon crossed the finish line within ten nerve-racking seconds of each other. They were followed a few minutes later by the final two competitors, concluding the informal event.

The Rubens spent a few minutes rehashing the highlights of the race with the other competitors and their cheering committees, then set to work unharnessing their respective teams. The well-conditioned animals showed no signs of exhaustion after the short twenty-five-kilometer race. In fact, they were barely warmed up and were eager to run again – to continue doing what they loved best. Although it was only 3:30 in the afternoon, 200 kilometres above Canada's Arctic Circle the late January sun was already sinking to the horizon. In twenty minutes, another brief Arctic day would once again succumb to darkness.

The Rubens worked together efficiently, and soon all sixteen dogs were off the gangline, out of harness, had wolfed down a snack, and were comfortably ensconced in their respective cubicles on the back of North's brand-new baby – a 1997 Ford F350 dually. He started the truck and cranked up the heat. The mutts, sensing another adventure, poked furry heads through their porthole windows, creating a comical picture: two rows of busy black noses, erect ears and bright, inquisitive eyes peered from masked faces.

North ignored the dogs and lovingly patted the shining white hood of his new prized possession; he still hadn't tired of admiring the converted vehicle. In place of a standard cargo box, the truck's 3-meter-long custom bed boasted a large, double-decker plywood box which was divided into individual compartments to safely transport up to twenty animals. A narrow aisle ran down the center of the box, creating a convenient place to stow gear and food, and two sleds could be transported on its top. Within the spacious four-door super-crew cab, a converter system provided power for a small microwave to heat drinks and meals while they were on the road. North loved his new truck almost as much as he loved his new wife.

He had purchased the costly vehicle for the upcoming Alaskan Iditarod Trail Sled Dog Race, fondly known to the mushing crowd as *The Last Great Race.* This year's event was even more noteworthy than usual; it was the 25th running of the famous race. Special silver anniversary celebrations and media coverage were planned for Sunday, March 2, and for the first time in his life North was registered to compete. The mere thought of racing against the best mushers in the world, in the most demanding race known to man, often made his heart miss a beat. Not that he would admit his weakness to another living soul.

"I told Margo we'd meet them at The Brass Rail after we get the mutts settled at home," Andi said as she climbed into the high cab of the Ford. She knocked snow from her heavy white boots before pulling them into the vehicle's warm interior, well-aware of her husband's infatuation with the truck. He spent more time cleaning and polishing his new toy than she did on housework.

"Sounds good to me," North smiled. "I could definitely go for a cold beer and a burger."

"It sounds like most of this crowd is heading over too. They all want to hear more about the Iditarod."

North groaned, but his dark eyes glinted with pleasure. "God, you'd think I'd already won the bloody race, the way these guys have been carrying on." He shook his head solemnly, not quite succeeding to contain a crooked smile. "It's great to see they have some degree of faith in me, though, because I sure as hell don't."

"You're going to do *awesome*," Andi insisted. "I just know you're going to give the world a race to remember."

"Oh, I'm sure they'll remember me all right. They'll be laughing forever about the crazy Canuck who tried to run the Iditarod with a pack of slow working dogs."

They bounced along the trail leading from the river's edge to the highway, no more than two tire ruts in the packed snow. Andi reached for her seat belt. "I thought you had more faith in the dogs."

North signed. "I do. It's just that ..."

"What?"

His glance was brief, but long enough for Andi to see the doubt in his dark eyes. Doubt, and something else. "Maybe I am crazy. Maybe I should be raising Siberian Huskies, or Alaskan Malamutes, like everyone else. Dogs that can actually *run*. Nobody has ever attempted the Iditarod with a team of Canadian Eskimo Dogs before."

"So you'll be the first. I've never known you to doubt your team before, so why now?"

North shrugged. "Ah, I don't know." They'd reached the highway and bounced over a small snowbank deposited by a grader before hitting the pavement. "I love my dogs, don't get me wrong. You know I do. They can pull anything you harness them up to and go all day, but they're just not really built for speed. Or climbing, for that matter. I'm probably going to look like a fool in front of the best mushers in the world."

"Well, you can still scratch from the race if you really want to."

"I don't want to scratch."

Andi sighed in exasperation. "Well what *do* you want?"

"I want a beer."

ABOUT THE AUTHOR

Joan Mettauer was born and raised in Alberta's heartland. Her love affair with aviation was sparked at an early age, and she dedicated most of her working years to the flying business. Living in various Northern communities, including Lac La Ronge, Saskatchewan and Yellowknife, Northwest Territories, she traveled throughout Canada's Arctic. Her final years in the aviation industry were spent in Inuvik, N.W.T., from where she bid farewell to the North.

Now retired, she has returned to her Alberta roots and lives in Medicine Hat with her husband. Her biggest joy is spending time with her eight grandchildren, who are scattered around the world in Canada, Australia and Switzerland.

Diamonds in an Arctic Sky is Joan's first novel in the 'Andi & North' series, inspired by her life and experiences in the Arctic, and fueled by her imagination.

You can find her at:
Facebook: Joan Mettauer, Author
Instagram: Joan Mettauer, @joanmettauer
www.goodreads.com
Amazon worldwide

Manufactured by Amazon.ca
Bolton, ON

40931352R00162